BALLARD REDOUBT

By John M. Hamilton

ISBN-13: 978-0-9913379-6-5

RIP Ballard

For my wife, always

Ballard WA 1995

1.

Sometimes the Norns are real bitches. They drown you in fresh water while still tied to the dock. But let's not get ahead of ourselves.

It was a slow night and the staff had started drinking, even the bartender was drinking and she wasn't a drinker. But the fall rains had come and everyone knew that the sun had left Seattle for a six-month vacation.

Anders had let the dishwasher and prep cook leave early and had already written full shifts on their timecards. He could have made them stand around to earn their pay but Anders respected work too much to insult it with lies or acting.

It was Anders' first night in charge of the kitchen. Only three orders crossed the counter. So, he drank cooking wine from a coffee cup. Anders had found a chef's knife with the tip broken off, the metal rolled to one side. Someone had used it as a pry. He slowly worked it on a sharpening stone, reprofiling the tip. Ten strokes on either side. It was the only sound in the kitchen besides the pasta water gurgling at a low boil. They were cheap Chinese knives made to be dishwasher safe and not really worth the effort but there was nothing else to do and working helped Anders think.

Anders took two garbage bags out the back door to the dumpster. He opened the lid and then swung the bags up and in like a hammer throw. Soon the seiners would head south to the Channel Islands off of Ventura for the squid season. Anders should be on one of those boats.

While working on his letter to the kitchen manager for the morning, what sold, what didn't, etc., the night's lone waitress swung by the counter.

"Anders?"

"Yes Amanda?" He replied without looking up from his letter.

"Is there anything left to eat?"

"I already turned everything off."

"But we're not closed," she said.

"Do we have a customer?" Anders asked and looked around with false interest.

"Is there anything?" she pleaded.

He continued looking at the letter, pretending to scrutinize a word of the finished product.

"What do you want?" he asked without looking up.

"I want a lot, but I'll settle for being satisfied," she said. Anders looked up. He wasn't the only staff member drinking on the job. It was too slow for the front room to make money. At least he was paid an hourly wage.

"I'll try," he said, and she hurried off. Anders went to the walk in and looked around. Something warm, he thought. That would mean turning the stove back on. The fryer was still warm. He would make something and then reclean the kitchen. It was something he could do as the lead cook. Something he would not have tried as a prep cook. Then Amanda would have got some bread and olive oil or butter and maybe some cold soup. He looked through the refrigerator shelves. There was a small steak, abandoned. It wasn't big enough to serve and needed a home after all. He gathered his ingredients. Anders sautéed an onion and pan-fried the steak. He mixed some grated horseradish with mayo and then cut the steak in slices and served it on a hamburger bun with provolone cheese and a small handful side of fries.

He placed the meal on the counter and then set about cleaning the kitchen for a second time. When he turned back towards the order window only an empty plate remained. Anders placed it in a wash rack and then went downstairs to the dry storage to think and wait for his shift to end.

He pulled the string that turned on the single overhead light and fished through an old plastic lard container for a cassette tape. He chose *Meat is Murder* by the Smiths and put it in the boom box. His boat had always been a fan of the Smiths and after he rewound the first side images of Southeast Alaska came to his mind with the first notes of the album. It was music for transiting from cannery to fishing grounds or back. Music for sitting in the wheelhouse drinking coffee with your mates and talking about shore life. Anders wondered if he was missing something that hadn't yet gone. He sat down on a fifty-pound bag of rice and troubled over one of the big questions of life, the biggest he had ever dealt with.

Anders thought about how he had gotten there, other than a sidewalk. Anders had learned to cook as a boy on the boats. He was twelve when he first left home. At an age when other kids in the neighborhood spent their summers chasing girls and bagging groceries Anders went to work with his father and uncles. Those first few summers were spent staying out of the way and trying not to get killed. But by fifteen years old he was given the cook's position.

Skippers helm the boats during the day and exclusively while fishing but the crew drives the long shifts through the black night. These are the passages from fishery to fishery or to and from harbor. A fresh crewman can safely navigate a boat alone in the dark while the rest of his crewmates sleep. This is done by the green glow of radar and red map lights for stretches of four hours. But a crew coming off a two-day opener with two or three hours sleep over 72 hours might have to double up and pull watches as short as one or two hours. Then the cook will have to make sure sandwiches and coffee are readily available. Most crashes are caused by sleeping at the wheel and it happened every year.

Boat cooks live in a special and turbulent world. They are not required to drive the boat, to pull wheel watches. That separates them from the rest of the crew. Cooks still work on deck during the setting and pulling of the net but they don't drive the boat. Cooks are expected to provide four meals a day and snacks in addition to their regular duties on deck when fishing. They must cook when other crew members are sleeping. Because they are not responsible for the safe navigation of the boat it is a position often given to junior crew members. Greenhorns must learn quickly how to fish, how to cook and how to live with four other men who might not be happy with their performance of either task.

Anders could still taste the humiliation of that lowest rung. When Anders was seventeen his father retired and moved from skipper to owner. His uncle Knute took over the boat. It was the first year he had fished with Karl and Tommy, long before they were roommates. They had been shifted over from the third Brekke boat to give the new skipper a solid crew— Karl as skiff man and Tommy as engineer. Anders remembered the humiliation of climbing the wheelhouse ladder with a breakfast for his uncle, how his uncle, in front of the other crew members, in front of Tommy and Karl, had slid the pilot house window open and thrown the breakfast overboard, plate and all, because the eggs were not over-easy. In hindsight, his uncle may have been making the point that although Anders' father owned the boat, his uncle was the skipper. But that didn't occur to the young man as he returned to the galley and cracked six eggs hoping to flip at least two without breaking the yolk. A few minutes after the first breakfast was unceremoniously buried at sea Tommy descended the ladder and helped Anders with the breakfast. Tommy showed the boy how to turn over the eggs and how to use a pan lid on the flat grill to achieve the same effect. And at that moment Anders did learn something important and lasting— that his Uncle was an ass. Treason starts small. That first siding with the crew against blood was small but it enabled this later desertion of family duty.

By eighteen he could cook and bake. He made breakfasts to order and was known within the small fleet for his garlic pot roast. Anders never completely handed off the cooking duties even as he graduated from the bottom position. He continued to do most of the cooking even though he pulled wheel watches and as a future skipper was trained in all other aspects of the trade from navigation and tactics to engineering. In the off season, back in the neighborhood while still in high school, he worked nights and weekends at a variety of restaurants in the neighborhood.

Anders knew what he wanted but had not yet said the words that would make it happen. The tape flipped over and Anders set the coffee cup of wine next to his boots between sips. Footsteps descended the stairs. Anders stood and picked up his clipboard feigning interest in the supply of chickpeas.

The waitress, Amanda, turned the corner. She let out a short sharp scream and jumped back both hands waving uselessly in front of her face. "Fuck Anders, you scared me." She was breathing quick. She put one hand on her chest and reached the other out and grabbed Anders' upper arm. "I should kick your ass," she said squeezing his muscle. Her breathing calmed and she let go. She fished in her purse. "Do you mind if I...?" She held up a little brass pot pipe.

"So, you're the new boss man?" she asked.

"I don't know about that. I'm the cook."

Anders resat on the rice bag. He watched as Amanda lit the pipe and turned from him towards the tape player. He tried to ignore the woman. Anders brushed some dirt from the toe of his boot. The kiltie was curled up and he tried to push it flat. He was the only one in the restaurant that wore boots. He looked up at Amanda. Her back was to him and she danced slightly to *Rusholme Ruffians*. She was thin and muscular. She looked over her shoulder and lit the pipe again. It was obvious that he was watching and her eyes smiled. Amanda exhaled and put the pipe away.

"Look at you, laying around like you own the place. Eating and drinking for free, fucking the waitresses."

"I don't fuck the waitresses," Anders said defensively but not sure against what.

"Why?" Amanda stage pouted. She walked the two steps between them and then straddled his lap. Anders was confused. "You don't like us? You don't like me?" She rocked her hips forward, hands on his shoulders, her gray eyes staring straight into his. She rocked her hips just a little but a little can go a long way. Anders was less confused. He looked at her eyes trying to find an answer. She had been too nice to him all night. "I asked you a question," Amanda rocked her hips again with a quicker and authoritative movement. So, he kissed her. She grabbed the back of his head and kissed him hard. She ground on him some more and then quickly stood up. Anders worried that he had done something wrong. But Amanda kicked off her shoes and pulled off her jeans and underwear in one quick motion. Anders struggled with his belt and then moved to untie the laces on his boots. He thought maybe he should get some shoes. "Don't bother," she said and helped him slide his jeans to his ankles. "Do you have a rubber?" she asked.

"I didn't..." Anders said as he looked around like there would have been a supply amongst the other dry goods.

"Tsk, tsk," she said and went to her purse. Amanda helped him. She restraddled Anders on top of the rice bag and whispered, "you're going to be good," in his ear. Anders held her just above the hip bones and concentrated on the number ten cans of corn on the shelf over her shoulder because he was a young man and didn't like baseball. Why would they stock so much corn? He struggled for an answer. Morrissey crooned, *"I might walk home alone but my faith in love is still devout"*. She ran her hands over his close-cropped head. "Why don't you grow some hair? It would look good." Amanda again brought her mouth to his ear and he could feel her hot breaths. "I'm getting close," she said. It was too much and Anders came. Amanda frowned and dug her fingernails into the muscles that ran from his shoulders to his neck. Anders went board stiff, his body paralyzed by the unexpected pleasure. Amanda leaned back and ground a punishment on him and came with a grunted, "fuck!" And then she slowed to a stop. She kissed him once on the lips.

Amanda stood and pulled her jeans back on. She picked up her purse and looked at Anders lying on the bag of rice, his pants still around his ankles. She pointed at him and said, "you owe me one." And then she left and Anders listened to her climb the stairs. He reached up and touched his shoulder under his shirt. Her fingernails had drawn blood.

Anders stood on wobbly legs, pulled off the rubber and tossed it in the garbage. He wiped his cock on his discarded cook's apron and then threw it in the laundry hamper. Anders walked over to the stack of Heineken cases piled high against the wall. He ripped the cardboard on the top one and pulled a bottle out. He opened it with the side of his pocketknife. The warm beer was delicious. A thought that had been fermenting in his head for weeks was finally born into reality. "I'm not going to fish," he said aloud. It was treason against his family, mutiny against the neighborhood and blasphemy against his life. And it was so easy after a waitress had just left your lap. It was a life changing event. For his family, life changing events usually happened at sea— a dragging anchor or a loss of power during a storm. For Anders it was sex on a fifty-pound bag of rice. That is how Anders Brekke left the boats.

2.

Red lights flashed on the Ballard bridge and Tommy slowed his truck even though he could have made it across before the traffic barricades dropped sealing the neighborhood from the city. He wasn't in a hurry. Tommy was returning from the Teamster Hall where they had just authorized a strike. He still hoped for common sense to prevail.

It was Friday night and he wanted to see if someone was stupid enough to be leaving. Tommy set his brake and turned off his engine as the bridge opened. He could see a white mast light coming from the east, headed the wrong way. "Dumb ass," Tommy mumbled to himself. "I wonder who it is?" he asked as he stepped from the truck, into the rain, but he already knew the answer. There was a large class of boats that fell between skiff and work boat. It didn't matter if they had sails or engines, or were worth one dollar or a million. They were yachts. The word was foul, it was a curse and a hex. Sure enough, a large sailboat motored through the bridge. Any mariner, someone who made their living on the water, would have known not to leave on a Friday. Well, Tommy thought, you'll probably find some wind, maybe too much.

He turned right on NW 52nd and pulled up on the curb in front of the little house. The mercury vapor light in the crane yard had gone out and the street was dark. The house lights dimly poked through the swirling mist. His roommate had mounted ship's lanterns, red and green brass lamps, on either side of the porch. It looked like a boat was emerging from the block. They had talked about mounting a white mast or anchor light on top of the flagpole to complete the illusion but never got around to it. The Norwegian flag snapped in the stiffening wind. His ex used to call it, 'The Ballard flag'. Tommy liked that. She wasn't all bad.

Tommy pulled his lunchbox from the truck and climbed the weathered wooden steps. Their sometimes cat, a very large and vicious black tom was frozen in a pre-pounce. Somewhere while still a stray it had lost an eye. That eye was milk white and useless. They, of course, named it Odin.

"What you got?" Tommy asked the cat. "Rat?"

Rats. Fucking rats. Tommy hated rats and Ballard always had a rat problem. But it was a port neighborhood in a port town.

The cat chirped at a pile of orange chafing net abandoned on the corner of the porch. His white teeth and long white claws exposed. Tommy nudged the scrap of salmon seine with his foot. The rat flushed and ran along the edge of the house, past Tommy, to the row of fisherman boots next to the front door. The right boot of Tommy's pair lay on its side and the rat sought refuge inside. Tommy knew that they were his boots because he had spray painted the toes orange to make them easy to find in a pile on a boat. Odin pounced on the boot closing the exit. "Where is he?" Tommy asked again. He nudged the boot with his toe and Odin hissed. It disgusted Tommy that a rat was hiding where his toes would go. He grabbed the boot around the heel and shook it sharply, violently, towards the house sending the rat bouncing off the siding. Odin pounced but the rat escaped the porch and scurried up the leg of their barbeque. Tommy's anger was naturally slow to rise but it had passed annoyance. Rats in boots and grills definitely crossed the line. Odin stood on his hind legs his claws scratching the paint on the burner dial. He yowled and snorted. Tommy walked over. "Fuck that guy," Tommy said and he turned the propane valve on. "Take a nap or talk to Odin," Tommy told the grill. While the rat faced the gas chamber Tommy let himself into the house. Neither of his roommates were home. Tommy grabbed a beer from the fridge and returned to the execution. Odin paced around the hissing grill. Tommy shoved him off

8

with the toe of his boot. Odin hissed again, his ears flat and teeth shining white in his black face. "Let's see if he's sleeping yet," Tommy said as he opened the lid. Unfortunately, the rat wasn't dead or even slowed. It ran straight for Tommy's peering face. He slammed the lid and jumped back, heart racing. "Motherfucker!" he swore and reached for the red striker button.

Time slowed— one of those rare moments of life distilled through danger like the time he saw the skiff come loose on the back deck during a storm. He had opened the galley door and looked out on the work deck awash with green sea water. He watched one chain go slack and then the other three slacked and then the skiff was sliding sideways and went over the rail. Tommy wanted to yell something but he had no words. The skiff rolled into the waves and then was caught by its tow line still attached to the deck winch. It became a giant sea anchor and pulled the seiner to a listing halt. Tommy thought they would capsize, disappear in a storm on the Georgia Straight. He was thrown out of the galley door and fell on the fish hold hatch. As he felt the boat heel over he thought of Anders asleep in the fo'c'sle, still just a boy.

All this he remembered in that moment between the trigger push and click. Luckily Tommy was still crouched in fear and only felt the warm wave of fire pass over his head. Just a moment of heat, an outward expansion of burning air. The lid landed ten feet away on the sidewalk. He spotted Odin crossing the street at a full gallop before disappearing into Dantrawl's net yard.

Tommy stood and looked around, feeling his head with his hands, amazed that he still had hair. Then he saw the burnt rat, its body still smoking, crawl under the fence into his neighbor's yard. He gathered the lid and put it back on the grill. Tommy turned off the gas. Before going inside, he lowered the flag and stored it in an ammo box on the porch.

Tommy sat down in the chair next to the door and unlaced his boots, inspecting them. He slipped his feet into a pair of Portuguese fishing shoes and carried his boots to the kitchen sink. He grabbed a stiff brush from the hook underneath the sink and knocked off all the mud and concrete residue paying attention to the welt and stitching. The boots spent every night on a boot dryer and then on Sundays he worked a fresh layer of wax into the leather, the heat of his hands warming the leather and wax. Tommy could make a two-hundred-dollar pair of Danners last a couple years.

Next door the explosion startled Werner. He was an old man sitting at the table of his breakfast nook working on a poem and the pen flew from his hand. He felt his old heart strain, fragile, and his hands tingled. He hoped his heart would stop, that he would die. But he didn't. His heart calmed. There was nothing to do but return to work. His once-a-day poem was the only thing he did that could be thought as constructive. He pushed the blank sheet of paper away and then opened and closed his weathered hands. They were worn from a lifetime of work. They were ill suited to the task of poetry. He thought of the war and regretted not dying with his friends. He was old and wanted to die. He had nothing to live for but wouldn't take his own life out of spite for God. He would not quit, he would not admit defeat. He had done it before and did not care to do it again. He got up and retrieved the pen before sitting back down at the table. The blank sheet asked for its due. Forty years of poems had been written at that table. One a day, always on the same subject, Signe. She was his one love. She was the reason he was in Ballard. She had ruined his life and she had given it purpose. He looked at the blank sheet. His poems had gotten shorter and shorter over time. Haikus, single line stanzas, they kept shrinking. Often, lately, he was down to one word. He thought of the word 'whore'. No, he was saving that one. Not today. Instead he wrote 'calve'. He looked at it and then crossed it out and wrote 'calf' underneath. He no longer thought in German yet some things about English still made no sense. Either way he thought of Signe's lower leg, of how he had held it in his hand and felt the muscle roll up and down as she flexed her foot. It was long ago and they were children in a war neither of them understood. Norway was far away from America. The poem was good enough for his ritual. The poem wasn't the important thing. It was the ritual. He stood and walked to the front door.

Werner changed out of his house slippers into a pair of galoshes. He went out into the swirling Seattle rain. He had built a brick fireplace, a stove really, in the corner of the yard. It was for burning trash. A brick walkway led to it. All built with his own hands. Werner pulled his pipe zippo from his pocket and set the single sheet alight. He placed it in the firebox and watched it turn black and the embers float toward the short chimney. Another day complete.

3.

Monday morning Tommy was awake at four listening to his clock flip over the little panels that made the numbers. At 4:30 he got up and made his bed. He pulled on a pair of boxers and went to the bathroom to brush his teeth and take a piss. He turned on the living room light and saw that Anders' boots were by the front door. The door to Karl's room was open meaning that he was still at sea. His housemates were accounted for. Tommy put the kettle on the burner and ground some coffee. While the French press steeped he took a shower. He drank his first cup as he dressed.

As he made two turkey sandwiches Tommy looked at the back door leading from the kitchen to nowhere. The chain-link fence surrounding the crane yard was only a foot past the door. A cut piece of truck mud flap covered the lower right pane, duct tape created a top hinge. The middle leg of a white raised W pointed towards the door handle. It was a Kenworth flap. Tommy had fashioned it. He let the knife hit the side of the mayo jar, sounding a slight 'tink'. The mud flap pushed up and Odin's face looked in, his one milky white eye visible in the darkness. The cat stood on the outside trim looking in. Odin pushed through and dropped to the floor. The cat was heavy, strong. No feline was ever truly domesticated. Tommy thought to be domesticated an animal had to perform work or obey commands. Odin wasn't even close. He was violent, selfish and unpredictable. Tommy lacked all those qualities and admired them in the cat. "The Terrible One!" Tommy greeted the cat with another name for Odin. "Good morning rat breath," Tommy said. "You survived the blast, huh?" Tommy reached down and scratched the cat's head. Odin responded with a growl instead of a purr and then stood on his hind legs, the long, curved blades of his fore claws digging into the heavy denim of Tommy's double front logger pants. It was their ritual. Tommy said, "put those things away," as he pulled a slice of turkey from the package and gave it to the cat. Odin snatched the sheet of turkey, retreated to a corner of the kitchen and loudly made it disappear. Tommy packed his lunch box with an apple, a banana and a bottle of water. He then poured what was left in the coffee press into his travel mug and let himself out the door. It was raining. He zipped his reflective orange coat to his neck and drank some coffee under the porch. Winter was coming. It was stupid to negotiate a contract in the fall. They should have bargained in the spring or summer when the demand is highest. It was another thing they had traded away during the bad times of the late 80s. Tommy wondered if they would really go out over strike language.

It was before six but the neighborhood was awake. Next door, in the crane yard, two big trucks idled. One was already hooked to a flatbed full of counterweights. The air dryers spit an irregular accompaniment to the diesel rattle.

Across the street, at the net builders, a man pushed open the large sliding doors to their building. The mostly Vietnamese crew walked into the light. Orange and black pieces of trawl hung from the ceiling. Tommy walked to his truck and waved to men also carrying their lunch pails. "Ciao," Tommy said. They returned the greeting. One of them had taught Tommy the Vietnamese for good morning. He forgot what it was but it sounded like ciao. And now they spoke Italian to each other in a Norwegian neighborhood.

Tommy liked living amongst work, more importantly he liked waking up surrounded by work. He understood it and it immediately centered him. It made sense. If he woke daily in a sleepy neighborhood where everyone drove to office jobs he would start his day with doubts. He understood why suburban people were so pointless. It was how they woke. There was no recovering. He had some simple rules: anything considered work requires boots, a man should own a pickup truck and a motorcycle. But he wasn't daft enough to believe that his opinions were valid for all people. Only college students and the religious were that daft.

The truck was sluggish to turn over but eventually cracked to life with an overzealous roar. Tommy tapped the accelerator until, eventually, the choke calmed the RPMs down. The mildly built three-fifty had embarrassed him when he lived in Shoreline with his wife, surrounded by houses instead of work. No neighbor likes a race boat fired up at five each morning. While the truck warmed, he climbed back onto the porch and pulled the Norwegian flag from the ammo box, clipped it on the flagpole line and raised it. Raising and lowering the flag was a chore shared by all three roommates. The day had begun.

He left the house at 5:50 even though his start time wasn't until 6:40. It took longer to warm his truck than to drive to work but Tommy was still too much of a mechanic, an engineer to boats, to mistreat an engine. It was 5:57 when he backed his pickup into his spot against the fence at the precast yard. He shut the engine down and could hear some fighting coming from the blackberry patch that had overrun the chain link fence surrounding the precast yard. "Campers" lived in shacks made of pallets and blue tarps, squatting on company property. The drivers ignored them until something was stolen from the company or workers and then a phone call to SPD instigated a sweep of the patch. But a few weeks later they would return and the cycle would continue. Tommy could hear muffled hard words and an occasional woman's curse, she seemed to be winning whatever the fight was about. There was still a faint glow from the night's campfire and the smoke smelled toxic like plywood or pressure-treated lumber. Tommy listened some more. It didn't sound like violence, only misery. How did they get there? A few bad decisions? Or worse, no decisions.

The trucks were parked twelve blocks from the plant at the pre-cast yard. It was where the extra from each load was recycled into one-yard concrete blocks. Tommy pre-tripped his truck before starting the engine. He swept a flashlight underneath the engine, making sure there were no new puddles of oil or coolant and then stood on the bumper and pulled the hood open. He held the dipstick up to the dull light from the mercury-vapor lamp on the power pole. He stuck his finger in the radiator. It was too dark to see. He smelled his finger and then rubbed it against his thumb. Antifreeze has a different viscosity than water. He wiped his finger on his pants— the same spot every day. The fan had two belts and the hoses were attached so he was okay to make the pistons go up and down.

Tommy pushed the starter and the truck rocked back and forth, finally rumbling to life. He turned on the running and marker lights. He tuned the radio to KPLU for the morning news and waited. After the engine had warmed for a few minutes, Tommy pushed the drum control forward just enough to get the drum turning. He let the hydraulic system warm up. Tommy loved machines and he treated them well. Tommy drove a concrete mixer, not a cement mixer. Cement is an ingredient in concrete, along with water and aggregate— the sand and gravel that gives the mix its strength and workability properties. People often confuse this. Normal people had almost no knowledge of concrete despite it being, literally, foundational to modern civilization. But Tommy knew little about plumbing or medicine and they were pretty important too.

Being a Union shop, everything was determined by seniority. From first pick on the vacation calendar to the assignment of trucks— seniority ruled. Tommy's truck, number 34, was nicer than most trucks but lacked the comforts of the more senior trucks. It was a five window— it had two extra windows on the back corners of the cab which meant that Tommy could see more. He could look over his shoulder in traffic and could look straight back if his mirrors were obscured by trees or folded in to access a tight alley. The trucks above him had power windows and air conditioning for the two months of Seattle summer.

One by one the trucks crawled out of the pre-cast yard into the darkness of a sleeping neighborhood, a sleeping city. The plant could load a truck in seven minutes if everything was working right- a rare occurrence. Because of this start times were staggered at five and ten-minute intervals.

Tommy was the shop steward and he represented Halibut Flats Sand and Gravel on the bargaining committee. The contract would expire in two Sundays. Today Tommy would work like every other driver. Tomorrow Tommy would be at the table. He would rather work than be in the hall. Across the table would sit professional negotiators representing the companies. They tried to intimidate from the first handshake. Tommy's natural inclination was to find middle ground. It was frustrating.

"Thirty is back," the radio crackled breaking the silence. The first human voice of the day. Number 30 truck was pulling into the plant.

"Thirty is back," dispatch repeated. "You're under Mike." They were ready to load him.

Five minutes later, "Thirty-three is back."

"Thirty-three is back. Brian you can follow Mike."

Finally, it neared Tommy's start time. He pulled his hand brake and turned on his four-way flashers and headlights— everything that could light up or blink. Walking a second time around his truck, Tommy checked the tires for rocks stuck between the duals and thumped each tire with a two-foot piece of hydraulic hose. It was a formidable weapon. The steel mesh lining gave it a punch. By hitting the duals, he could feel or hear a low tire. He examined the frame and suspension. He drained any accumulated water from the air tanks and looked over all the air and hydraulic lines. With no reportable problems Tommy headed for the plant.

Tommy's first load was ten yards of quick setting, high-strength curb and gutter concrete for the city. He liked working with the city crews. Tommy knew everyone's name and knew something about each person's life. He liked checking in, finding out how a child was doing or how long someone had until retirement. Tommy liked people.

The job was downtown on the edge of Pioneer Square, the historic downtown, on the corner of Third and Washington. The crew was still building the wooden framework that would form the mud into a curb and wheelchair ramp when Tommy pulled around the corner with all his lights flashing and his tag and pusher axles slowly rising to discharge positions. When the bridge axle folded up like a giant jackknife it was a mechanical spectacle that made pedestrians stop and gawk. Inside the cab Tommy checked the slump meter that measured hydraulic effort to spin the drum and figured the concrete could use a couple more gallons of water. As he coasted to a stop in a no parking area against the curb Tommy pulled his hand throttle out and the tachometer needle swung hard over to the right. The Cat diesel screamed and Tommy pushed his drum control all the way forward until the orange and white striped drum became a strobe rotating at maximum rpms while he counted the seconds and added water with a valve held open in the cab. It dumped water into the spinning drum-roughly one gallon per second. Once mixed he throttled down and set the parking brake. He climbed down from his cab and walked over to talk with the crew. They were still fifteen minutes from being ready so Tommy walked down the street to a little bodega. The Indian proprietor was rolling up his night gate. Tommy waited and then bought a copy of the Post-Intelligencer. He would not read the Times, Seattle's other paper. The Times had a very noticeable anti-union bias that was dictated from the owning family. Tommy always thought that two papers were the mark of a legitimate city, along with professional teams in all three of the big sports. Eventually the crew was ready. They poured the wheelchair ramp and curb with stiff mud. While they worked on those more difficult features Tommy added water to make the flat sidewalk easier to finish. He was at a point in his career where he knew what the crew would want. Tommy always read his dispatch tickets carefully noting the address and mix make up, deciphering each for clues and trying to think ahead of his arrival. You didn't bring wet mud to 535 Queen Anne Avenue. Or at least you shouldn't.

Tommy cleared the job with a yard of concrete left in his drum. Dispatch told him to head for the pre-cast yard and make an ecology block. He did so and then washed down the inside of his drum before heading back to the plant for his next load.

4.

In a neighborhood that dreamt of sinking Werner woke again, for the thousandth time, from his dunking. Always the dream was of sinking not of drowning. It always ended the same. In it he left the black hull of the stricken submarine and rose through the increasingly green sea. It was a long ascent and he did not know if his lungs would last but after so many years he also knew that it was a dream unlike the first time and more and more Werner did not care if he broke the surface. But he always did and always the same shock of brightness. The sun and blue sky and the white snow on the mountains, blinding. And then he was on the surface spitting salt water and not ten feet away was a mountain trooper in a fishing dory, his arms outstretched to welcome Werner back to the land of men. Werner stared at the edelweiss pin on his forage cap and thought what a strange world this was and then blood filled his eyes.

Werner's first patrol didn't go well. It lasted only eight days before they were sunk. U-64 had left Wilhelmshaven on the North Sea in April of 1940 after their initial workup and then headed north to participate in the conquering of Norway. They toured around a bit and failed to see any enemy before being surprised by a British biplane while at anchor in a side fjord off of Narvik. It was early in the war, long before the U-boats became iron coffins for two-thirds of the force. On that spring day, eight of his comrades were killed, but thirty-eight were able to escape. Those like him in the engine room rode the boat to the bottom and had to make a free ascent to the surface. The boat lay slightly on her side and when it was Werner's turn to escape he judged the angle wrong and when he pushed off he ran his face into the combing surrounding the hatch. He broke his orbital socket and cut his face badly.

Werner was first taken to a field hospital where he lay next to a lot of boys that had been machine gunned or sniped by the Norwegians or French Foreign Legion. He was an odd case— a sailor with a cracked skull. When the invasion stabilized a bit, he was transferred to an Army hospital in Bergen. There had been a mistake when Werner was processed and they had listed him as an officer instead of a petty officer. Werner only realized this later, after he had been given a private room. That is where he met Signe. She was a sixteen-year-old nurses' aid with long golden braids and a woman's body. She had a harelip scar and this made her shy. She turned away or kept her head bowed as she straightened up Werner's room. She too had thought him a Naval officer.

The war wasn't going well for the young man. The doctors had tried to fix his skull but the bones had set badly and this gave him a slightly staved in look. He was barely eighteen, an orphan, an ex-commercial fisherman and already a wounded veteran.

But then Signe walked into his room to change his sheets. Werner had never been with a woman. He had never had a girlfriend. And then, a young Norwegian girl, a girl from the country, was reaching under his blankets teaching him that there was more to life than the sea. He could remember it vividly. He was in bed, his head wrapped in bandages, only one eye free. He wore cotton pajamas and the sheets were cotton. Two wool blankets covered him. He didn't want to heal. Werner wanted to stay in that room and be visited by Signe twice a day, forever. Communication was difficult but maybe just a little more so than any couple. Through pantomime and simple words she had told him that she had gotten pregnant in her little town and was sent away to Bergen after miscarrying as a result of a peasant remedy.

Before he left for Germany to join another boat she had given him a postcard with a picture of fishing boats on it. On the back was printed, "The Fishing Fleet at Ballard Washington". There, in the postcard, they would start their own life away from family and war. He would go back to being a fisherman and she could have their children. And like children, they made plans and believed in them.

It was not to be. Instead, Werner woke up alone in a little house in Ballard. He got out of bed. He was still alive.

So many of his friends had died and he couldn't understand why he had survived. He had no right to demand anything from life. He had been given length but not happiness. Werner couldn't remember the last time he woke with an erection. His body was useless but it persisted. Ever since he was forced to retire from the shipyard the days had passed with a Sisyphean monotony. His own murder or stiff dick would be a welcome anomaly.

Werner put the kettle on. He couldn't drink coffee anymore, it tore up his guts, so he drank three glasses of hot water every morning before his walk. As he waited for the pot to sing Werner watched the men working in the crane yard. They were preparing trucks for a job. Giant yellow counterweights were being stacked on a flatbed. They were going to lift something heavy today. The men ignored the rain and threw chains to each other across the load. Werner had always preferred to work inside. Not inside an office like a bureaucrat but inside a boat like someone with brains. The men who worked on deck were nothing more than trained monkeys. The smart men were in the engine room. That was another reason that submariners were the superior mariners.

Werner got ready for his walk. It was his 'constitutional' as the English called it. He donned his old oilskin and hat and left the house. In the middle of his lawn was a burnt rat. It didn't shock him. Nothing shocked him. Briefly he thought it was a gift, a message, from his old co-workers. Before he was forced to retire he had sided with management in a labor 'question'. It had made him unwanted by all parties once it was settled. He had found a dead rat on his car in the shipyard parking lot. But that was years ago and everyone he worked with had to be retired by now. Werner looked up. Where could it have come from? Why? He picked it up with a paper bag and put the body in the garbage. His yard once again orderly and neat.

Werner was convinced that he always chose wrong and more so that choosing right was impossible. From his branch of the military, to love, to leaving his country after the war, he had chosen poorly. Every choice ended in disappointment. That was the key to his not killing himself, because death must surely be a disappointment. Instead, he had made peace with disappointment.

Werner walked up 11th past Gilman Park. A drunk lay sleeping in the little league dugout. Werner spat on the grass as he walked by but the sleeper didn't move. Werner had no sympathy. There was nothing terrible about poverty. He had been extremely poor. Poverty was a state like rain. It was temporary or enduring. But there were actions that could be taken. The most important action was mental— how you saw yourself. These people, the campers, had ceased to struggle. Their war, their catastrophe, was with a bottle or with a needle.

Werner continued on and as he neared Market Street his stomach felt like it was dragging anchor across a rocky bottom. His body was trained by years of habit. Even when he still worked in the shipyard he stopped by every morning for a sausage biscuit from McDonald's because it reminded him of the time he spent in Ruston Louisiana as a prisoner of war. His second boat was as lucky as the first. They were caught on the surface and were strafed and bombed until the boat was useless for a dive. The dive alarm sounded but it was quickly drowned out by the sound of shells hitting the boat. Two large explosions followed. They were the bombs from the plane finding their mark. The lights had gone out and everyone in the engine room had been knocked to the floor. Abandon ship was sounded before the plane could turn for another run. This time Werner wasted no time getting out. They were in the North Atlantic and he knew he couldn't ride that boat to the bottom and hope to escape.

The American POW camp had lent the prisoners out to help the local farmers as their own sons were away fighting. A couple of the men protested that they were being treated like black slaves but Werner enjoyed it. He had never worked in the earth or been around animals. He liked the Thompsons, the family he was loaned to. They were good people, hard workers if only a little too religious. Mrs. Thompson always had biscuits every day when Werner arrived from the camp. The Thompsons ended up sponsoring Werner when he immigrated after the war. He stayed in Louisiana for a couple years but always looked northwest towards Washington state. Through prison camps in Northern Louisiana and later in Britain, through Germany and back to the United States he had carried that postcard Signe had given him.

Werner had grown up in the Rhur, a surprise only child to parents in their 40s. His father was killed in a mining accident when Werner was thirteen. He was old enough to understand that he wasn't good at school and he didn't want to be a burden so he went quietly when his mother found him a spot as an apprentice on a commercial fishing boat out of Hamburg. Those first three years were tough. The skipper treated him badly and didn't trust him with anything except cooking for the first few months. He sometimes missed his mother but accepted his life. He sent most of his money to his mother and kept a little for himself. In early 1939 his skipper died of a heart attack while they were fishing and that left Werner without an apprenticeship. Three months later he was in the Kriegsmarine and three weeks later they were at war.

When he emerged after his biscuit the sky was dark with heavy black clouds. It felt like a February morning and promised more than the usual Seattle rain. Werner opened his umbrella and stood just outside McDonald's. The passing cars threw wakes across the asphalt. A young girl with a shock of copper colored hair passed on a bicycle. She wore black jeans and a black sweatshirt and was soaked to the bone. She turned and made eye contact with Werner. Her smile was defiant, uncaring and beautiful. A bus passed and the storm of dirty rain chasing it enveloped her. She disappeared. Werner watched the single passenger in the lit interior, a young man, head bowed. When the bus crossed 14th the power pole jumped and a shower of sparks fell in the rain. His heart stopped. He recognized that spark. It was the pain of leaving Signe, of young love against the world in flames. He had believed in it as he stood on the troop ship headed back to Germany to join a new boat, his face still in bandages, the smell of her still on his hands. As they pulled out from Bergen a trolley on the city street caused the same shower of sparks, the one light in a dark city seen from a darkened ship and to Werner that spark was his love for Signe flaming in the darkness of a continent at war.

5.

Anders had the dream, the nightmare. He woke alone in the fo'c'sle. He woke alone with only panic accompanying the main engine and genset droning through the bulkhead from the engine room. Anders couldn't remember why he should be there. What season was it? What fishery? He climbed the ladder to the galley. It was empty. The boat rocked from side to side working its way through an off stern swell. Where was the crew? Who was the crew? He took the next ladder up to the wheelhouse. The bridge was empty. The boat drove on. It headed towards a harbor. It looked like Sitka. Confused he climbed the outside ladder down to the deck. The stern rode low in the water. She was tanked down. But the deck was clear. No net and no skiff. Where was the crew? A broken line swung from the power block. Why was the boat like this? Where was the captain? A wave washed over the stern and knocked him down and then another picked him up and carried him overboard. He floated in the sea and watched the boat, pilotless, plow on into the harbor. It was the dream he had often. There were minor variations but always the boat driving itself towards a crash. Anders thought it meant he should never skipper. He didn't know that the other two men sleeping upstairs also had this dream, often. That it was the dream of all fishermen. He woke in the low ceilinged basement and turned on his light. It was too like a bunk light. The room was too like a fo'c'sle. He needed to get out.

Karl sat in the skipper's chair of the ocean tug. He used large binoculars to scan the Seattle waterfront as they left the Todd shipyard at the south end of Elliot Bay. He watched the little people scurry around the sidewalks and streets. Karl was fascinated as a sociologist or a naturalist might be. He wondered what they were doing, what they were thinking. As he moved ships and barges around, they moved dollars or words. Karl had never worked in an office or even in a building. His life had always been on boats. He had started fishing early and then moved to towing, to tugs. They had just returned from a four-week trip to the Aleutians and back. Unfortunately, the barge they were towing was damaged by a storm while crossing the Gulf. It was not company owned so they dropped it off at Todd shipyard to be repaired. This created more paperwork and Karl piloted the boat as the Skipper filled out his report. He drove them past the tall buildings downtown. Karl held a Master license. He had earned it three years prior and would soon have his own boat. They were building a new one in the company shipyard. Once it was finished everyone who wanted to move up one boat would and the leftover boat would be Karl's. It was nice not to be towing and they pushed a wasted bow wave out past the two Liberian flagged freighters lying at anchor waiting for their turns at the grain terminal. They rounded the light at Discovery Park and headed toward the Chittenden Locks that separate the salt water of Puget Sound from the fresh water of the ship canal connecting Lake Union and Lake Washington. Seals crowded the buoys, sunning themselves or barking. As the locks came into view Karl shut down the radars so he wouldn't blast the Corps of Engineers workers who ran the locks.

"The bridge is yours Cap. Half mile out," Karl said.

"Thanks Karl," he said without looking up from the paperwork.

Karl went out on deck to prepare the lines. The locks, one small and one large, were Ballard's trump card over every other west coast port. They enabled boats to berth and repair in fresh water but work in salt. The boat went through the locks smoothly and professionally with a minimum of noise and movement and then they were in fresh water. He knew the lock operators by name and chatted as the tug was raised in the larger lock. Karl liked to tease them about their snappy outfits. They looked like park rangers. Tourists stood by the fence taking pictures. Karl didn't mind. He liked that they were impressed. Seattle natives ignored boats like they ignored bad weather. Both were permanent fixtures of the skyline. It was good to be back in Ballard and as they traveled up the ship canal he eyed for any changes in the neighborhood. There were always changes and they were rarely good. At least Fishermen's Terminal hadn't yet been pushed out. There had been talk about mooring yachts. The city had changed. It had moved from tough to smart. It had become bold in thought but mincing in step. Karl's people were disappearing, people of the woods and sea. Maybe Ballard could hold out with its maritime and industrial base, a redoubt against flaccid progress. More likely, as with other redoubts, like Dien Bien Phu it would fall or like Khe Sahn, it would be abandoned. The evolution of war made redoubts untenable. Wealth made working neighborhood redoubts untenable. Karl looked to see what fishing boats were in before they crossed under the Ballard Bridge. He spotted his roommate on the back of the Saratoga mending net. His boat continued on. Their yard was further up the canal.

Anders looked up at the bridge. A Halibut Flats truck headed south across it towards downtown the stipes on the barrel rotating quickly, still mixing its load of concrete. It wasn't Tommy. The truck was a short, squat Mack with an off-centered cab. Another truck passed it headed north back to the plant. It was a square Peterbilt. Tommy drove a locally built Kenworth with a long sloping roman nose.

At least it wasn't raining and, at least, it wasn't Alaska. Those thoughts percolated in Anders Brekke's head as he stood on the back deck of the Saratoga under a low Seattle sky. It was a fall sky, a sky that hugged you and made you think of neighborhood and of small vistas. It was a sky that made fall work possible. The gray didn't lead his eye from the needed maintenance and repair. The Saratoga, or Sara, was a fifty-eight-foot limit seiner with a high bow and a squat house. She was a beautiful black steel killer. She had just returned from her Spring and Summer fisheries in South-East Alaska. She was of one of his father's three boats and she was Anders' birthright.

The original Brekke boats built by his great grandfather were named after family matriarchs in the traditional style but after World War Two his grandfather changed the family's naming convention to honor warships instead of women. Anders' father, Don, had continued the practice with the boats he built. The Lexington, the Lex, and the Yorktown, the Yorky T, were moored next to the Sara.

His grandfather was denied a Navy commission because he lacked a proper education, although he had been schooled in the sea since before his birth. In spite he joined the Navy as a Seabee and was sent to Ulithi to build the forward shipyard facility. But after talking boat construction with the ship fitters over beers he was Shanghaied and spent the remainder of the war fixing the battle-damaged fleet.

The main engine hummed with the hydraulics engaged. Anders worked a plastic sewing needle loaded with tarred twine. He ran another six feet of salmon seine through the power block hanging from the boom overhead and quickly examined the net from left to right throwing the curtain of mesh from hand to hand. He mended the holes, tying each knot by hand.

Anders was readying the boat for its voyage south to Southern California. The Brekke boats fished year-round. Anders had fished year-round since graduating high school four years earlier. His family's calendar didn't have months. It had seasons. Herring, halibut, salmon and squid. The fishing never stopped. He had skipped out early from the fall salmon season to fly home for his grandmother Signe's funeral. He had always been close to her and was her acknowledged favorite. That summer she had moved into the Norse Home on Phinney ridge from her house on Sunset Hill. In March, before he left for spring herring, before she got really sick she had held his hand tight and told him, "be your own man. It doesn't work out— living other peoples' lives. I tried it. It didn't work." Anders didn't understand what she meant but knew that it was wisdom and tried to apply it to his life.

Now he maneuvered, he navigated to stay in the city. In the winter they fished squid at night in the Channel Islands off of Ventura. There were always more fishermen than slots for the winter fisheries and squid was considered a nice way to warm the bones so he wouldn't be short handing the boat if he could say the words aloud, to his father.

It had been the best salmon season since the miracle year of 1989. They had flown the broom almost every opener and crew shares were twenty-nine thousand dollars. Anders had plenty of money to experiment at being a landsman.

He again looked around at the city and across the canal towards the neighborhood. Here he could walk off the boat and see people, see girls. He could go to a restaurant or a bookstore. Here his last name wasn't, "from the Saratoga." Here he was safe from his own last name.

Anders went back to work. It was the afternoon and he was the only one working on dock three. Occasionally a crewman or a vagrant, it was hard to tell the difference, would walk up or down the dock most likely headed somewhere to get drunk or high. Anders held a strong disdain for almost all other crews. The Brekke boats were different. They looked different. They were steel boats, painted black. They fished in a pack and only talked to each other on encrypted radios. And most importantly their crews were different. They didn't accept druggies or long hairs. And they fished harder. They attacked. Because of that attitude they made more money. They were the highliners.

Net mending is basic work, it is one of the first useful things a greenhorn can learn. Net mending wasn't bad work. It could be fun. During the season, between openings, the crew stood on the work deck all searching and sewing together, telling stories, maybe sipping beers. But this was the solitary fall work of a skipper's son. His father told Anders to mend the salmon seine before swapping it for the squid seine in preparation for the trip south. He also said, "I shouldn't have to tell you these things." It cut Anders. Anders was proud of his skill in a job he no longer wanted. He paused from his knots and looked around Fishermen's Terminal. Almost all the boats were in. The trollers and seiners were lined up and the crabbers had yet to leave for the Bering. Only the longliners were out. Anders loved those high bowed, hundred-year-old wooden schooners. They were the most beautiful vessels in or out of the harbor. Maybe it would be different if I were a long liner, he thought. No. "I'm not going to fish," Anders said aloud, again to himself.

A bell started rInging as if his words summoned a prize— clang, clang, clang, clang— a sign, an omen. Anders looked up at the bridge. The lights were flashing and a couple drivers punched it to get over before the barricades dropped. A Halibut Flats truck coasted to a stop and set its air brakes, the drum still spinning. Anders wondered if it was Tommy.

Anders looked around and then said, "I'm not going to fish." He said it aloud because he needed to say it aloud. He was practicing. His voice still did not sound sure. He practiced again. Soon he would have to say the words to others. Anders pulled another section of net towards his chest looking for holes. He found one and pulled the plastic needle from the side tool pocket on his pants and began to mend. He tightened the knot and his mind went for the thousandth time back to the night before. Did Amanda really fuck him in the dry storage? He wasn't young enough or stupid enough to think she wanted to be his girlfriend. No, he knew it was a transaction— a power play. That is what he told himself— that he was smart, that he was in control, that he knew what she was thinking and that he was strong. Young men and old men lie to themselves when faced with love— or what they imagine as love. Hamsun said it would make the king lie in the dirt with his tongue poking out. Anders was no king. Well, she could have whatever she was aiming at. Anders wondered if it would happen again. He smiled to himself like an idiot. Fuck! That was living! He ran the memory through his head again. He could feel her hips grinding on him, their jeans getting hot. He let the net hang and went inside the galley. There was a box of polaroids behind the spice rack. They were pictures of every woman and girl fucked aboard the boat. It was an offering to the sea god Ægir to keep the crew out of Ràn's net. Women were bad luck on a boat and this offering excused their presence. They became communal, a sacrifice meaning more than momentary sex. Anders selected a close-up of some giant tits cupped by a woman's hands and offered to the camera. He went into the head to jerk off. As momentarily satiated as a young man can be he was back on his father's boat, looking for holes and mending a stinking net. "I'm not going to fish," he said again. He rehearsed the words. In his head the words were useless. But he was alone.

Anders heard the big ocean tug pass. He had been thinking about how he would break the news to his father and to his family. He needed to talk to his roommate Tommy first and ask his opinion. Tommy was good at advice although he rarely gave it. Maybe that's what made his advice worth listening to. He didn't want to tell his other housemate. Anders looked at the passing tug and Karl stood next to the giant tow winch, arms crossed, and staring at Anders from a hundred yards away. It was unnerving, another omen. Anders didn't wave but went back to work.

Fifteen minutes later his housemate stood on the dock. Karl went without sleeves even though it was a cool day. He wore a hickory shirt, the blue and white striped shirt with a zippered neck popular with loggers and fishermen. The sleeves were cut off high on the arm and it looked like the alteration was made with a hatchet or a knife. Sweat pants with 'Dutch Harbor' printed down the left leg ran tucked into a pair of well-worn Xtratuf rubber boots. He was a short muscular man with a shaved head and tattoos covering both arms. Karl was 100% boat. He looked like a killer.

"Permission to come aboard," Karl said more than asked and then passed a half rack of beer in cans over the rail. Karl was a student of history, well read on everything maritime and a stickler for etiquette.

"Welcome home," Anders replied as Karl climbed over the rail. Karl walked into the galley and dug through the canvas bag holding the plastic sewing needles until he found one with his runes carved into it. The Saratoga was his last fishing boat and it still bore his mark— fancy lashing on the handrails of the inside ladders and a coffee grinder. He loaded the needle with twine and then stretched some net away from Anders looking for holes. The two men worked in silence accompanied only by the soft hum from the exhaust stack, occasionally sipping beers. Below deck, the main engine— an 8V71 Detroit ran with the PTO engaged.

"You get everything?" Karl asked.

"I think so," Anders said without enough confidence.

Karl looked at the pile of net and could see that Anders was barely started. "We might as well roll it back and start again." He went to the hydraulic controls mounted on the bulkhead and fed the net through the power block while Anders struggled to do three men's jobs stacking leads, corks and net. They began again and progressed from bitter end to sack, mending as much as they could reach before running a few more feet through the power block hanging from the boom overhead. Karl could sew in any direction but Anders could only tie his knots right side up. Karl made quick movements to his belt and unsheathed the Victorinox knife, the small, serrated plastic handled ubiquitous fishing knife known as a Vicky. He pulled a flap of net towards him that had been stretched out of shape. The knots disappeared, pop, pop, pop as he ran his knife through them. He threw the piece on the wooden deck and started sewing a patch. He tied quickly, professionally, measuring each knot against one of three tattooed marks on his left hand before pulling them iron tight. Karl had made the hash marks himself with a piece of wire and the ink from a ballpoint pen. They were modifications made at sea to increase efficiency and production. The other two marks measured the smaller holes of the herring and squid seines. Soon the hole was mended.

6.

Tommy got off the Viaduct at Western and drove 15th back to Ballard. The bridge lights flashed and Tommy pulled the truck out of gear and let it coast to a stop as the gates came down. He reached up for his radio and keyed the mic. "34. I'm caught by the bridge."

"Roger 34." The dispatcher paused for a moment and then came back, "You'll be done Tommy. Get fuel."

Tommy set his brake and then climbed down from the truck. When it wasn't raining, drivers waiting for the bridge got out of their cars and talked or went to the rail and watched the boats cross under. It only happened on the Ballard bridge and sometimes on the First Avenue bridge over the Duwamish— in the neighborhoods that were more invested in marine traffic. In a cold city it was a moment of solidarity. Tommy crossed the southbound lanes and looked down into Fishermen's Terminal. He looked down on the fleet. He looked at his past. Tommy was a fisherman, past tense. He had been a fisherman and probably still would have been one had life been different. He had been good at it. But he left the boats in an attempt to save his marriage. It didn't work. He had left fishing slowly. Moving from three seasons to two— at first only driving fuel trucks in the winter and still heading north in the summer for the herring and salmon seasons. When his marriage turned terminal, he started driving for Halibut Flats full time. He had been driving mixer trucks for six years.

He loved looking at the boats. His eyes followed the docks and he tried to remember the names of skippers and crews. It got more difficult with time. He looked at the Nadine over on dock six— his boss' new toy.

And then he saw his roommates working on the back deck of the Saratoga. They were net mending, sewing. Tommy didn't yell or wave his arms. He watched and was suddenly tired of a strike that had not yet begun.

"You're not supposed to idle on the bridge," the lady said.

Tommy turned. A concerned citizen, a true Seattleite. Tommy raised himself to his full height. At 6'2 he was too tall to be an engineer. Engine rooms were for trolls. Tommy thought as he removed his earplugs. It was his genius— he didn't spout words. He was the best steward in the city.

"That's true," he said nodding at the lady. Giving her a victory. "But that's a concrete mixer and they can't be shut off. The drum agitates the concrete and keeps it from hardening. It really just slows down the process. Eventually the concrete will become solid. Do you want to see how it works?" Tommy walked towards the truck waving the lady with him, not giving her a choice. He gave a quick tour explaining how the drum and fins worked, the chutes and water and air tanks. At the rear of the truck he coaxed the woman to push the control lever all the way forward to feel the machine work. The truck started to buck. Her eyes grew child wide. "Pretty cool huh?" Tommy said. "Now pull it back until the drum stops. Good. Now just a little forward to keep it moving. Alright. You could be a Teamster."

The lady smiled. "My husband is a civil engineer and he says you guys are going on strike."

"Well, your husband knows more about it than me." He stood next to the Local 174 sticker on the chute cover as he talked. "Halibut Flats is a good company. It's been in the neighborhood for a hundred years. No one wants to strike. We like working. It's really about the strike language— about our ability to honor other workers' picket lines without being fired. It's about honor and respect." He watched her digest his words. Maybe she would tell her family or someone in her neighborhood. Maybe she didn't understand at all and would tell no one.

"It's loud," she said.

Tommy laughed. "True."

When Tommy got back to the house from work he found a note on the kitchen table. "F/V Saratoga— bring dinner" written in Karl's pen. Christ, Tommy thought, like I don't know she's a fishing vessel and would go looking for an aircraft carrier. Tommy drove north on 15th to Ivar's and picked up three orders of cod and chips. Dinner secured, he crossed the Ballard bridge towards Fishermen's Terminal.

Tommy walked up the dock with the large paper sack of greasy food. He was somewhat of a health nut and proud that his body ran from nipple to knee in one almost unbroken plane but he had a weakness for fish and chips and it was a tradition. Karl spotted him. "Oi, now there's a man. The Nice Guy takes care of his fellow crewmates." Tommy smiled at the compliment and the dig. Hazing Anders was a team sport. The older men had spent years making Anders tougher, smarter, more confident. They were proud of their protégé but still jabbed him to keep the softness at bay.

Tommy handed the food to Anders and then swung over the rail. It was Anders's boat yet the other two men supplied the food and drink, in addition to their labor. It embarrassed Anders and he swallowed the words 'I'm not going to fish' deeper in his stomach.

"How much more?" Tommy asked as he climbed the rail.

"We're almost done," Karl said. "But his old man wants this net stored and the squid net brought on board."

"No shit? And he wanted you to do that all by yourself?" Tommy asked Anders.

"I don't think there was thought behind it. He just told me to get it done."

"Bullshit," Tommy said. "There's always thought behind it. He knew you'd get us to help. Me, at least." Tommy switched effortlessly to the fact finder, the steward. Tall and thin, Tommy had the look of a farm hand, someone from Kittitas or the Palouse. His slow movements belied the efficiency of his actions. He hated wasted, meaningless work. But most importantly he didn't rile. Be it bad weather or bad bosses Tommy's crewmates and union brothers knew they could depend on his sober judgment. The worse the conditions the calmer Tommy became.

They ate their cod and french fries sitting on the rail of the back deck and sipped beers before they finished mending the net. The squid net was staged for the swap on a large wooden pallet near the edge of the west wall. The west wall of Fishermen's Terminal was an open workspace that enabled work boats to get close to trucks or cranes for refitting and repairs. The Saratoga needed her squid seine put in the fish hold and the salmon seine taken off the deck and put onto a pallet for storage in the city-owned net sheds.

Karl climbed over the stern and started the smaller 671 diesel that powered the skiff. It was similar to the main engine. The genset, or electrical plant, was also a 71 series Detroit, a 471. They were two-stroke diesels with blowers displacing 71 inches per cylinder. The 471 had four cylinders as the 671 had six. The main was an 8V71 with eight cylinders in a V configuration. It was a brilliant engine, sharing components across the models. Pistons were interchangeable and heads came in two sizes. A 16V used 4 four-cylinder heads and a 12V used two sixes. Modern engines were more efficient but more difficult to maintain and almost impossible to fix at sea. An initial puff of blue smoke from the engine changed to white and then gray. After warming the skiff for a couple of minutes Karl untied and backed away. He rafted the small boat off the stern of the Pillar Bay in the next slip.

He then walked back up the dock. "All right let's do it," Karl said to Anders. Tommy sat forward on the rail next to the bow line. Anders moved towards the stern. "What are you doing?" Karl asked. Anders stopped.

"You're driving shitbag. Get up there." Karl pointed at the wheelhouse and Anders did as he was told and climbed the outside ladder.

Tommy smiled at Karl and said, "it's like he doesn't want to be skipper." Karl just shook his head.

Anders sat in the captain's chair and slid the wheelhouse side window open. He looked out at the two men.

"Let go stern. Let go bow," he said quickly and quietly.

"Stern away!" Karl shouted back.

"Bow away!" Tommy howled.

Anders slid the reduction gear into reverse and the boat created gentle turbulence along its sides. The two older men made the lines ready for docking on the west wall. The Saratoga steered with a small rudder joystick on a pedestal to the left of the captain's chair. Two buttons on either side of the stick moved the rudder by single degrees left and right. The crew steered by push-button when traveling or fishing. The joystick was only for the quick rudder movements of docking. The boat had a traditional wooden wheel in the center of the bridge as a backup but none of the crew could remember ever needing to use it. The throttle and reduction gear were controlled by a lever. Seiners were single engine, single wheel boats which meant you needed a small amount of skill to land them unlike twin screw boats that could tank turn by running propellers in opposite directions.

Anders sat in the chair that was his bloodright— the skipper's chair. It was comfortable. It would be easier to succeed than to choose otherwise. He knew Tommy and Karl never faced such choices. Both their fathers were dead, leaving them nothing but a name. Anders' blood tasted of salt. He had generations of fishermen behind him. His great grandfather had immigrated from Northern Norway and was one of the pioneers of the modern Northwest fishing fleet. His family had been fishermen, Lofotens fishermen, for generations before that. As long as anyone's memory.

Anders adjusted course to the left and throttled down. He piloted the boat close to the wall and Karl jumped from the rail midships to a ladder attached to one of the pilings. It was a move that would get a greenhorn killed or fired. Most fishery injuries happen between the dock and deck. But Karl was not a greenhorn. He caught the bow line from Tommy and took a bite on the cleat. Anders put the rudder hard over and walked the stern in, positioning the boat so the nets could be fed through the power block— the squid net from pallet to hold and the salmon net from deck to pallet. Karl secured the stern line.

"You're not a bad boat driver," Tommy said.

Why would he say that? Anders wondered. Did he know? Was it obvious?

"Yeah, no more..." Karl threw his body back and forth, back and forth in a pantomime of overzealous shifting. The two older men laughed.

Tommy removed the stainless hatch bolts and recoated the threads with anti-seize to protect them from the corrosive and galling effects of salt water. Karl attached a two-way picking sling and pulled the hatch off the hold with a winch on the main boom and then lowered the hatch onto the salmon net. They then fed the squid net through the power block and into the hold. Karl used poly straps to gather the net every twenty feet. It would keep the net from tangling around pillars and bin boards if the hold was tanked down in rough weather. Transforming the net into a giant sausage was a lesson learned from earlier voyages south, something that would save the squid crew hours and hours of repair work.

They had all made previous trips south for squid and under the low gray Seattle skies they talked fondly of the flip-flop life that awaited Anders, an idyllic vision of fresh fish tacos and Mexican girls with dark eyes and shiny black hair. They recalled the lights of the oil platforms Gilda and Grace at night as they left Ventura Harbor for the Channel

Islands. Karl reminded Anders how important it was for the slow moving fishing boats to watch the radar and listen to the radio when crossing the north-south shipping lanes. Container ships cruised those highways at twenty knots.

As they stored the salmon seine on the pallet Tommy sprinkled Borax soap between layers of net to guard against rot during the six-month storage. Anders wanted to talk about not going south but he couldn't, not while they worked on the boat. He wasn't afraid that his roommates would walk away leaving him shorthanded. It was a matter of taste, of respect. It seemed the wrong place for such a subject. Like a priest admitting his doubt on the altar— better to save it for the garden. Especially wrong around such a crew. If they sailed together they would have all demanded more than the usual top of ten percent. They could navigate, weld, wrench, sew and cook. In years past, when canneries would still back loans for new boats and permits, they would have all been skippers. But it was a different world.

Work done, nets transferred they secured the boat again in its slip and reattached their skiff to the proper stern.

7.

The three men sat into the night on the front porch sheltered from the fine mist blowing from the north sipping beers and passing a pellet gun between them to shoot at rats. Between shots and sips Anders worked up the courage to admit he was no longer going to fish. Although he was the only remaining commercial fisherman of the three it was what united them. It was how they had met.

At thirty-eight, Karl was the oldest and he had fished since he was sixteen and had only moved to tow boats in his early thirties. Karl was by far the most experienced and able crewman. He had fished Bristol Bay salmon, South-East Alaska salmon and herring, crabbed in the Bering and long-lined cod and halibut through the Gulf, along with squid in Southern California and tuna in the south Pacific. He had crewed on coastal tramps out of Ballard and now worked on towboats making the same Alaska supply run.

Tommy had started fishing at eighteen. He was not as ambitious as Karl and only fished spring, summer and fall fisheries. But he had a real talent for boats and was by nature ambivalent to discomfort. Always an engineer, it was an even money bet if more of his fishing career was spent below deck than on it. Tommy was forced to shore by love or a forgotten condom. He left the boats six years before to stay in the neighborhood. Since then he had been a construction Teamster.

But Anders was born into it. He was a fourth-generation Alaskan fisherman. His father and grandfather were retired skippers and his family owned three boats. So, the other two were surprised when Anders finally said, "I don't want to go fishing. I don't want to do squid this year." The other two men just looked at the boy. "I want to try something else before it's too late and there are always enough guys looking for squid slots." Still no reaction from his housemates.

Karl and Tommy looked out into the mist. Karl opened another beer. He had always suspected Anders of being a coward. Karl had never, until now, witnessed the cowardice but it was something in the Anders' eyes. When things were bad, weather was rough or a decision was to be made. Something in Anders' eyes hesitated. When Anders was still a boy Don Brekke, Anders' father, had asked Karl to look after the boy because, "he's got too much of his mother, and worse, his grandmother onboard. There's cowards' blood on that side". Karl still didn't know exactly what that meant but the conclusion was proving itself and it angered Karl. It was desertion. He thought about throwing Anders out of the house.

Tommy drained the last of the Rainier from the can and threw it at the recycling bin using the crane yard fence as a backboard. He pulled another from the cardboard twelve pack between the two older men and opened another can. He took and long pull and was deep in thought. Karl and Anders both looked at him. "Have you told your father?" he asked. Tommy wanted the facts.

"No," Anders said quietly. "I thought I'd tell you guys first."

Karl grew angrier. "Who's the girl?" Karl asked. "Someone suck your dick and now you want to wash dishes for the rest of your life?" Karl wanted the reasons.

"No!" Anders said too quickly. "There's no one. Well, there's a waitress but she hasn't blown me."

"What's her name?" Karl demanded.

"It's no one. That's not the point. I want to try something else. I just don't want to fish." Anders wanted the two other men to understand but couldn't think of a reason that would satisfy them. Tommy handed him another beer.

They sat in silence for a long time. No longer even shooting at the occasional rats that crossed their fields of fire. Through the gray misting night a work boat sounded one long horn blast followed by one short asking the bridge to open. It received four short blasts in reply from the bridge operator, the signal for hold tight. Tommy and Anders looked at Karl and Karl checked his watch before announcing that the boat was, 'not one of ours.'

Anders had made the classic mistake of youth. He had wished that it would be easy. The boy had yet to learn that easy might save your life but it killed your soul. Tommy found it difficult to concentrate on a young man's freedom. He had more important things to worry about. Karl had the orphan's anger at watching someone given an opportunity because of family and then failing at unwrapping the gift. Everything Karl owned was earned with his brain and his muscle, and often his blood. Karl had the gift of naming. He had given Tommy the forename— Nice Guy. Now the word "squander" came to his mind.

Tommy was tired and he didn't need this newest development upsetting his happy home life. At least he didn't have to wake up early in the morning. The next day he wouldn't be in a truck. Tommy was on the negotiating committee and tomorrow was more bargaining at the Teamster Hall. He hoped the owners would cave on the language issue.

They had two days left on the contract and after that loomed the possibility of a strike. But negotiations were not progressing well and for the first time in seven contracts or more than twenty years it looked as if they might actually go out on strike. As steward all this weighed on Tommy. He needed sleep. He slept six hours in perfect conditions but he knew that night he would be lucky to get four. He could fall asleep soundly and fast but it never lasted. Dreams and worry conspired to wake him a few hours later. It was eleven when he left the porch.

Karl and Anders remained.

"You want to be a cook?" Karl asked as an insult. Karl didn't understand. The usual answer for feelings of preseason dread were quick trips to Amsterdam or Costa Rica for booze and hookers. Not to quit fishing. "Anders the squanderer!" Karl announced to the Ballard night.

Anders remained silent. He had wanted to talk to Tommy not Karl. He thought he knew how Karl viewed the world and he was tired of it. Life didn't have to be constantly tough, violent and dangerous. It could be better. Anders finally got up without saying anything and disappeared inside. He reappeared wearing a jacket and donning his helmet. Anders kicked his little motorcycle to life. It was a 1974 Yamaha DT 125 that Anders had bought for fifty bucks. They all called the machine Ring Ding Ding, an obvious onomatopoeia. A blue cloud joined the swirling Ballard mist as the boy rode away, headlight turned off to the conserve battery.

The noise had caused Tommy's head to poke from the doorway. "Why does he ride that thing at night?" he asked

"To live dangerously I guess," Karl said flatly.

"It's not smart."

"He's not smart."

Karl was left alone on the porch of the house he owned. He stared across the street at the long low warehouse. He could smell salt water or maybe it was just the neighborhood. Occasionally a rat would scurry from one pile of net to another looking for sea snacks on the dirty repairable mesh. Karl had bought the house six years earlier for seventy-nine thousand dollars cash. It was his crew share from a successful king and opilio crab season. He'd bought it off another crew member. It was a deal grown from an idle comment as the men pulled loaded pots from the floor of the Bering Sea. Karl hadn't even meant the offer in earnest. He merely said, "my share for your house," when they started to get into the crab, to make money. "No shit?" the other man asked. Karl looked around at the waves and replied, "no shit." As the loaded pots broke the surface of the cold water the men knew it was going to be a good year. They were going to become blue-collar rich. And Karl's offer got better with each pot. To the former owner it was a thought that couldn't be escaped or ignored. On a boat, there is nowhere safe from an idea. Thoughts come onboard across the wind or through the radio but once they are aboard they don't depart until the boat is once again tied to the dock. Thoughts can fly in but can only walk off. If you suspect your wife or girlfriend is fucking around— you either have to make peace with that idea or jump overboard because you won't forget it and it won't give you a moment's peace. And to the house's former owner every crab that went into the hold became two, and in his mind, he began spending that money. Indeed, by the end of the season he viewed himself as better than his crewmates because he was making skipper share, twice the deckhand wage. Karl never knew what his crewmate did with the money. The next season he showed up the same man, without a house. It probably went up his nose but with crabbers that was to be expected. And in the end, three months of Karl's life for a house seemed like a pretty good deal.

Karl finally went inside and sat on the couch. The first night back blues were setting in. His roommates were busy with their lives and no woman was waiting. The walls of their little living room were adorned with ship paintings from yard sales and junk stores. There were aesthetic rules that had to be followed. The painting had to be oil and it couldn't be kitsch. No yachts were allowed, only working boats. It was a decorative style borrowed from a bar. Karl got up to examine a painting. It was of the power scow Deer Harbor passing in front of Mount Edgecumbe leaving the port of Sitka. He had bought it in a second-hand store in Juneau on a work trip. He knew the boat and had dinner several times in the galley with the crew while waiting for salmon openers. The power scows were built for supplying Alaska during World War Two and many were still working as tenders. Karl was impressed by how comfortable the Deer Harbor was inside.

"What do you think?" Karl asked Tommy as the steward returned from the bathroom.

"It's a mistake but what can you do? He wants to be his own person, someone other than just his father's son. And, he's at the age when the city seems to be the center of the world. He looks around and sees beautiful women and every night there is something happening that doesn't include him. He wants to be part of it. I wish I had never left fishing but I made a decision and no one could have convinced me otherwise."

"Should I have tried?"

"It wouldn't have worked. Might have made things worse. Anders has never seen any other way of living and he needs to reach the right conclusion for himself. We know the right answer but he has to find it on his own," Tommy said and went into the kitchen.

Karl moved to the bookshelf looking for something to read, something to distract. Boats created readers. You could either work or read. They had a lot of books— page turners, biographies, history, literature. The bookshelf was full and there were overflow piles of books in each room. Boats birthed fo'c'sle philosophers, men with the arrogance to read good books and decide for themselves. No working man reads Hegel, Kant or Wittgenstein. But boys and young men read Nietzsche, Rand, Camus and Lao Tzu. They read Jack London and Charles Bukowski. All commercial fishermen should be able to quote from *Moby Dick* and *The Sea Wolf*. Tonight, Karl wanted something not tasting of salt. He pulled out *The Centurions* by Jean Lartéguy, long out of print and hated for being sexual, violent, colonial and anti-communist. The paperback was worth a hundred bucks on the used market but Karl's copy was for reading and for pressing into other people's hands. It was the story of French paratroopers from the fall of Dien Bien Phu to the war in Algeria. It was Karl's favorite book and he had read it a dozen times, underlining meaningful passages. He flipped through the pages looking for some wisdom. He thumbed to the back where the rebel leader has been caught in the city. 'I've made two mistakes, gentlemen. I've confided in a woman and I've slept in a bed.' Karl closed the book and put it back on the shelf.

In the breakfast nook, written on a yellow legal pad next to the phone was a record of all incoming calls. It was written in the style of a boat's log. Karl looked through it hoping for a name that he knew would not be there. There were a couple calls from exes. Tammy Peters called at 2200 on 13OCT. That one was obvious enough. Carol Sanderson called at 0945 on 15OCT. She was a nurse who worked nights. Karl heard she was getting married. Odd. But no Lily.

He sat on the couch and wondered where Lily was. Karl's thoughts always went back to her. She was the one that he couldn't have, the one that got away.

Karl met Lily in 1989 at the Buckaroo Tavern over in Fremont. It was between the crab and herring seasons, before the Brekke boats began making the trip south for squid in the winter. Karl was enjoying his shore time and often rode over to Fremont to patronize the Buck and talk motorcycles. One night he was coming out of the bathroom and was stopped by a tall full-figured woman with a Betty Page haircut. She was wearing a dress which was very unusual in that time of flannel fashion. She blocked the narrow hallway that led to the bathrooms and pay phone. She kissed him full on the lips and then said, "we should be together."

Karl thought this woman was either crazy or strong. Karl bet on strong and said, "ok."

"No," she said. "Not tonight. I mean for real, as a team."

Karl said ok again and reached out and grabbed her hand. They were together as a team for a little more than a year. Within two weeks Karl had moved out of the room he rented in Ballard and moved in with Lily. She lived above a fish market in the University District. Her apartment was above the market's neon salmon sign. Karl thought it an auspicious omen, something he could navigate by.

When Lily kissed Karl she didn't know that he fished. And when she learned that he fished she didn't know what that meant. She learned that his career paid well and then she learned what it cost. The first three months were tough. The second three months were painful. She pulled the plug after the third three months. Lily's father was a firefighter. He had died in a fire. She watched her mother slowly die over the next year from heartbreak and booze. Lily knew that life could end suddenly but that love separated was worse than death. She couldn't handle Karl being gone for more than a year. That was her limit. She didn't want to practice at being her mother. Lily gave Karl an ultimatum. It was boats or her. Karl read it wrong. He thought she wanted freedom. He thought she'd be back. They became chess pieces floating through the Seattle night, known by everyone. Everyone had an opinion of them, either by themselves or against each other.

She had one small tattoo when they started dating. Karl had let her know that he didn't think women should be tattooed. He thought only working-class men should have tattoos and they should relate to strenuous professions— pictures of boats, military symbols, etc. When Karl returned from his first trip away she had an anchor tattooed on her thigh. By the time he returned from his third trip she had gone to his tattooist and gotten the exact three master Karl had across his chest. On her ample chest the boat rolled and flowed. The banner under Karl's boat read, "ANY PORT IN A STORM". Lily had improved her banner. It read, "I AM YOUR PORT".

Tommy made an herbal tea hoping it would help him sleep. Odin pushed through the window and dropped to the floor. "The terrible one," Tommy addressed the beast. The one-eyed cat sat on his haunches and looked up at Tommy slowly blinking, the eyelid over the milky eye opening and closing a little slower than the other. Odin stretched, his right paw reached out, long white claws extended. Tommy took a step back. His pajamas were no armor against the All Father. "Put those away," he said.

Karl took a long hot shower, his first non-boat shower in three weeks. The first night back sadness growing deeper. It was a feeling of purposelessness instead of freedom. He dried the mirror and then shaved his beard and what hair still grew on his skull. He looked in the mirror. He was the tattooed sailor. He looked down at his hands gripping the porcelain sink. Anchors weighed the top of each hand. 'AMOR FATI' ran across the fingers.

From the anchors on his hands ran golden yellow lines, ropes to landsmen. They wrapped around his wrists. It was the traditional symbol for a deckhand. The line continued up his arm through the illustrated gear and fish and then circled his neck before running back down the other arm. His left elbow was wrapped in a seine where a biker or convict's spider web might have been. That arm had a sockeye salmon, a halibut, true and black cod and a small school of herring. Mustad hooks and longline crossed through the scene. The right arm had different species of crab and pots with buoys and coils of line. Across his chest sailed the doppelgänger of Lily's tattoo.

His left foot had a rooster tattooed on it, the right a pig. These barnyard animals were supposed to protect sailors by running back to dry land if ever plunged into the sea. And maybe these talismans did work. Karl had been dunked and survived. He pushed the skin around on his stomach. There was no fat but the skin seemed to be detaching from the muscle. His aging depressed him. The opportunity to die well, to die in a fight was fading— not a bar fight but a fight with the sea, with society, or with the gods.

Karl put on a clean pair of sweatpants and lay on the couch. He flicked through the channels on the TV but was disappointed at the quality of choice. Finally, he found an hour-long documentary about the French Foreign Legion on the Military Channel. Although never drawn by the idea of fighting for the American army which he considered a tool of the ruling classes, Karl was intrigued by the idea of fighting for the legion. Legionnaires did not swear allegiance to France but to the Legion. Their motto was 'Legio Patria Nostra'— The Legion is Our Homeland. All this sounded interesting to Karl. He could see swearing loyalty to a group, a tribe, or a gang but never something as large as a country. And then an officer said, 'When you come through the gates you leave your politics, your religion outside. Here the mission is sacred." After fulfilling a five-year contract, the legionnaire was rewarded with French citizenship and benefits. He could grow old fishing the Mediterranean. Karl wondered if he was too old and he fell asleep to dreams of Africa.

8.

Anders rode the old two-stroke motorcycle through the mist towards the bar only turning on the headlight at intersections. The magneto was bad and the bike lived off the battery. He could ride it three or four times between charges. When he turned on the lights the ignition failed and he lost power. So, he played a power management game. He felt he had made a break with his roommates and that wasn't his intention.

Anders had been cooking at the Hat since returning early for his Grandmother's funeral from the summer salmon season. He had worked the prep side of the line for two months and then ran the grill and hot side. It surprised him when the head cook, Sara, called him down to her basement office. She was a lesbian with limited social skills and she asked his intentions like she was a parent and he was dating the restaurant with the possibility of giving it a social disease. "We need another cook and if you plan on staying around I was thinking of giving you the position. It will be more responsibility. You'll have to think- not just do what you are told. You'll run the shift, be the boss. You'll have to call in the next day's orders and stay on top of inventory. But if you're planning on fucking off to Alaska in a couple of weeks I'll hire someone else." That was a week ago and truthfully, Anders had been looking for a reason not to be on the boat. "You can have Monday and Tuesday nights. You'll still prep Thursday through Saturday," she said. After that he studied the menu and preparations for each dish. He switched places with the cooks for an hour or two each night to gain experience under their eye and advice.

The Hat was busy when Anders parked his bike at the edge of a no parking zone in front of the bar. He grabbed a beer from the bar and retreated to the kitchen to avoid the crowd. He stood back by the dishwasher and talked with the kitchen staff. The atmosphere of a working kitchen soothed Anders. He drank a couple beers while talking shop with the cook. Finally, the clock made it to midnight and the last orders came in. The kitchen staff started their cleaning duties and Anders migrated out to the bar. If Anders remained he would have had to grab a mop. He took a stool next to where the waitresses brought in their orders for the bartender. It protected him from the customers on one side and he could chat with the waitresses.

"Why the fishing boots?" Amanda asked.

Anders looked at his own feet. His Xtratufs were rolled down but still on his feet. He hadn't noticed. That was a bad sign. He needed to get away from fishing. Anders tucked his feet under the bar stool.

"I was working on the boat today and forgot to take them off."

Amanda put her hand on his forearm and leaned in close. She sniffed him. "You don't smell like fish," Amanda said and then went back to her work. She was smart. She knew the power of touch, of the warmth of a woman's skin in a cold climate. Anders didn't realize that every half hour she would touch him, lay her hand on his forearm or brush against him in passing. Just enough touch to rekindle the little fire that smoldered up and down his spine.

Amanda worked the back room and she finished her night closing tabs, doing side work as she talked with Anders. All Amanda's movements had purpose. She didn't waste effort and she didn't hesitate. Anders had been like that on the boat and he hoped that someday he could be like that in the kitchen. He knew that day would come, with time. Amanda was older, in her thirties, she was a professional working at a couple of different restaurants in the city. And she was thin, smoker thin without the cigarettes. She had long, muscular arms that could weave dishes off and on tables without disruption. Her loyalties were to the customer because she lived off tips. Anders thought she special ordered too much but in truth she was competent and didn't tolerate the opposite. He was a little afraid of her.

"Don't get weird about last night," she said.

"Of course," he said. Anders didn't know what to think so he thought about the words 'of course'. A course was a line on a chart that the boat followed. Was 'of course' somewhere on that line? Was getting fucked by a waitress somewhere on a chart? Possibly it was the Seymour Narrows where tides trumped will. It was a place where a boat could run full throttle for hours and not make a foot of progress until the tide changed and sucked the boats through. But even worse approaching the narrows at a full following tide where the current ran faster than the boat rendering rudder and engine little more than good intentions. Amanda might be that following tide. For a moment Anders doubted the wisdom of leaving fishing, where even the unknowns were known. Seasons, charts, weather and luck. Here was a different system, a system without charts. Anyway, what was 'weird'?

Amanda took off her half apron and poured herself a glass of red wine, her shift drink. She stood next to Anders and massaged the back of her neck underneath her shoulder-length brown hair. It made her short bangs rise and fall.

"So, are you ready?" she asked.

"For what?"

"You'll do fine Anders."

Why did she talk that way, cryptic? It was bizarre and he couldn't tell if it was meant to be insulting or mysterious. She was only a few years older than him. Then he realized it was positional. She was a professional and he was an apprentice, an amateur. All his work experience ended at the kitchen door. He wanted to claim years at sea and a skipper's name but he had left that on the porch just an hour earlier. It was a new life and for the first time in his life, he had chosen it.

"I'd appreciate any advice or pointers. If you see me doing something stupid— please tell me," Anders said.

She laughed and shook her head. He knew that Amanda's new attention was work related. Who cares what a dishwasher or prep cook thinks? But the cook, that could make a difference in Amanda's life, a difference in her wallet. She was smart to try and win Anders's affection and it wasn't difficult.

A group of young neighborhood punk rockers came in and rounded the corner into the bar. Anders recognized a couple of them from high school. "She looks a little young," Amanda said pointing to a girl that couldn't have been more than five foot two. The girl had tattoos covering both arms and hair dyed copper orange and black. Instantly Anders dismissed her as a fake, as a pretender. Anders thought only working-class men should have tattoos. It was Karl's thought in Anders's head. Anders had yet to realize how much of his vision was through someone else's glasses.

The waitress left and Anders asked the bartender for five dollars worth of pull tabs to gauge his luck. He won two dollars and Amy handed him a Jefferson, negating a tip. His effort at reading the tea leaves was a failure.

Amanda returned from the back room and again stood next to Anders. Without saying anything she put her arm around his waist and bounced her hip against his. She seemed to be measuring. All the air disappeared from his lungs and Anders struggled, suffocating. Was that weird? What was weird? Things were so simple on the boat.

"Are you leaving?" Amanda asked.

"I don't think so," Anders choked.

"Good, then I'll see you in a bit. I'm going downstairs." And then she released him and walked off towards the door to the basement.

A bead of sweat ran from Anders's armpit. He reached over and patted it into his shirt. Could she have wanted him to follow her downstairs? Possibly, but no. Anders knew he was being manipulated. If they were bargaining he had to keep his price high. Anders ordered another can of beer and Amy brought it over to him slowly shaking her head.

"Be careful," she said.

"Of what?" Anders asked.

"Of whom," Amy corrected.

"Cops," someone said and Anders turned towards the door.

Bruce came through the door. He was the neighborhood cop whose beat was to walk up and down Ballard Avenue past the many bars keeping order.

Anders got off his stool and rounded the corner of the dividing half-wall. "Someone rob a bank?" Anders asked, beer can against his chest and blocking the way.

"No, just making the rounds," Bruce said. He was the good cop, not looking too hard but always near. He liked to talk and would even carry on long conversations with homeless drunks.

Around the dividing wall that separated the restaurant from the bar proper, unseen by Anders or Bruce the cop, the young girl with orange and black hair casually got up from her table and walked towards the wait station at the end of the bar. Amy could only think of the coming fine. She didn't want to explain it to the owners. And then the young punk turned into the wait station and pulled a full tray of dirty glasses from the rack and walked off towards the kitchen. Amy smiled. Anders was still blocking the way. "Working!" the young woman said with the practiced passive-aggressive tone of a professional and he automatically moved forward to let her pass. Anders took a long drink from his can of beer to hide his smile. Bruce may have noticed.

"Your roommate really going to take those guys out on strike?" Bruce asked.

"Tommy thinks the odds are good," Anders answered refocusing on his immediate task of protecting his workplace.

"I remember the last strike. '79. They lost their asses. But times are different. I wish 'em luck although officially I'm neutral and want no problems. But I am a guild member… So."

Anders looked down at his beer thinking of the labor history he had learned from his roommates. Seattle was a union town. It was heavily influenced by the large Scandinavian population, Anders' people. The labor hero Joe Hill was really Joe Hillstrom or Joel Hagglund. And Seattle had a fighting history since the Wobblies and the general strike of 1919. They even wandered off into radical paths enough to cause the liberal FDR administration to refer to the country as "forty-seven states and the Soviet of Washington."

"Do you mind," Bruce said and gently moved Anders to the side. Bruce rounded the corner and looked into the bar. He waved at Amy and she smiled. His work done Bruce turned and took the police presence further down the street.

Anders went to the kitchen. Inside the young girl was standing next to the running Hobart machine. "You know how that thing works?" he asked.

"Of course," she said. "Sorry about that," she pointed out towards the bar. "I had to do something."

"I thought it was brilliant." He stood not sure what to say. "Dish dog, eh?"

"I am. It's the only honest position in a restaurant."

"Oh yeah? What about cooks?"

"Cooks want to be chefs or managers."

"Don't dishwashers want to be prep cooks?"

"Not all of them. Not the smart ones."

And even though he had no management status and wasn't even really a cook, yet, Anders asked, "You want a job?"

"Maybe," she said and opened the door to the machine, its cycle done. "Where do these go?" she asked.

"Just leave it," Anders said as he dug through a pile of menus and receipts looking for an application. He found one. "Here fill this out." Anders put the paper on the counter and pulled a pen from his pocket. In the remarks section on the back page he wrote, 'Recommended by Amy and Anders.'

Amanda had returned to the bar and Anders leaned in next to her. "I thought you left," she said with a smile.

"Just taking care of some kitchen business. You know," he said.

Amanda noticed the young girl come out of the kitchen and turned toward Anders unsure that he was as foolish as he acted. "Who is that?" she asked.

"Our new dishwasher," he said staring ahead at the bins of pull-tabs.

"You can walk me home," she said.

"I have my motorcycle."

"You'll figure it out." They walked three blocks towards the bridge. Amanda lived in an apartment above a machine shop.

"You have a girlfriend Anders?" she asked.

"No. I was always fishing, and young girls don't like waiting."

"No, I suppose they don't."

They continued walking. Outside her door Anders again said he would be thankful for any pointers in the kitchen.

"Oh, I'm sure there are a lot of things I could teach you," Amanda said with a smile and then she let herself in the door and disappeared.

Anders walked back to the bar and kicked Ring Ding Ding to life with a cloud of blue smoke. He rode home through the mist smiling to himself under his helmet, sure that he had made the right decision. He let himself into the house quietly not wanting to disturb Tommy. Karl was sleeping on the couch. Sure, Anders thought, the one man with a decent bedroom and he sleeps on the couch. Karl had written 'Aubagne' on a piece of paper next to the remote. Anders thought it might be a name of a boat. He switched off the TV and opened the door to the basement. It wasn't much but you couldn't beat the price— free.

9.

"Nice Guy Tommy," another steward greeted. "How goes life with the little guys?"

Torger Torgersen was known as Tommy or Nice Guy Tommy or NGT but never as Tom, Thomas or Torger. The other steward was referring to Tommy's employer, Halibut Flats Sand and Gravel. It was the smallest shop in the bargaining unit.

"Good, good. Can't complain." Tommy said, locking his pickup's door. "I hope this shit doesn't go sideways."

"What's the bottom line for you guys?"

"Strike language... and a little money but the guys really want their strike language back. You?"

"Same," the other steward said. "We probably want more money but it's the language."

Tommy leaned against the bed of his truck and looked at the gray Seattle sky. The rain couldn't be seen, only felt. He ran his hand through his hair working the rain in. "It doesn't cost them a fucking dime."

The other steward grunted in agreement. "Remember, they have principals too."

"That's what I'm worried about."

They walked into the hall and within a half hour they were back in the parking lot. The owners weren't at the contract meeting. In their place was one HR executive bargaining, or not bargaining, for a united front. The HR man tripped over his own ego. He was a small man who mistook his placeholding for power, like a clerk left in charge of a store. The meeting was insulting because it was a waste of time. All the drivers would have rather been delivering concrete.

"Can you believe he used the word 'quotidian'?" Tommy asked as they returned to their pickups.

"I know," the other steward laughed. "What a douchebag."

Anders made Amanda her shift meal. Unlike the other staff she liked to eat at the end of the night. He wondered how she stayed so skinny. Maybe she didn't go to bed after work. Maybe she did but burned the calories... Anders watched her eat at the prep counter. She bounced from foot to foot like eating was some physical exercise, some pleasurable workout. He was staring at her when she turned and spoke to him.

"You like this," she said. He thought she was talking about herself, but she continued. "You like the kitchen. You like the pressure, the heat, the business. I can tell. You should come work for Jules at Le Canard and learn how to really cook." Anders knew the restaurant. One of the best French places in the city was on a little Ballard side street. He knew Amanda waited there also but doubted she hired kitchen help.

Amanda took another large bite. She held up one finger for Anders to wait. He did. When she had an empty mouth, she continued. "Most cooks are just trained monkeys, pumping out the same meal after meal. Which is good because customers want consistency. But the good ones know when they can make something better without altering its core. You know what I mean?"

"I think so," he said. He studied her. He liked her professionalism. Anders knew her skills would pay more at Le Canard or any other fine restaurant. "Why do you still work here?" he asked.

"Number one— the money is good," she said and reached over for his coffee mug of wine. She took a drink to wash down her meal. "But I like working here. I like the people, the staff and the customers. At a nice restaurant you only serve rich people and that's what it feels like, serving. Here a group of fishermen will include you in their stories, flirt with you and overtip. They are different worlds. I like that rich people appreciate quality or at least they pretend to." She turned to leave but swung around. "As a cook, to make a living you should really be at a nice place. And you should go to culinary school."

"Yeah, one step at a time," Anders said.

"I can introduce you to Jules at Le Canard. They're looking for a new day cook."

Anders was wise enough to recognize opportunity. "I might take you up on that," he said.

Amanda drifted away to finish her side work and Anders finished his duties.

10.

Tommy was on lunch at the precast yard. They had a breakroom in a converted storage container, SEALAND still painted on the side. He struggled with the crossword puzzle. He hated to ask the other drivers for the answers, to admit needing help. But his mind was unable to focus, the contract negotiations buzzed in his brain behind every other thought.

Mike, one of the yard guys, poked his head in the breakroom door. "Hey Tommy, some dude is hassling Phil."

"What?" Tommy asked looking up from the paper confused.

"Yeah," Mike pointed with his chin out into the precast yard. "Looks like a blackberry camper."

"Fucking shit," Tommy said as he stood up and donned his hard hat. He rolled the paper tight like a baton and grabbed his lunchbox. Tommy strode with purpose across the gravel lot towards two men engaged in argument. Phil, the Halibut Flats driver, was obviously on his heels. A second man, dirty and drunk, waved his arms around and yelled at Phil, continuing to close the distance even as Phil back-peddled.

"Hey!" Tommy yelled. Both men turned towards him. Tommy's face was hard and he was closing fast. The intruder in the dust half pivoted to square his feet towards the on-rushing steward. "Get the fuck out of here!" Tommy said evenly, not open to question.

"Why don't you mind your own fucking business!" the man said. It may have been his only move.

Tommy swept his arm, claiming this corner of the neighborhood. "This literally is our business." Tommy recognized the man. He was a camper who lived either in a car or tent in the blackberry bushes outside the fence, depending on the winds of fate and fortune. He was not old but had already turned that corner, the drugs and alcohol boring holes in his brain. Tommy used to see him with a junkie lady but lately he'd seen her with someone new.

Phil found his voice. "He says I called the cops on him. Got his car towed."

Tommy smiled. "Seriously?" He shook his head. "The cops don't need our help to find your camp. Maybe I'll call them right now."

"Maybe I'll make *your* cars disappear," the young man threatened. It was a bold threat.

"Maybe we'll make *you* disappear," Tommy threatened straight-faced.

The junkie knew he was beat. He switched tactics. His threats and overacted craziness were effective on office workers and housewives but not on the hard hat crowd. "Hey, come on. We don't fuck with you. Just leave us alone." He pleaded, it was a weakling's bargain that offered nothing.

"Fuck off," Tommy said as a command and pointed out of the yard. The junkie walked off mumbling. The three workers watched the defeated man leave. Tommy turned to Phil, "You alright?"

"Yeah," Phil said.

Tommy climbed into his idling truck and pushed the brake valve. He let the clutch out on third gear and climbed out of precast. Tommy keyed his radio mic as he pulled into the yard. "Thirty-four is back from lunch. Empty."

"Go ahead and park it and come up and see me," the dispatcher said.

Tommy wondered if it had to do with the bum in precast but was sure he hadn't done anything wrong. He climbed the stairs to dispatch two steps at a time. Inside was the usual hum and chaos of phones ringing, dispatchers bumping into each other and constant changes on the status board. In the corner was the doctor or 'doc', the batchman. He sat in front of a bank of switches and scales and like a cook or baker mixed each load to order with their differences in aggregate size and cement ratio. Halibut Flats was a dry batch plant and it used the trucks for mixing. It was cheaper than a wet mix plant but led to problems with consistency. The batchman was a union operator. He was a spy in management land. The dispatchers could edit what they said to each other but customers demanded answers and the batchman was there to hear half the phone call. Several times he was told that the conversations he heard were confidential and should stay in the plant. Doc agreed, "of course," but all knew he would tell his brothers anything of use.

The head dispatcher, Doug, was talking on the phone and writing an order. He held up one finger for Tommy to wait. Doug hung up the phone and then stepped on a switch mounted on a pedestal just off the floor that controlled his radio to the trucks. He told a truck in the field to go to the second address on his ticket.

"You got to be fucking kidding me!" the radio spit back.

"Language," Doug responded quietly.

Tommy was looking over Doug's shoulder at the ticket. The driver had a legitimate gripe. He was down in Madison Valley and was just told to climb back out. He would have to take a long route up the hill not to spill. Tommy laughed thinking of the driver on the receiving end of such a transmission. Seattle is a city of hills and mixer trucks haul a liquid load in a drum with an open end. Some neighborhoods have only one entrance route that wouldn't cause spillage. Some can only be entered and not exited with a full load. Plenty of streets had to be backed up, keeping the open end of the drum pointed uphill. Doug turned to Tommy, "Harold wants to see you across the street."

"Roger dodger," Tommy said and headed to the main office.

"Hey Cathy," Tommy said to the receptionist. She was in her sixties and had worked for Halibut Flats for decades. She was a bigger lady who could drink with all the boys at the Christmas party. Tommy always surmised that her husband was lucky. "That's a cute sweater. Is it new?" Tommy couldn't resist flirting with older women. Cathy just smiled and shook her head, dismissing his feeble foray.

Tommy sat down and waited. There was a pile of industry magazines and he caught up on the latest ready-mix technologies. He looked at an ad for a front discharge mixer. Tommy never understood why they didn't drive front discharge mixers. All the plants were on the waterfront because they received their aggregate via barge. Everything else, every job was uphill.

Cathy's phone rang. "You can go in Tommy," she said.

"We should get a drink sometime," Tommy said with a wink.

"Thanks Tommy but you should concentrate on work."

"You make it tough."

"Tommy, you're the only one who's made your life tough."

"Damn Cathy. Brutal."

She smiled. Tommy rolled his sleeves up to flaunt the four-inch rule and went into Harold's office.

"What's up boss?"

Harold stayed seated behind his desk. He pointed at a chair with an open hand. "Take a seat Tommy." Tommy followed his direction. "I hear you guys authorized a strike."

Tommy leaned forward. He didn't expect Harold to lead with small talk. "We did. Unanimous."

Harold frowned. "That's not what I heard."

"Close enough," Tommy said with a 'fuck you' smile.

They were both on the negotiating committee. Harold represented his hundred-year-old family business and Tommy represented his workers. Two of the three other companies under the contract were large corporate businesses with professional negotiators, either HR representatives or hired guns, black souled lawyers paid bonuses to take every penny possible off the table and if possible, to break the union. At least Tommy's side of the table had dirty clothes in common.

"Are you guys really going to go out over language?" Harold asked.

"That's up to you."

"Your guys are really willing to lose thousands of dollars and possibly their careers over not having to cross a grocery worker's line?"

"Absolutely," Tommy said.

"When will you be finished with the Nadine?" Harold asked. Tommy had been doing a side job for Harold. His boss had bought an old fishing boat, the F/V Nadine, and wanted it turned into a Puget Sound cruiser. She was a 48' wooden seiner built in 1947 by Olaf Hansen. She was too small to compete anymore. She couldn't pack enough, couldn't fish hard enough. Maybe if salmon was on a quota system like crab, she could take her time to get her share but Salmon was run on derby openings where it was get all you can grab and do it quick. Tommy would hate to admit it but Harold had shown great style in choosing to convert her. Two months earlier he had asked Tommy to go through the engine room and remove anything not needed in the Nadine's new life. That was quite a project and Tommy had been spending his nights uninstalling the RSW, refrigerated seawater system. Eventually, the fish hold would be converted to berthing. She would make a nice cruiser. Tommy lusted to get back in the engine room. He loved driving trucks— being out in the city every day, being part of the city. But he missed boats. Nothing on land replaced it.

"It's close. A couple weeks but you know I can't work on it if we go out."

"Why not? The two jobs aren't related."

"Everything's related. It's the principal— just like the language."

"You guys are idiots if you strike over language."

"Maybe. It's up to your side of the table not to let it happen."

They had both said too much, had broken too many negotiating rules.

"Don't let this get out of hand Tommy."

"You too boss."

Tommy retrieved his trip ticket from the pneumatic tube that led to and from dispatch. He knew it would be bad when he read the address and saw the red 'COD' stamped on the ticket, Cash On Delivery. Shit, cod fishing in the Rainier Valley, Tommy thought. The delivery was going to a 'Mr. Tran Newin'. Four yards. Tommy took the ticket and climbed back into his truck. The loading hopper came down from the plant and mated with his truck. Tommy pushed his drum control all the way forward and set his hand throttle to max. He felt the load slam into his drum. "Jesus doc. At least buy me a drink first." There were three trucks in line behind him. The batchman was loading as fast as possible. The buzzer went off and Tommy exited the plant.

Tommy drove south on the viaduct and then crossed over and climbed the hill on Columbia. He wove through the neighborhood and glided up to the address. The driveway was framed and ready but Tommy didn't see any workers only an old Vietnamese man without shoes. He set his brake and then wrote his arrival time on the upper tear-off strip on the ticket. To make a short load work you had to be ready when the truck pulled up. The customer got six minutes per yard but had to pay $1.25 per minute after that. That worked out to an hour of work time on a fully loaded ten yard truck. This old man had 24 minutes to place his four yards and his crew wasn't around. Tommy climbed down from the cab.

"Ciao," Tommy said.

The old man smiled. "Chào," he said.

Tommy showed the man the delivery ticket. "COD," he said and pointed at the subtotal. The old man nodded his head and waved to Tommy indicating where the concrete should go. "Yes. Do you have the money? Where is your crew?" But the old man just continued to smile and waved at the target. Someone had prepped the job. The sides were framed and a two by four screed board lay on the lawn. Tommy pointed at the board and asked, "who?" The old man continued smiling and nodding and then he pointed at his own chest.

Shit, Tommy thought looking at the old man's bare feet. He held one finger up and then went and climbed back into his cab. He grabbed his radio mic.

"34. I've got a problem here."

"What's wrong Tommy?" dispatch answered back.

"Well, my customer is an 80-year-old Vietnamese man with no shoes. Seriously no shoes, bare feet."

"Can he pay?"

"I think so. Listen, I don't want to kill this guy or burn his feet off." Concrete is chemically very base and burns exposed skin.

"No. Don't do anything unsafe. Collect for the load and return fee."

Tommy looked at the speaker and shook his head. He rehung the mic and climbed out. The old man was still standing in the worksite. Tommy pointed at his feet. "No good. You need boots." He pointed to his own feet. "Boots." The old man smiled and waved towards the driveway. He was ready to work. Tommy shook his head. "Not without boots." Tommy made a lighter with his fist. His thumb was a flame that burnt his other hand. He then pointed at the old man's feet and then back at his own. "Boots." The old man continued smiling and waving. This wasn't going well. Tommy pointed at the old man's feet and then at the truck and shook his head no. He then pointed at his own feet and the truck and nodded yes. Something clicked. The old man scurried away to his house. He quickly reemerged wearing white tennis shoes. Tommy was ready to leave but then the old man pulled a black garbage bag from his pocket and stepped one leg into it. He secured it above the knee with a rubber band. He did the same with his other foot. Now Tommy smiled.

Tommy helped the man. It was against the rules. He was a delivery driver, not a finisher. They worked quickly, efficiently. They worked without a shared language but communicated perfectly. Tommy grabbed his magnesium trowel from the cab and finished the edges of the driveway. It wasn't a pretty job but this old man had obviously done concrete work. Probably without boots.

Tommy sat in the cab figuring the bill. He looked at his watch and then subtracted 27 minutes and wrote that time in the arrival slot. Close enough. 'Nice guy' wasn't an ironic nickname. He gave the old man the total and was amazed when the concrete wizard pulled a wad of hundreds from his pocket. The old man tipped Tommy with a Vietnamese Red Bull.

11.

Anders went to his appointment. Le Canard was even closer to the house than the Hat— less than five minutes by bike. Anders found the back door and peeked in the kitchen. A sullen young man stared into a stock pot. "Jules?" Anders asked. The stock watcher looked up surprised and then pointed. Jules was in his office writing in a large ledger. "Jules?" Anders asked again.

Jules looked up and smiled. "You must be Anders. Amanda said you'd be coming by but I won't hold that against you." He stood up and shook Anders's hand with a strong and friendly grip. He did not look like any cook Anders had ever known. Jules was tall and thick. He had a black beard and looked more like a fisherman or a logger than the thin pale cooks Anders was accustomed to. Jules led Anders to a couple bar stools next to a workstation between the stoves and the dining room door. It was the 'plating' station Anders would later learn.

"Sit down," Jules said. He tore a couple of chunks of bread from a baguette and put a bowl of soft butter between them. He then poured two cups of black coffee from an ancient machine against the wall and set the cups down. Anders thanked him. The man at the stove continued working.

"What do you know?" Jules asked and then tore a smaller piece of bread from his chunk and swept it through the edge of the soft butter.

"Amanda said you might need some help during the day."

Jules waved and swallowed hard on the bread. "No. No. What do *you* know? I know what I know. What do you know about cooking? What do you know about French cooking?"

Anders talked through a short history of his experience thinking it was what Jules wanted to know.

"So, you know how to hold a knife," Jules said and then gulped some coffee. "But that's good. I don't want someone who knows anything about anything. It takes too long to break them of bad habits. Like Seth here," Jules pointed at the stock stirrer. The young man nodded and smiled. "When he came here he couldn't crack an egg. But now he wants to be some scientist— fuck with chemicals instead of life. After all I've taught him." The young man smiled again. Anders would start the next day.

Anders got to the restaurant fifteen minutes early. He tied on his apron. Jules looked at him. "Where are your knives?" he asked. The question put Anders on his heels like a jab. He had always used the restaurant's knives.

"I'm going to assume you know nothing," Jules said. His carefree mannerisms were gone and seemed never to have existed. "This is how I want the carrots julienned. Not any other way. Just like this. All of them should look like this." He held up one thin, rectangle of carrot. "All of them like this." Anders julienned for forty-five minutes. Jules came back and pushed his hand through the pile. "No," he said. He took and carrot and instructed again. "Like this." Jules then took the pile of unsatisfactory carrots and dumped it in a stock pot. "Try again," he said. His manners might have produced tears in a fragile soul but Anders had been raised on a boat.

12.

Thursday morning was Tommy's last day ever driving a concrete mixer. But he didn't know that. Most drivers arrived well ahead of their start times, to read or eat or drink coffee or talk. Tommy didn't show up early for Union duty alone. The industrial aesthetic pleased his soul. The visual poetry of the trucks crawling out one by one ranked in his mind second only to fishing boats at anchor, swinging around their hooks in unison through the night, the dance choreographed by tide and wind. It was industrial beauty full of meaning.

All that week the plant had been run at capacity and been completely sold out. Every contractor was trying to pour anything they could in anticipation of a concrete drought.

Tommy's first job of the day was a good one. He was the second truck on a trench backfill for Seattle City Light. The low cement content in those loads meant they could wait hours as long as their drums kept turning. It was on the west side of First Hill and Tommy watched the daylight break over a downtown filled with low fog. The tall buildings stood out of the mist like morels from a pine floor after a shower. Tommy watched the city come to life. A homeless man walked up out of the brush that bordered I-5, affectionately known as 'the jungle'. He was wearing a Gulf One era desert field jacket and his pants cuffs were wet from the dew.

It was nearly ten-thirty before Tommy started the long back down the alley. From the driver's seat ten feet up he peered into the hidden worlds of backyards. Most people stored their crap out back but occasionally he passed a secret Zen garden in the ghetto. Today only an old lady glared down from an attic window. When Tommy fixed his eyes upon hers she quickly pulled the curtain and disappeared. Alleys of mystery in the city.

In the afternoon Tommy was sent to a large foundation pour in the Broadmoor neighborhood. It was every driver's least favorite destination, a gated community, filled wall to wall with assholes. At least in the hood there was a possibility of getting some good takeout food. He took Northlake to look at the boats and then Pacific and crossed over the Montlake bridge. He waited in the right lane for the light to change. Tommy looked down into the car next to him. It was an older but well cared for BMW and he could only see a woman's legs, her skirt bunched at mid-thigh. An elegant hand guided the stick into first. Tommy loved to watch how women held shifters. It took skill to drive a manual in a city of hills and he imagined she drank whiskey on the rocks, wore nice underwear and could shoot a gun. The light turned and she was gone. Tommy let his clutch out and the old Kenworth torqued over to the left with the effort. The hill on 24th loomed ahead and he knew he'd only get to fourth gear. The load was wet and needed to be slammed to the front of the drum to keep from spilling. Tommy pulled the hand throttle out and let the machine work. Other cars passed him. They zipped up the hill unaware of their own machines. They would never know, especially those who drove automatics, the joys of operating a machine at work, the joy of pulling 76,000 pounds up a steep hill.

The light at the top of the hill turned. Tommy shifted down, trying to maintain his momentum. He got down into first and let the truck walk. A dirty dented car covered in stickers cut in front of him, corked him, stealing precious territory. "Fucking idiot," Tommy growled and stomped his clutch. The truck quickly lost speed. The stickered car began to disappear beneath the hood of the mixer. Tommy could 'feel' his truck's bumper. He knew exactly how far he could fill the car's rearview mirror. The light turned green and the car sped off. A car, a driver like that said so many things, spoke a language if you knew how to hear it. It was a proclamation of uncaring. That driver did not care for his machine. The driver did not understand it. He definitely did not master it. Tommy wondered how many other things that person did poorly. Probably had a sink full of dishes, dirty maggot filled trashcans and struggled to parallel park. The opportunity for mastery was precious. There was no punishment for incompetence in modern society. Tommy watched the car disappear around a corner, turn signal unused. Tommy shook his head as he forced his shifter against the spinning teeth of first gear.

Again, he was the second truck. He drove around the park and pulled up to the back gate, the service entrance. He gave the guard his name and destination and was let through. Billy was ahead of him at the pump but everything was on hold. The pump had blown a deck pipe, split cleanly at the weld, and they were waiting on the mechanics. Billy had called dispatch on the radio but four trucks were already loaded. Soon Larry pulled up with the third truck. The drivers stood around talking about the contract. If anyone was afraid no one showed it.

As they talked Tommy noticed a neighbor's curtain fluttering back and forth. Someone behind was looking out every thirty seconds to confirm something. Soon a lady left her front door and quickly walked to the jobsite. She talked briefly with the foreman and then returned to her lair. Tommy had no doubt whatsoever what was happening. In rich neighborhoods it was to be expected. They continued debating the idiocy of management while the general contractor, the general, walked over.

"Hey guys. This neighbor," he pointed toward the curtain flutterer, "is having a meltdown because of the noise. Can you guys go out the gate until we're back up and running?"

Concrete mixers are loud. That wasn't debatable. But in a rich neighborhood where everything was constantly upgraded, remodeled, tore down and built up how were these jobs to get done? Mrs. Sensitive Ears' house must have dropped from the sky complete, noiselessly landing by parachute. They went out the back gate and parked along a commoner's street until they were fetched by the foreman's pickup.

If you drive a truck long enough some interesting or even bad things are going to happen. Tommy thought of the time he watched Robbie's whole truck disappear in a sinkhole in Madison Valley, of the lady who threw eggs at the paving crew working through the night to resurface Second Avenue and the cops who visited her. And Tommy thought of the mistakes he made, always while thinking of something other than driving. He once merged into a car and pushed it into a bridge railing crossing I-5. That probably cost Halibut Flats more than a penny. His biggest mistake was caused by good intention. Tommy was driving the boom truck and delivered a load of palletized block down in Georgetown. The jobsite was very busy so once Tommy had his load on the ground he centered his boom and raised the outriggers to pull out of the way of other workers. Then he stored his outrigger mats and straps and all the other accoutrements of crane. Maybe he was thinking of Kim, or the job, or of fishing but as he headed north on Airport Way everyone in oncoming cars waved at him. Odd, Tommy thought, Seattle isn't really a waving town, and then he looked in his mirror and saw a row of dancing streetlights. He had forgotten one thing— to lower his boom. Luckily, he didn't snap any of the wires, only had given them a good smack. The memory still made Tommy embarrassed.

Then they were up and running. They fed two trucks at a time into the pump's hopper and the pump ran without pause. After discharging Tommy pulled forward to let the next truck in. He parked and went up his ladder to wash down the inside of the drum before returning to Ballard. His chores done he stepped off the ladder and was almost run down by a large champagne colored Mercedes driven by an old lady with too much white hair, driving too fast and reacting too slow. Tommy swung off the ladder onto the rear step next to the discharge controls. He watched the car pass within inches. Tommy yelled "slow down" and flew her the bird before he remembered where he was. She braked hard and then continued on. Probably drunk, probably returning from the private country club secured inside the neighborhood gates. A woman who never worked a day in her life except to offer her ass to the wealthiest caller, Tommy thought. Her grievances were addressed by husbands and lawyers. The phone was her fist.

Tommy waited for the reprimand that never came.

Every customer asked about negotiations. Universally they seemed resigned to a strike. Tommy tried to reassure them but wondered where they got their information. Was management putting out warnings? That was not a good sign.

It hadn't happened for twenty odd years and naturally it should happen like cicada hatches. As Tommy signed out, Doug, the dispatcher, approached him off to the side.

"What do you think?" asked Doug.

"About what?" Tommy considered Doug management, which he was.

"Are you guys really going out?"

"That's up to the other side of the street. They keep walking away and we're not asking for much. The economics are very reasonable."

"It's the strike language," Doug said.

"Language is our right and that's not negotiable."

"But you haven't had it for twenty years. Why now?" he said admitting that he knew what was what and that he wasn't standing in the middle of the road like an idiot waiting to be hit by a bus.

"Because one year was too long," Tommy said hardening his face.

After work Tommy went straight to Fishermen's Terminal. He knew his roommates were replacing antennas on the Lex. When he walked up the dock he could see Anders high above the wheelhouse. Karl was shouting directions from the back deck. Karl and Tommy shared an interest in radio theory. It had served them well. They had even toured the Navy radio station at Jim Creek in the North Cascades. It was the most powerful transmitter in the world that broadcasted a miles long wave, a very low frequency, and could talk to submarines across the globe. Most people didn't even know that antennas were sized to wavelengths. What the average person didn't know about what was working around them was astounding. But then, neither Tommy nor Karl knew anything of sports or Hollywood.

Work done, the men decided to get a beer at The Highliner, a bar inside the Terminal. Tommy said he would join them there and peeled off to walk out dock three and secure his tools. Returning from the Nadine Tommy was surprised to see Harold coming up the dock. His head was bowed, lost in thought.

"What's up boss?" Tommy asked.

Harold seemed just as surprised to meet Tommy. They had just talked a few hours prior and they would both be at the Teamster Hall in the morning for the final day of negotiations.

"What's going on Tommy?" Harold replied. "I thought you said you weren't going to work on the Nadine."

"I'm not. We were getting the Lexington ready for the winter fishery, new antennas," Tommy said.

"You know something I don't?" Harold asked. "Or are you going somewhere?"

Tommy smiled his nice guy smile and shook his head. "Not me. I'm not going anywhere. Just helping my friends."

They parted, their brief conversation laden with subtext and a sprinkling of spite. Harold continued down the dock towards the Nadine. The boss thought Tommy was too clever to be a Teamster. The smart move would be to promote him out of the steward position. He'd be a good salesman. He knew the industry and all the customers liked him. Harold swung on to the Nadine and stopped at the galley door. There was a brass lock on it with the initials 'NGT' scribed across its face. "Fuck me," Harold said. He was locked out.

13.

Werner worked on his nightly poem. By the time Werner made it to Ballard, Signe was already married and had given birth to Anders' mother and uncle. Family shame sent Signe to the United States right after the war. Werner hadn't been her only German lover. He had seen Signe several times in the neighborhood. He didn't think she would leave her family to be with him, but he wanted to talk to her, to let her know that he had made it, that he had kept his word. One day he spotted her alone. He had convinced himself that she no longer held his soul but when he approached her from behind his heart threatened to explode.

"Signe," he said in his German accented English.

She turned and squinted, unable to place him in her new life. "Werner?" she asked in her Norwegian accented English.

"Why are you here?" she asked.

"The postcard."

Signe looked around. She seemed concerned that someone might see them talking. "No, no, no," she said in a low voice. "This is no good."

Werner didn't want to upset her. He didn't want to scare her. Their meeting wasn't going as he had thought. He wasn't sure what he had thought but it wasn't this. "I didn't... or rather I don't..." he stammered.

"No, no Werner. I have a new life now. Please never talk to me again," Signe said and quickly walked away.

Over the years he had seen her several more times. Sometimes their eyes would meet and hers would be as cold and dead as a day-old fish. He thought of the Goethe quote, 'if I love you, what business is it of yours?' He wrote that on the paper. He could be called a plagiarist but soon the evidence would be ash.

Anders and Tommy followed Karl across the bridge back into Ballard proper. Fishermen's Terminal is considered to be a part of Ballard even though it was on the Magnolia side of the ship canal. They took a right on 52nd and pulled up in front of the little house.

They lived in the flat or what was legally the Ballard Industrial District. They lived in the middle of a six-block area filled with warehouses, small manufacturing facilities and storage yards. On their block two houses sat next to each other surrounded on three sides by working property. There was a net builder, a crane yard, a marine cabinet shop and an industrial laminator. Everything either smelled of fish or the sea. The houses were both small thirty by thirty World War

Two bungalows but they were very different. One was immaculately maintained. Karl, Anders and Tommy lived in the other.

The house looked like it could have been a net shed on the Wrangell Narrows south of Petersburg. It had always been owned by fishermen. The porch lights burned port red and starboard green. And it had a dock that jutted out of the porch and ran two feet above the concrete yard all the way to the sidewalk. It was handy for loading a motorcycle into a truck but was still a dock in the middle of a city. The porch rail was an old seine cork line, with real cork floats. Karl's addition to the house was a flagpole with yardarms from which always and only flew the Norwegian flag. Rarely they raised a small bravo flag (the danger flag— fueling or loading dangerous cargo) on a side line if a serious party was to commence.

Tommy turned off his ignition but the truck ran on and on. He released the clutch while holding the brake and killed the engine in a long final sputter. Karl looked down from the end of the dock.

"That's not good," he said to Tommy. Almost every other kind of negligence was excusable, except mechanical. Machines either saved your life or ended it and most times that depended on maintenance.

"The choke was still on. I didn't let it warm up enough. It was still running rich," Tommy explained. "I don't know why they ever switched to automatic chokes..." Tommy would continue talking about engines for hours if anyone seemed slightly interested. Anders climbed the dock and could see across their concrete grinder into the well-manicured yard next door. Werner, their neighbor, was at his burn barrel in the corner at the far end of the fence just as he was every night, burning some paper and trash. He had bricked in the barrel and made a chimney but it was still a barrel for burning trash. Karl followed the other two up the dock and spotted Werner. "Burning the code books?" he asked the neighbor. Werner glared back with red rimmed eyes but said nothing. He had heard Karl's joke a thousand times and never found it funny.

14.

The negotiation meeting wasn't until nine. Tommy woke at four and stared at the ceiling for an hour. When Tommy came out of his bedroom Karl was still on the couch and he woke looking confused and old. Tommy laughed at the rare sight but Karl recovered and was whole again.

"I dreamt I was dead," Karl said.

"How did it happen?" Tommy asked.

"Drowned."

"Sounds about right. You want coffee?" He moved to the kitchen and put the pot on the burner. He then went to the bathroom to take a piss and brush his teeth. Karl had decoupaged the room with Playboy centerfolds from the 60s and 70s. It was a nice way to lift the morning fog. Every day Tommy brushed his teeth and stared at the naked women wondering where they were now.

"I don't have the dream anymore," Tommy said when he came out of the bathroom. "I guess I'm safe."

"Hmmm," Karl said as he removed the whistling pot. He was thinking about what Tommy had admitted. Outside the window a crane was jockeying its way out of the yard. The ball and hook swung side to side. "That's a sad thing. You might as well live in Ohio."

"I suppose you are right." Tommy watched the counterweight truck follow the crane out of the yard. "I've been thinking about buying a little fishing boat just so I don't completely dry up but it's a mystery."

"What is?"

"Everything. Fishing poles?"

They both laughed. Neither of them knew how to work a fishing pole.

"When are you headed out?" Tommy asked.

"We are supposed to leave this evening but I bet there'll be some delays and we'll untie just after midnight. I swear they schedule Friday sailings just to fuck with us. They're probably waiting for that one crew that leaves on schedule so they can fire them for being unsafe."

Tommy laughed. "Makes sense to me," he said.

Anders came up from the basement unused to seeing both of his roommates sitting in the breakfast nook on a weekday morning.

"Morning Chef!" Karl chided him.

"Time to make the doughnuts?" Tommy asked. Both older men were tickled by their own humor.

"Jesus," Anders said. "At least let me get some coffee before you start busting my balls."

"You talk to your Dad yet?" Karl asked.

"No, but really, let me get some coffee first."

After a shower and coffee, Anders rode off on Ring Ding Ding to start another double shift. Tommy dressed in work clothes even though his day would be spent at the negotiation table and headed down to the Hall. Karl was left alone. He didn't need to be to the boat until the afternoon so he decided for a little more bed vice bunk sleep. As he lay looking at the ceiling he thought of Tommy's admission, of his drying out and being safe. That admission was something that scared Karl. He hoped he would never die on dry land. He had been dunked once and didn't find it too terrifying. Karl had read that drowning was not a bad way to die and he thought of the time he sank.

There are always many reasons for a boat sinking. The rock punching through the hull is just one of them. Lies, truths, decisions made and decisions unmade are all rocks. When the Ingrid II disappeared in two-hundred fathoms she had a fo'c'sle full of guns. The assault weapon import ban of 89 was also a rock. Karl saw an opportunity and bought a dozen eastern bloc guns from a dealer in Anchorage.

68

Other rocks were the genset going down and bad batteries that took the radar with it. But the real rock was a real rock and it tore open the side of the Ingrid II and she turned over and disappeared, guns and all, never to be raised. She had been due for some maintenance but it was the end of the season and they had all the time in the world to work on the boat back in Ballard.

When the radar went out the skipper called everyone to the bridge. They sat with their survival suits within reach. When the wheelhouse went dark Karl and the skipper pulled a chart out and quickly went about dead reckoning. Unfortunately the only flashlight they had wasn't a red light and every time they used it their night vision was destroyed. They knew they were just off Bella Bella but the rain was blowing sideways and no lights from shore or obstacle were to be seen. The skipper kept mumbling 'fuck' almost resigned to what he knew was coming. "Get your suits ready boys. If it happens— Karl, you'll deploy the raft and I'll grab the EPIRB."

Danny, the apprentice and cook, was terrified and already working his feet into the neoprene survival suit. He said, "we should tip that thing over right now. It'd give the Coast Guard a head start."

"The Canadian Coast Guard," Karl said, all too aware of their location.

"No," the skipper said. "We aren't lost yet. We're just not exactly sure where we are."

"Two three five," Karl said looking up from the chart.

"Two three five," the skipper said looking at the luminous compass rose as it swung gently to the course.

They continued on for forty minutes. The initial terror subsiding. Danny even thought about removing his feet from his suit because they were getting hot. And then they hit the rock. The bow raised and then veered right. The men all continued forward into the wheelhouse windows. They could feel the boat lower down off the rock and settle. She didn't settle upright but with a port list. "Get 'em on," the skipper said and all the men scrambled with their suits. "See if you can make a call Karl."

Karl was already at the radio but the dead batteries gave only a brief flicker of illumination and then faded back to black. "Nothing," he said.

The skipper pulled the EPIRB from the rack and turned it upside down. The beacon started flashing giving a slow-motion film effect to the tragedy. Flash— Danny's terrified face, a cut on his forehead leaking blood down his face. Flash— the skipper's disappointed countenance, disappointed that he had lost his horse from underneath him without any valor. Flash— Karl's Mona Lisa smile, wondering what was next.

The boat started to roll over and they moved to the deck outside the wheelhouse. Gear tubs had already fallen overboard adding thousands of Mustad hooks to the inviting North Pacific. "Stay together," the skipper said. "Karl, go ahead and release the raft." The beacon flash was blinding everyone and the wind and rain stung the eyes. It was tempting to just keep your eyes closed.

"You guys get in and I'll wait a little longer. Stay together and I'll try and swim the painter over to you."

"No, release it now. We will swim to it," the skipper ordered and Karl obeyed. He yanked the release and the life raft came out of its cocoon with a hiss. The Ingrid II was settling on her side. They would have to jump soon. Karl struggled with the raft, it was tangled in the antennas and stabilizer poles. And then the wind grabbed it and the storm claimed it as booty. The little orange igloo was picked up in one beacon flash and disappeared into the sky in the next.

"Mother fucker!" the skipper shouted at the storm.

"Yep," Karl said. "Time to jump, Skip."

"I know. Everyone overboard." He looked around doing a quick head count. "Is everyone here?"

"Yep," Karl said.

"Alright, let's go," the skipper said and he led the procession overboard like lemmings to the sea. Karl was the last one in. Before he jumped he cut a twenty foot piece of line so they'd have something to hold on to in the dark and could keep together. The water was coated with diesel from a torn bunker tank and their first gasp of air tasted of fuel. The beacons on each of the suits were water activated and three other strobes joined the larger one still cradled in the skipper's arms, the churning storm surface turned into a disco of survival suit dancers. Before anyone could wonder what next, Danny announced, "I touched something!" with a little too much obvious panic. Everyone had their own thought of what it could be. "Again!" he shouted in the wind. "It's a rock." They all swam the short distance towards the cook. Toes reached out until all the men could feel the obstacle.

Karl handed his makeshift lifeline to the others. It was a piece of hope in the darkness. "This way," Karl shouted. He was following the rise of the rock. It wasn't above the water level but he was almost standing. The waves kept pushing him off his feet.

"Over here is flat," the skipper shouted. The men moved to the new position and could fight the waves, be pulled back with the line. Karl moved toward the skipper, losing his balance and being washed off his feet a couple times during the transit. "Skip, if this is L-18 then the big rock should be close but I don't see the light."

Almost a smile came across the skipper's face. "I like it," he said. "Everyone, cover your beacons and look for the light." They used their oversized gloves to muffle the strobes and a hundred yards away two long flashes and a short fought against the storm.

They swam to the light, each man holding onto the line that kept them together. The navigation aid was built into the rock with a concrete base. It was washed with seawater and kelp and barnacles added an unpleasant texture but it was above water. Karl tied a quick bowline around one of the steel legs of the light and the men huddled in the lee. Two hours later the Canadian Coast Guard rescued them and took them to the village. They didn't meet lotus eaters, a cyclops or Circe but Tlingits who after clothing the crew in Salvation Army duds put them on a bus for Bellingham.

15.

Tommy drove to the Union hall but it was a waste of time. The negotiation meeting was a farce as both sides seemed resigned to the coming strike. They sat down at the table and then there was an uncomfortable silence. "Any change?" the Union lead asked. The management team shook their heads and it was over. As a member of the negotiation committee Tommy got paid a full day's wages for attending. It felt like a scam.

Tommy drove by the precast yard to break the news to the guys. He pulled his pickup through the gates and parked. Two mixer trucks were discharging the remainder of their loads, creating ecology blocks. The drivers stopped their drums and set their brakes before climbing out of their cabs. The two men who ran the yard, members of the Operators' Union, a union with strike language, also came over. Tommy got out of the cab and leaned against the bed.

"How'd it go?" asked one of the drivers. Bill was smart. He owned several rental properties and read the paper front to back every day. He was always investing, turning his hourly wage into a real wealth. Tommy waited for the other three men to be within hearing range. He knew that he would be having repeat conversations and worked to minimize it.

"Not good. They offered us the same thing. No strike language." The other men either frowned or looked away. "We'll vote on it Sunday morning at ten in the hall."

"What do you think?" Bill asked Tommy.

"I think it sucks. Language doesn't cost them anything but a strike costs everyone. There's a chance that something may change by Sunday but I don't think any of the other companies are going to accept the contract as it is." The little meeting broke up and Tommy pulled the keys from his pickup and walked over to his mixer. He turned the electricals on, waited for a break in the radio traffic and then keyed the mic. "Hey guys, vote is Sunday morning at ten. Clean out your trucks tonight. Spread the word. I'll be at precast for a while if you have any questions."

The responses came back— copy, copy, alright, thanks Tommy.

He cleaned out his truck. Tommy knew a couple things about leadership. As steward he needed to be an example. Even cleaning out his truck— he stayed positive, confident. Phil said he was going to leave his sandwich under the seat. "By the time they hire scabs it will be rancid. Give the fuckers the bubonic plague."

"What if they don't hire scabs?" Tommy asked.

"Then I'll get bubonic plague."

There was lots of talk between the drivers. Most thought that management would cave before the Sunday deadline. There was joking and camaraderie. They weren't on strike yet, options still existed. Over months and years of work a truck cab becomes a rolling warehouse of work supplies— map book, chip hammer, clipboard, rain gear, two hard hats and a dozen pairs of gloves added to the usual load of lunch box and coffee mug. Tommy stacked all his gear in his pickup.

The ringing phone woke Karl. He heard Tommy answer it and looked at his watch. It was only 11:30. Tommy was back early from his negotiation meeting, Karl wondered if that was a good or bad sign and then Tommy knocked on his door.

"Karl, Port Captain is on the phone."

"Alright, coming." Karl hustled to the phone. "What's up boss?"

"Would you mind giving up your Dutch run? Eric blew out his back and I could really use you for some harbor work. Unfortunately, that boat doesn't come back on call until Wednesday so you'll have a few days off."

"Yeah, no problem. I'll find something to do."

"Karl, you've got a ton of vacation built up," the Port Captain reminded.

"I know but a few days will be fine. I'll take the harbor work. I need to come get my stuff out of the stateroom though."

The Port Captain chuckled. "I'm sure they won't leave until after midnight."

The fall rush was over. The far north had been supplied and the fish from Bristol Bay had been brought south. Many guys took a month or more off in early winter. Karl's seniority would allow him to bump others if he wanted but he was flexible and respected the limits of the family men.

16.

Tommy spent every Saturday with his daughter. After coffee he drove up to his house in Shoreline and usually did some chores for Kim before taking Lottie somewhere to get her out of the house and give Kim some free time. They went to parks if the weather was nice. Sometimes they rented canoes from the University of Washington or borrowed a friend's rowboat. In the summer they would drive up to the mountains and wander around. Lottie was too small to really hike but Tommy wanted her to see things outside of the city.

Tommy got to the house early and pulled a ladder from the side of the garage. The girls, his ex-wife and daughter, wouldn't be up before nine. The rainy season was upon them although that day was sunny and crisp. He set the ladder against the eave and began cleaning the gutters. He threw the leaves and pine needles, or more properly fir needles, in neat little piles that could be cleaned up easily. As he passed his ex's bedroom, their former bedroom, he could see Kim sleeping face down with one bare leg protruding from the blankets. She was alone but someday there would be someone else. When that happened, he wouldn't clean their gutters. His niceness had its limits.

As he finished sweeping up his daughter emerged from the house still in her pajamas.

"Hi Daddy," she said and gave him a hug.

"Good morning Princess," he said and gave her a loud kiss on the forehead.

"Do you want pancakes?" she asked.

"I've already had breakfast," he said.

"But Mommy made you pancakes," his daughter said.

"Oh," Tommy said standing up straight. "In that case I better have pancakes."

They loaded up in his pickup and headed downhill towards Ballard. "What do you want to do Sugar?" he asked.

"Boats!" she said. She was his daughter.

They borrowed a dingy and rowed around the ship canal looking at the tugs, a couple of big catcher processors and a lot of ducks. Tommy had a brown paper sandwich bag three-quarters full of duck food from the feed store in his pocket and he handed it to Lottie. He always had a few of these bags in his pickup. It was enough to feed the ducks on one loop around Greenlake. His first couple winters of working at Halibut Flats Tommy lacked the seniority to work every day. Those days, especially in the winter, he would sit by the phone until nine a.m. waiting for a call from dispatch to come in to work. On days that he didn't work he drove to Greenlake and walked a loop, at first with Kim but later with Karl. It was Karl that started the habit of carrying bird food. Ever the bird man he was angered watching people feed the ducks bread. Karl went to the feed store and bought bird seed and duck food, which was like chicken scratch but floated. They walked the lake with pockets full of the feed and after a few weeks all the ducks and birds recognized the two men and would come to them for snacks. The red-winged blackbirds that lived on the Aurora side of the lake would land on Karl's hands and eat. Tommy was never able to pull this off. Karl could stand on the trail with arms outstretched and let the birds feed from his hands like some punk rock version of Saint Francis of Assisi. The young women pushing strollers would always stop and watch. Often, they were new mothers with full boobs and a new perspective. Their faces showed a mixture of love and regret, the beauty of young motherhood. It was the truest countenance, more true than pain or fear, and especially more true than joy.

Tommy handed one of the bags to Lottie. He rowed along the concrete bank and she fed the mallards. They passed under the bridge and skirted the boat ramp on 14th. Tommy spotted a female, missing a flipper, hobbling down the ramp. He tried to focus his daughter's eyes elsewhere but she noticed the Ahab stump.

"Daddy, she's hurt," Lottie said, concern and sympathy in her young voice.

"No sweetheart. She was hurt. Now she's healed." He dreaded when the real world would touch his daughter. "But give her some extra food."

Tommy had heard that largemouth bass would eat baby ducks whole. Tommy had never seen a largemouth bass other than in magazines. The interior of the country was a mystery to him. He had never been beyond the smell of salt water.

17.

Sunday the real world touched Tommy. The vote was scheduled for ten. Weekend votes used to be scheduled in the afternoon but that had been changed after the pipefitters went out on strike for three days just because they gave their members too long to get drunk before the vote. Weekday votes were always at five a.m. so the guys could go to work after they ratified the contract and not miss a day.

Tommy arrived at the hall early. Soon, the rest of the negotiation committee was there. They all suffered from an unease, a nausea, like the feeling that sets in after swallowing an oyster that didn't taste right. What these men said would guide the lives of hundreds of their brothers and all their families. It showed on their faces. "Anyone want to change their vote?" the Business Agent asked. The four bargaining team members just shook their heads slowly. They all would have liked to recommend the proposal but the owners never came close. Management wouldn't budge on the strike language and now it looked like the men would be walking the picket line. None of them had ever been on strike and none of them looked forward to it. By nine-thirty the hall was almost full. The Business Agent looked out at the crowd, now mostly sitting according to company. The two largest, corporate owned shops filled most of the room. The two smaller, family-owned businesses including Halibut Flats, sat to either side. Tommy nodded or waved as his guys found their seats. He kept a roster in his head and noticed that not everyone was present. It would be the first of many disappointments.

Each of the four companies had one member on the bargaining committee. For Halibut Flats it was Tommy. One company had their most senior driver as their representative instead of their steward in the hope that his age and experience would give the committee some wisdom or at least institutional memory. It made sense. Stewards are not paid for their service and often they are too young or too motivated. Nothing was worse than a Steward who fancied himself an activist. A steady hand was needed. Tommy looked out at the gathered crowd. The disparity of size was immediately apparent. How one or both of the big companies voted would take the rest along for the ride. It reminded him of state politics. How Seattle voted decided for the whole state. Halibut Flats was the Palouse of Local 174. Had the contract been better, been something they might have lived with, he would have been worried about the power of numbers. The two corporate units had an adversarial relationship with their employers that was addressed by HR departments. Halibut Flats didn't have an HR department. They had Harold and Tommy. But the proposal wasn't good and no one would recommend it for ratification.

"You guys ready?" the BA asked and the committee moved towards their seats in the front of the noisy room.

The Secretary-Treasurer of the local, the top-ranking leader of 174 went to the center podium. He tapped the microphone. "Brothers, take your seats. We have a lot of work today." With that the crowd settled in. Tommy opened one of the water bottles on the table and downed half of it. He didn't like being in front of crowds. He didn't like speaking in public.

There is always a level of distrust between the different shops or bargaining units that make up a Local. Men who drive garbage or recycling trucks don't understand the grievances of port or freight drivers. The Secretary-Treasurer, the top Teamster of a local, always came out of UPS which made up the bulk of the membership. Known as Big Brown, UPS birthed some real fire breathers and they were seen as somehow smarter than the average Teamster, possibly because of their snappy uniforms. The Secretary-Treasurer was a good leader. He wanted the men to work and make a good living. Most importantly he didn't view the local as a stepping stone to some national level position. At least Local 174 was all truck drivers and had that in common. Some Teamster locals represented everything from clerks to train drivers.

"I want you to know," the Secretary-Treasurer told the crowd, "that whatever we— or rather whatever you— decide today, the Local and International will support with all our strength." There was some polite clapping. Then he continued, "Truthfully, if there was one unit of this local to go out— I would have to pick concrete. You are the most militant, most informed and most involved of all our members." This was naked flattery but true. Tommy had been on the political action committee and the volunteer organizing committee and each had a disproportionate contingent of ready-mix drivers. It was job related. Throughout their day ready-mix drivers had short bursts of time to read the paper, to discuss with other drivers whether while loading or waiting to discharge. Freight drivers had to run, run, run. Dump truck drivers never got out of their seats, which also led to obesity amongst that unit. At Halibut Flats, a third of the drivers completed the crossword in the newspaper each day. "But in the end it is up to you if you vote to accept this proposal or not," he concluded and then turned and handed the meeting over to the Business Agent.

"Brothers, before we start I'd like to acknowledge the hard work your bargaining committee has done for you. These men bargained in good faith for the good of all of you sitting out there." There was more polite applause and Tommy felt a little sick. He wished he could be sitting with his friends. And then the real work began. A draft proposal was handed out and the men dug through it. The BA hit the wave tops going down the page. There were some shouted questions from the crowd but the BA deflected them saying, "there will be an open question period next. Same as always, line up for the microphone."

Unions are Jeffersonian democracies run amok. Instead of yeoman farmers, men with thick hands and stolid minds lined up to have their opinions heard. Some made valid points, some talked of personal grievances and others just talked to be heard. No single speaker swung the crowd. A resignation built up with each empty plea for patience or angry cry for action. Finally, someone asked the bargainers at the table, "Do you recommend it?" The question would have been asked formally after everyone had a chance to give their opinions but the Business Agent could feel the same wave building. He looked at Tommy and the others and then handed Tommy his microphone. Tommy said one word quietly but clear, "No."

The men still in line to speak returned to their seats and the ballots were handed out.

By noon it was over. They were on strike. It was official. But it was Sunday and there were no lines to man, no doors to shut, so they made plans for the next day. All pickets would commence at eight in the morning. That would give the other trades a chance to clock in and get ready their belongings before walking. The membership drifted off to get drunk or play golf or have a quiet Sunday afternoon with their families. The stewards stayed and again discussed the rules and strategies of work stoppage.

18.

"Better get something to eat tonight. Let's go to the Hat. Anders is working," Karl said.

Tommy drove his truck because it looked like rain. Karl rode his motorcycle because it wasn't yet raining and he had been on boats so long that he didn't recognize rain anymore, didn't recognize its reality or authority. He had spent years either too hot in PVC rain gear or soaked through in cotton that it didn't matter because he knew the opposite would soon arrive. It was the kind of environmental numbness that allows men to wear Xtratuffs with shorts as the pinnacle of practical attire.

Karl parked his motorcycle in front of the bar in a no parking space but Tommy had to drive around the block twice because the only open spaces were in front of the Halibut Flats office and he didn't want it to look like he was somewhere he shouldn't be. The morning's vote had changed the declination. North wasn't the same. From then on, appearances would be very important. He needed to start thinking and acting like a leader of men. Although he didn't look forward to the fight, the responsibility didn't scare him. It was the job he was born for.

Karl waited for Tommy and they entered the bar together. Anders was back to his position of number two prep man and they waved to him as they rounded the wall into the bar. Amy was bartending and she slid them two Jack and Cokes before they sat down. She was a curvy thing with much style and humor but she knew the three roommates too well to ever be naked with any of them. They sat on stools at the end of the bar and started drinking. Karl said, "it's on me tonight." But that was nothing new or special because it was always on Karl. He had more money than god. You couldn't begrudge him that though. Since fourteen all he had done was work. And, he had never let one slip up an ambitious hairdresser. Carved into the bar in front of Karl was his name in runes. It had got him 86'd for two months when he was twenty.

They clinked their glasses and said, "Vanebo!" They drank and then drank some more and then ate a couple orders of chicken fried chicken. They drank more liquid catharsis and talked. They talked about the labor history of Seattle and of Ballard because they were history buffs. They talked about the Seattle General Strike of 1919, the Stimson mill strike and the 1906 shingle weaver strikes in Ballard. They compared Dave Beck to Harry Bridges and the Teamsters to the Industrial Workers of the World and the Longshore Union. Karl's union, the Inland Boatman's Union, was a subset of the International Longshore and Warehouse Union. The unexpressed underlying theme of all the strikes was that labor always loses in the end. But that wasn't a nice subject to talk about going into a strike.

"Hey Karl, I think this car is going to hit your bike," Amy was looking out to the sidewalk through the little one by one foot peep window behind the bar. Karl sat his drink down and ran around the wall to the door. Tommy followed at a slower pace. Other patrons stood up to look out the other two windows.

As Karl exited the bar a black Mercedes bumped his bike. It didn't go over but rocked on the center stand. The driver was trying to squeeze into the red painted no parking space that Karl was parked in.

"Whoa bitch! No parking!" Karl shouted stooping down so the woman driver could see him in her mirror. She threw up her hands in disgust and the white reverse lights went out as she inched forward. Tommy watched from under the canopy over the bar's front door. "Stupid rich cunt. Doesn't she know this is a no park zone?" Karl said, his irony dripping like the rain. Tommy just pointed back at the car. The reverse lights were lit again and the driver made a second attempt at the illegal spot that was obviously too small but apparently convenient to her destination. She hit Karl's bike a second time. Karl walked back to the car and put a steel toe solidly through her tail light assembly. The plastic exploded and the incandescent bulbs popped like little shots. It was a well-placed kick destroying only plastic and glass, not touching the sheet metal. It was easily fixed pain as a negative

80

reinforcement, a training aid like a choke collar on a dog. Karl bent down so he could be seen in the rearview mirror and gave her the finger so she would understand what had just happened. He went forward to the passenger door and tried the handle. Luckily for everyone it was locked. The driver finally grasped the situation and drove away spinning her rear tires across the wet brick pavers. She wouldn't let off the gas until she was over the 520 bridge but maybe she was only going to Queen Anne.

"Wow," Tommy said as he came out into the rain. Karl still stood in a fighting stance, knees bent, hands raised to the world. "She do anything to your bike?" he asked. And at that Karl changed. His arms went down and his knees straightened. He went to his bike and gave it a brief glance. It was no show bike, an airhead BMW more than twenty years old. It had lived outside and rough. Another scratch wouldn't have showed. Karl barely looked.

"No, I don't think so," he said.

"Cause you fucked her car," Tommy said calmly.

"Really?"

"Oh yeah."

A smile came to Karl's face. It was hard to tell if the smile was guilt or pride or embarrassment. He stood up straight and looked around surveying the lay from five feet seven inches. "Maybe I better go park in the marina. I'll meet you back inside." And quickly he jumped on the bike and was gone, helmetless in the rain.

And the discussion in the bar quickly turned to the events outside the window. Thought broke into distinct camps. Amy, the bartender, and Amanda, the waitress, thought Karl "psycho." Kate, the dishwasher, was impressed and enthusiastic in her punk rockness. Tommy and Anders were embarrassed.

Later when Karl reappeared soaked the assembled staff and clientele wondered each in their own head about the scars that crisscrossed Karl's skull. Fishing or fighting? Karl had ridden his bike all the way back to the house, six blocks through a couple lights. Not smart.

Karl and Tommy moved to a booth in the bar. Anders came out of the kitchen a couple times and would sit with them for a bit. Amanda came up to the bar. She was finishing her night of waitressing the back room. Karl noticed the way Anders looked at her. That's it, he thought. She's the reason. She was the woman that was going to fuck his life. Anders went back to the kitchen to finish his chores.

The next time Amanda passed Karl stopped her. "What's your name darling?" he asked. "You a friend of Anders? You trying to get him to quit fishing?" He patted the booth seat next to his thigh.

She pushed Tommy on the shoulder and slide in next to him, facing Karl. "I don't try to get him to do anything. He's an adult. He can decide what to do with his life," she said.

Tommy cocked his head and smiled. He was impressed with her moxie.

Karl threw up his hands in mock frustration. "Everybody just do what you want!" he said to the general din of bar noise. "Shit, I thought this was Ballard."

"What are you guys celebrating?" Amanda asked, not snared by Karl's theatrics.

"Tommy's going on strike so we are celebrating the fight. Join us," Karl said, a smile returning to his face.

"Why strike?" she asked. "I thought you guys made good money." Amanda knew the basics about Anders' roommates.

"No one wants to strike but you only get to negotiate every three years. We gave up some important language in the early 80s and need to get it back. Truthfully, the money is fine. But don't tell anyone that because we are asking for a little more." Tommy winked a conspiratorial eye. Amanda giggled at the lanky steward. She rose and went off to finish her side work.

Tommy and Karl returned to their labor discussion. Tommy believed in the system even though he knew it was rigged so he would fail. He understood the rules.

Later, Amanda returned and sat next to Karl. She listened politely to Tommy's diatribe about the importance of rank-and-file leadership at the local level. He was vehemently against outside agitators, professional troublemakers or anyone educated in a college labor studies program.

"Don't you guys talk about music or movies or anything else?" she asked, a little bored.

"We talk about life not consumerism," Karl said. She rolled her eyes because Karl was being honest. Karl went to the bar and got three more drinks.

"Why don't you become a criminal if you don't believe in society?" Amanda asked. The men were good and drunk and the conversation was easily derailed if not steered.

Karl laughed. "You mean live for money? Drugs are for idiots and to be involved with them would be dishonorable. Prostitution? I do like to fuck but I couldn't own someone. People are meant to be free. Freedom is responsibility. Modern man is a cunt scared of the dark. Prostitution should be legal. If a woman wants to sell her pussy who am I to tell her not to? I've meant plenty of ladies that that's their most valuable skill. They could basically be professional athletes. But somehow it's scary because bodily fluids are involved and little precious babies might appear with their precious little souls. So, we tell these ladies that they can't work. So, they have to find husbands who only pay them to be pretty and fuck well. Same thing isn't it? I say let's be honest. Let them work. Isn't that freedom?"

"Did you just say that work was freedom?" Amanda asked.

"Hmmm," Karl paused and tapped his lips with one finger and then took a drink of the whiskey. "I guess it did."

"What about drugs then? Shouldn't people be able to do what they want?" Amanda asked. She liked to drink and smoke pot and do a little coke if someone had it.

"That's poison. That's the same as not letting people burn garbage or dump oil overboard."

"See?" Tommy said pointing at Karl and referring to their earlier conversation. "You believe in the rule of law. You don't want some Hobbesian anarchy bullshit."

"Of course. I just want some honesty." Then he pointed at Amanda. "Work is honest lady." Amanda pointed at both of the men and to Amy, behind the bar, it looked like a Mexican standoff, each pointing at someone else. Everyone slowly lowered their hands.

"I still think you should be a criminal," Amanda said.

"Truthfully," Karl said. "I believe in the strict rule of law. Laws must be obeyed even if they are not agreed to. Look at prohibition. People didn't agree with the law so they ignored it and then breaking the law became socially acceptable. Once this happens it's a cultural green light to pick and choose your laws. Taxes, stop lights, even murder becomes a rationalized choice. It's no way to run a civilization. Shitty culture leads to shitty citizens. I don't even like the glorification of criminals. Gangster movies and shit like that. It appeals to office workers. That's shallow thinking. That's the myth of the rebel."

"Karl tried to be a gun runner but it didn't work out," Tommy laughed.

"That was never proven. There's no evidence," Karl argued.

"Yes, there is. It's just hard to see."

"Too deep," Karl nodded.

"You guys think you are too deep but I'm not so sure," Amanda commented misunderstanding the concepts of shallow and deep like a person of the land. She was looking at the tattoos on Karl's hands. She reached over and tapped his fingers with hers. Karl felt a pleasant electricity. Amanda had a power. "What's that?" she asked touching the AMOR FATI tattoo.

"It's the Nietzschean concept of eternal recurrence," Karl said.

"Huh?" she asked.

"It means he likes fat women," Tommy said.

Karl laughed. "Yes, that's much better." He saluted Tommy with his drink and then started singing, "some girls are bigger than others, some girls are bigger than others," in his best Morrissey.

Someone at the bar responded to his call with, "Some girls' mothers are bigger than other girls' mothers."

Karl clapped and said, "Damn, I love this place."

The mood in the bar improved. A little faster music was played and smiles flashed between the drinkers. Only Tommy sunk the other way. He had nothing to feel jovial about. Going into a strike was sober, calm, cold business so he left around ten. He had to be on the line at eight. Everyone wished him luck but to him it sounded hollow and he felt very alone as he left, carrying Karl's helmet the two rain soaked blocks to his truck.

84

Anders closed the kitchen at midnight and cleaned. Kate pulled the mats from the floor and took them out to the alley to rinse off. Amanda poked her head in the kitchen and seeing Anders alone came in. He was cleaning the grill with a pumice brick, pushing it back and forth and bending at the waist like a supplicant to the God of short order.

She brought him a beer and they leaned on the cold station next to each other. "Your roommates are crazy. You should find new friends." It wasn't an original thought. "You should get away from them. They're going to get someone killed."

"Not Tommy. He means well."

"Those kind of people are the most dangerous. They will lead you off a cliff because it's the right thing to do." She reached out and grabbed his belt on his hip and then gave him a tug back and forth.

Kate pushed through the swinging door struggling with a large black floor mat. "Think about it," Amanda said and then passing Kate said, "that looks heavy." Amanda returned to the bar. Karl sat alone in the booth thinking of sunken guns and a tattooed woman.

"You like her?" Kate asked after the door quit swinging.

"I don't know. Why?"

"She's duplicitous."

"Huh?"

"Two-faced. Only in it for herself."

"Isn't everyone?"

"She doesn't even have a team."

"Well, I may have just turned a free agent and she got me into Le Canard. I'm just trying to make my way. Don't you want to move up?"

"I like being a dishwasher."

"Yeah, but forever?"

"What's forever?"

Kate joined Anders and Karl in a booth and they drank and told stories and laughed at the lies till closing time. Amy pushed the randoms out at one-thirty and locked the doors on the chosen few. Anders and Karl remained. And so did Kate. A threesome of graphic designers from Nordstroms stayed, friends of Amanda.

A bar with locked doors has no laws, except respect, which should be the law that governs all other laws. No one served themselves and no one upgraded drinks.

Anders watched Amanda. He wanted to talk to her but she was laughing with her friends. He sat next to Kate.

"Have you ever read the Dishwasher zine?" Kate asked.

"There's a magazine for dishwashers?"

"No, it's about a dishwasher. This guy from Portland named Pete travels around the country, working at different places. He's trying to go to all fifty states. It's really good. I'll lend you some issues."

19.

Tommy woke early on Monday. He turned on the light and took a framed picture from his nightstand. In it, his young family sat next to a bonfire on the beach at Golden Gardens park and Kim held their toddler daughter. Tommy's arm circled them both. He set the picture back on the table and picked up the frame next to it. It was his first boat— the Yorktown.

He wasn't born into fishing like Anders. Tommy's father had worked for Seattle City Light as a lineman and Tommy could have followed him into the IBEW apprenticeship. In his senior year at Ballard high school he considered the construction trades, Boeing and fishing. He figured an apprenticeship could wait a year and he wanted to try something away from home so he focused on fishing. He walked the docks at Fishermen's Terminal in the spring, before school was even done. He tried volunteering to do gear work for free, an old and solid ploy, but no one wants a greenhorn. They are the unknown. They might suffer from sea sickness or stay for only one or two seasons. The skipper never gets the return for training them. Tommy graduated without a job and in June the boats began leaving. One by one they transited the locks and were gone for Alaska. He resigned himself to construction work but then his mother secured him a ride north on a boat skippered by a family friend from church. It wasn't a job, only a ride. The boat already had a full crew but at least he'd be able to get to Alaska and continue walking the docks.

He bought a set of rain gear and a pair of Xtratufs from Seattle Ship Supply and packed one duffle bag. The F/V Pillar Bay was a 58' Delta limit seiner, a fiberglass boat built on the Duwamish in South Seattle. She could pack a hundred and twenty thousand pounds of fish. A tall bow led to a stout wheelhouse before dropping off to a long work deck. She carried a skipper and a crew of four. It was a family boat. The skipper's son and daughter working as crew. They were loading groceries when Tommy walked up the dock and he immediately fell in to help with the work. The engineer showed him where to stow his gear. The fo'c'sle held six bunks and the two extras were filled with provisions and supplies. Tommy cleared the oil and fuel filters off the top bunk and spread out his sleeping bag.

Two hours later they left the dock in Ballard and headed north. His father had told him to keep his mouth shut, stay out of the way and try to learn from each crew member. It was good advice. The Pillar Bay's crew had been together steady for six seasons, which Tommy would come to learn was a very long time. They were a well behaved, subdued crew, professional in every way. They read or watched movies and tapes of television shows on the small set in the galley when not working. Tommy went up to the bridge with each crew member as they did their wheel watch. He watched how they checked the radar against the map and how they noted all changes in wind, waves and weather in the log book.

They met up with two other boats in Friday Harbor on San Juan Island before heading north. Most boats grouped together in gangs based on blood, nationality or hometown. Fishing families, groups from Ballard, Petersburg and Sitka. The Haidas and Tlingkit. The Croats from Gig Harbor and Bellingham. The Norwegians from Ballard and Petersburg. These gangs shared intelligence and muscled for their share of the fishery.

They ran into weather in the Straights of Georgia. The boats were spread out beyond sight of each other. A half knot difference over two days equals a long way. It was night and they were plowing through eight-foot seas when a call came over the radio. The Jackie Bell's rudder was stuck hard over and she was turning circles in the straight. Tommy was in the galley when the skipper called everyone to the bridge. He said they were turning back to help, if needed. "Lower the skiff," the skipper barked.

The Pillar Bay turned into the waves and the crew rushed to unchain the smaller boat. The skiff man explained to Tommy as he manned the boom and winch hydraulic controls. "With the skiff up we are faster in the water but the center of balance is raised. We'll put her in the water for more stability." To put the skiff back in the water you first have to raise its bow off the deck. This raises the center of balance even further and adds a several ton weight hanging from your boom. But the Pillar Bay crew were all veterans and they did this quickly, timing the waves. They picked the skiff in the trough and as the Pillar Bay climbed the skiff slid off the stern and floated into the dark salt water. A line was passed through a snot hole and hooked to the bow of the skiff which was then pulled tight against the stern of the Pillar Bay using the deck winch. As the skiff man secured his line and then ran a second line as a backup, the rest of the crew stowed the chains and binders and wood blocking that had held the skiff on deck. The whole process took three minutes.

"We're good," the skiff man shouted up to the bridge and the skipper turned the boat south to look for the Jackie Bell.

"I wonder if their skiff is still up?" the cook asked as the crew reentered the galley. Everyone but Tommy knew what that could mean for a boat circling in waves. The crew hung up their wet jackets and climbed the ladder one by one to the bridge. Tommy followed.

The skipper was talking to the Jackie Bell. "Can you see my lights?" he asked referring to the Pillar Bay's crab lights.

A little while later the radio cracked and the Jackie Bell's skipper said a simple, "no."

"Alright, I'm turning them off so we can see you. We're headed your way. Out."

"Roger that. Out."

And with that the skipper flipped a switch and the bank of six 1000-watt crab lights faded to black. The difference was astonishing. Rain and waves were replaced by darkness. After a few minutes Tommy's eyes adjusted and the white crests of waves were visible again. And then someone turned on the red chart light and Tommy could see the water outside and the crew inside. The engineer sat in front of the radar clicking the range back and forth, searching.

Tommy could sense the sideways glances from the crew at the greenhorn. How was he taking the waves, the excitement? Luckily Tommy learned two things about himself that night. First, that he didn't suffer from seasickness and secondly that he wasn't any more frightened than any of the veteran deck hands.

Tommy strained his eyes and wanted to be part of the search for their sister ship. He thought he saw something. It could have been a white mast light. He saw it again. "I think I see something," he said breaking the silence.

"Where?" the skipper asked.

"It was right there, about two o'clock."

The skipper looked to engineer and the green radar screen. The engineer shook his head, nothing. The skipper turned back to watch out the dark windows.

A half hour later the radio cracked again. "Jackie Bell KV756 to Pillar Bay."

The skipper grabbed the mic. "Go ahead."

"We're ok. Steering ram was stuck. We popped the lazerette and hit the ram with a hammer and it freed up."

And that was it. Somewhere they couldn't even find a boat flirted with disaster and then was spared by a swift hammer blow. The skipper slowed the throttle and then turned back into the waves.

"Is our laz covered by the net?" he asked.

None of the crew responded because it was. The crew climbed back down the ladder to the galley. The engineer lay on the bench and gave voice to what he had been thinking through the radio silence. "See it's always the engineer that goes down with the boat, not the skipper. That's a bullshit myth. The engineer is below decks always trying to fix whatever is fucked up until it's too late. Their engineer climbed down in the steering box of a boat that could've gone over at any moment."

"That's his job," the skiffman said.

"Yeah, I know. I'm not complaining. I'm just saying it's always the engineer that goes down."

The next night at the galley table after dinner the skipper suddenly informed Tommy that he would be leaving the boat.

"We'll drop you in Petersburg. It's a good place to walk the docks and the canneries are there if you want to do that. Someone will wake you up before we get there." And that was it. No discussion. Just the skipper's word.

They negotiated the Wrangell Narrows before sunrise. It was a tricky stretch of navigation in daylight. Tommy was deep asleep in his rack when a hand rocked his shoulder awake. He could see land, rock and trees out of each port light. It looked like they were in a creek or a ditch.

"Half-hour," the skipper's daughter said.

"Ok."

He readied himself, brushed his teeth and put everything into his seabag. Snoring continued from two of the other bunks. The young girl was in the galley and she pressed him a fresh mug of coffee and asked how he like his eggs.

"Is there time?" he asked.

The cook went to the galley door and looked out across the back deck at trees and said there was time. Tommy set his seabag on the back deck next to the giant double-sided deck winch. It had two bits on top and one on each side, port and starboard. The deck boards were dry from the calm passage up the narrows. He climbed the back ladder to the bridge, its rungs tied with line and synthetic slings, endless loops rated for tens of thousands of pounds. He was there to learn a new trade, to start his apprenticeship, yet he didn't even know the names of the tools let alone their purpose. The skiff man was in the captain's chair and the skipper sat on the bench behind. The Narrows was a two-man operation.

"We'll drop you on the dock and then continue on. So be ready."

Tommy climbed back down the ladder. He faced forward as he descended, the safe way, the normal way, the greenhorn way.

"Be ready on the port side," the skipper shouted down which sent Tommy into a crisis of confidence. The town was on his right, starboard. A piece of ice off the Mendenhall glacier floated by. It wasn't an iceberg but Tommy thought he was really in Alaska. To his left was nothing but rushing water and Baranof Island beyond that.

The skipper didn't think it worth it to wake the whole crew just so a stowaway could step comfortably on the dock. The strong tide was running with them. Too swift to merely pass the dock. They would have to come about and face the current.

Tommy refocused and gripped his seabag in his right hand. He switched it to his left, freeing his strong hand and then thought what if I need to grab something, a line, a ladder? Quickly he swung the pack onto his shoulders and tightened the straps. He stood by the starboard rail thinking the skipper may have made a mistake. Docks passed a hundred yards to starboard. Tommy thought he knew what was starboard. He had been studying.

The boat turned hard to the right and blue smoke marked the early morning sky and the main spun up and roared. Tommy reached for the rail but fell over, the heavy pack bringing him down against the piled net. The cook came out the galley door and saw him tossing about on the net.

"Other side," she said. "Port!"

He found his feet and worked towards the port rail. The skiffman came down the outside ladder face-first his arms and legs working behind him automatically, instinctively. He patted Tommy on the arm. "Good luck. Now most maritime accidents happen between the dock and the boat, not fishing, so make the jump. Good luck." He smiled and punched Tommy in the shoulder. A dock neared off the port side and the skipper brought the speed down to a brisk walk. Tommy climbed onto the rail grasping the davit with his right hand and then jumped. He may have jumped too far and too hard but he made the dock. He landed five feet in. The weight of the seabag sent him to his knees and then to his hands and then to his face. He slid across the heavy planking which thankfully was worn so smooth by boot, truck and weather that splinters would have to be freed by crowbar. With his face against the wood he smelled creosote, diesel and fish. He was in Alaska.

Tommy rolled over and sat up. Over the engine Tommy thought he could hear laughter. He stood on the L shaped end of that dock and watched the Pillar Bay move away towards widening water. The cook waved from the galley door and he waved back before turning to face the town.

The sky was just turning pink and Tommy was eager to get a good start on the day. No one was about on the docks. Seiners, gill netters, power and hand trollers lined the docks. To his left was a cannery and to his right was another. Alone in a foreign world of men, Tommy had landed in a working port.

As he walked up the dock he recognized a couple of boats from Ballard but most were unknown. All the nervousness of the past month slipped away. He climbed the steep ramp from the floating docks to the shore and moved inland. Tommy asked the first person he saw for directions to tent city and moved off in that direction. It was less than a mile walk and Tommy made off at a brisk pace. He wanted to be back in town when the boats started to stir.

Tent city was a semi-regulated affair. It housed the seasonal cannery workers. For five dollars a day or twenty-five dollars a week, a worker could rent four pallets that formed a deck and raised the tents off the mushy muskeg. There was a communal bathhouse and cooking facilities in a permanent building. Neighborhoods sprung up by ethnicity. Philipinos and Mexicans claimed their ground and whites filled in the vacancies, they were mostly college kids on summer break looking for adventure and quick cash. Mixed in this village was the usual assortment of hippies and criminals.

Because it was early in the season, only the cannery maintenance workers had reason to rise early. Ordinary workers having secured positions in the plants waited for the first loaded boats to arrive back from the fishing grounds and the call to twenty-hour days. In the meantime, these workers drank, spent money they didn't have and tried to lay claim to the few women in their midst.

Tommy had no desire to join that society and quietly set his seabag in a large standing tent with a sign that read "Temporary." A couple of sleeping bags snored away in the stink and Tommy double-checked the padlock on his bag. He turned to leave the tent but stopped and unlocked his seabag. From the bottom he pulled a red Ballard Oil t-shirt and put it on. Tommy smiled. His mother didn't raise an idiot.

When Tommy made it back to the harbor, the sky was brightening and he was amazed that the docks should remain so silent. Tommy looked at his watch and realized that it was only half past four. He wasn't upset at the early hour. The foreignness of the bright sky added to his adventure. Tommy used the time to reconnoiter the harbor and town. He walked the harbor learning where seiners and trollers docked. He found the canneries, the grocery store, the bars, the restaurants and a laundromat, which also had showers for customers.

A small greasy spoon downtown didn't open until six. Tommy debated walking back to the tent city for a nap but decided against it because he wanted an early start. He wanted to rest for a half hour but didn't want to lay on a park bench like a drunk. Behind the Sons of Norway hall, he had spotted a viking ship. It was a parade float complete with a dragon bow and a skirt of wooden waves that hid the wheels. Tommy went back there. He looked around to make sure no one was watching and then climbed beneath it for a nap. His family had always been members of Ballard's Leif Erikson hall so he felt slightly entitled if not safe, mostly he felt ridiculous. He slept for forty minutes and woke up feeling pretty accomplished for an eighteen-year-old.

He woke to two pairs of feet. Men were talking and Tommy lay still. The arm he used for a pillow had fallen asleep and was numb. They were talking salmon prices and Tommy guessed they were skippers but he couldn't crawl out from his hiding spot and ask for a job.

After they walked off Tommy crawled from beneath the boat and headed downtown. He went to the diner and had a breakfast of biscuits and gravy. He listened to the conversation swirl around him hoping to hear some skipper say, "boy, I sure could use a greenhorn." It didn't happen so he walked the docks.

Instead of learning a new trade he learned patience and persistence. He made eye contact with anyone on or near a boat.

"You guys need any help?"

"Got any experience?" they'd ask.

"No, but…"

"No, we don't need anyone."

Over and over again.

Quickly, he got to know certain crews who were friendly to his search and they asked friends and kept eyes and ears open. He made sure to start and finish the day with visits to these boats. It only took one day to realize that you couldn't continually walk the docks. If you talked to a skipper in the morning you couldn't stop by again a couple hours later and ask the same question. You would be taken for mentally deficient not a determined worker.

Tommy naturally carried himself in a way that said friendly and strong. He was distinct from the college kids. They walked with a slink that said pot smoking thieves or someone looking for an adventure. There is no one as unsteady as an adventurer. They see life as a game and don't buy in with anything precious. A cheap ante might bring experience but it would never reward or make soul. Tommy needed a job, not an adventure.

"Hey Tommy, what are you doing here?" A large young man called from the back deck of a seiner. It was Knut Tallefsen. Tommy and Knut went to high school together.

"Hey Knut. Shouldn't you be in the weight room?"

"This is my weight room," Knut said waving his arms around at the boats and mountains. They shook hands. Knut was wearing a Ballard high school football t-shirt. He was a friend and former teammate. Knut was a lineman going into his senior year. They had played football together and Tommy never hazed the younger guys but always helped them understand things and navigate. The seeds of a steward already present.

"What are you doing?" Knut asked.

"Looking for a spot on a boat."

"Shit. I wish we would have known. My dad would have hired you on in a second. Any luck?"

"Not yet."

"You want lunch? We just made grilled cheese."

"Sure," Tommy said and he ate with his former teammate. They sat on the piled net on the work deck and Tommy's ass was wet when he stood to continue his hunt. Tommy thanked Knut for the sandwich.

"Alright. I'll keep my ears open," Knut said.

As he walked away he could hear Knut say, "That's Tommy Torgersen. He's fucking cool..." It was a little boost in confidence that Tommy needed.

So, Tommy spent the midday hours in the public library. It was a nice building with a large selection of commercial fishing books. On the second floor Tommy discovered Knut Hamsun. The library had a whole shelf devoted to Hamsun. Half of it was in Norwegian, beautiful old books inscribed with their owners' names, books with stamps showing they were bought in Kristiania. Tommy sat by an open door that led to the roof and started *Growth of the Soil*. Ravens gathered outside the door and talked their gravelly rasping language. He applied for a library card in the name Torger Torgersen. Petersburg was the only place that Tommy ever introduced himself as Torger. It seemed fitting in that other Little Norway.

After his evening walk of the docks Tommy went to the grocery store and bought a loaf of bread and lunch meat. He made sandwiches to last through the next day and stuffed them in the thigh pockets of his fatigues. The pants were his father's from Vietnam and he wore them for luck. He spent that night in the tent city. He listened to other residents tell stories in the cooking area but generally felt a disdain for the pot smokers and petty criminals. That night he bedded down again in the large transient tent. He unrolled his sleeping bag and crawled in. He hadn't brought a sleeping pad because he had no intention of living in the tent city but only on a boat. Before sleep Tommy put his wallet and knife in his boots but thinking better of it transferred his wallet to the bottom of his sleeping bag.

Again, Tommy made the walk to town before it had woken for the day. He scouted the harbor for any new boats and spotted the Pillar Bay. She was tied to the end of a dock, not in a slip. It was a work area without shore power or water, temporary.

No one was on the back deck and Tommy knew enough not to board without permission. The engineer came out of the galley, coffee mug in hand.

"How goes the hunt?" he asked.

"Nothing yet," Tommy said. "I'll keep grinding."

"Come in for some coffee." Tommy climbed back aboard the Pillar Bay.

The rest of the crew was seated at the galley table finishing breakfast. Everyone including the skipper inquired about his job search. Tommy learned that they had looped around and came back to Petersburg in search of a hydraulic hose, unfrozen milk and fresh vegetables.

Tommy was invited back for dinner and he returned after his luckless evening stroll of the docks. He sat at the galley table with the crew of the Pillar Bay and made everyone laugh with his story of that first morning sleeping under the viking ship.

After dinner and after ice cream the skipper surprised everyone by inviting Tommy along to Hidden Falls. It was the first two-day opener of the season and was really considered a pre-season warm up, a teaching grounds for new crews, not a full-fledged money maker.

"It might help to know how the job is done and there will be other boats up there, from Wrangell, Craig and Ketchikan."

It didn't take much convincing. "When do we leave?" Tommy asked.

"Oh, probably first light, you should sleep on the boat," the skipper said.

Tommy jogged back to the tent city and slung on his seabag and quick marched back to the boat. He chastised himself to keep his mouth shut and his eyes open and not to repeat that first night in the Strait of Georgia.

The next morning as they motored north towards the fishing grounds, Tommy followed the engineer around the boat. There was much to learn and he carried a City Light notebook in his back pocket and jotted down everything of interest. There was too much to learn. Tommy found his brain getting overwhelmed and shutting down. It was like filling a tank too fast without releasing the air. So, he scribbled what he could in the little waterproof notebook. He wrote down terms, and names and processes with crude little flow charts. Tommy was putting in the work to learn. He might not have understood what was going on but he focused until his mind ached. To anchor, the engineer asked the skipper for the depth in fathoms and then multiplied that by seven to get the correct slope so they wouldn't drag anchor during the night. The engineer had painted a red mark on the wire rope every five fathoms so he could judge the length as it ran overboard. Wire rope was called rope but all other rope was called line. It was confusing. Once the anchor hit bottom the skipper backed away slowly to set the hook.

The morning before the opener was a perfect day. Eighty degrees with no wind. They jumped from the top of the wheelhouse into the frigid water. Tommy didn't know there were sharks this far north. He would reconsider that swim months later when they pulled a blue shark on board. As it struggled on the deck, with eyes rolled back, its razor teeth cleanly cut salmon in half with every movement of its snapping jaw. The skipper had jumped on it from behind and neatly put a deck knife into its brain. Years later, Tommy watched another skipper grab a bull shark by the tail and send it back to the deep like an athlete throwing a hammer. Tommy still wasn't sure of the correct method.

The morning of the opener the crew woke at four. They moved about smartly, each getting their gear ready for the day. They pulled anchor at four-thirty and went to work. Tommy watched over the side of the bow for the rising anchor. He told the engineer when it was close and when it was free of the sea. They secured the anchor to a pad eye with a chain binder as a safety backup. The cook made breakfast and sandwiches for snacks through the day. Everyone had a known task and Tommy tried to stay out of the way.

The skipper motored the Pillar Bay out of the cove and towards the fishing grounds. At five in the morning, with two hours to go they started the skiff to warm. Fifteen minutes later the small boat died in a cloud of black smoke. The Pillar Bay was already on the prowl claiming its spot for the first set of the day. The skippers knew the best spots to set their nets. They played off the land. They looked for a spit or peninsula that would gather the salmon and would funnel them towards open water. That's where you wanted to set, the net would be a basket to catch the running fish. There were unwritten rules in commercial fishing as with all legitimate trades. Rules that were followed in deference to the profession not the competitor. The first boat on location claimed first set but boats anchored did not count. A motoring boat was an active boat. Boats wanting the second and following sets at that location could wait their turn, holding their positions just off the set. Setting in front of an active net was considered very bad form and was a purposeful insult. Tommy had heard the phrase, "to get corked," throughout his life but only now did he understand what it really meant. Getting corked was when another boat set their net in front of yours and took all your fish. Their corks floated in front of yours.

When the skiff died the engineer scrambled across the net to the smaller boat to investigate. He threw over the engine cover and diagnosed. The clear plastic fuel strainer was filled with black debris. Later they would track down the cause of the contamination but at that moment all that mattered was fixing the skiff. The skipper stayed at the wheel so as not to get corked but shouted down questions and orders as often as he could. Tommy asked if he could help and to his surprise the engineer said yes.

The man and the boy worked together. The engineer spun the filter off and discreetly dumped it overboard. They hoped that the strainer had caught the contaminants and that the injectors wouldn't be fouled. They ran a long hose and pumped out the skiff's fuel into one of the Pillar Bay's bunkers and then refilled the skiff with fuel from another bunker. While he did this Tommy changed fuel filters topping the new one off with fresh clear diesel and then cracked the fittings at the injectors and primed the system manually until no air bubbles came from the fittings. Tommy had learned basic diesel maintenance working in the woods of the Kitsap Peninsula for two summers in high school with an uncle who logged but never thought it unusual or special knowledge. Eventually they got the engine restarted and had a half-hour to rest before the seven o'clock opening horn.

During that first pull it all started to make sense, thought became reality with the sound of an air horn from an Alaska Fish and Wildlife boat signaling the start of the season. This was quickly followed by a bell on the back deck, the signal from the skipper to set the net. A deckhand pulled a short lanyard that released the pin on the 'beartrap', a mechanical latch that held the skiff tight against the stern. Then the roar of the skiff and main spooling up, two-stroke diesels quickly reaching their power bands, and finally the sound of the corks and purse rings bouncing over the rail as the net disappeared into slate gray sea. Tommy smiled, instantly in love with the spectacle, with everything about commercial fishing, his blood forever to taste of salt. He watched the skiff and main boat pull the ends of a u-shaped net trying to corral as many salmon as possible, the curved line of corks marking the top of the net. The skipper called Tommy up to the bridge. He asked Tommy how he knew about engines and what he knew. After that, he ceased to look at Tommy as another child in the way and took an interest in finding him a boat. Tommy stayed on deck and rotated with the three hands. They taught him how to pile net, corks and lead line. How to purse. How to brail. Anything a greenhorn could learn in one day. Of course, he worked too hard, inefficiently. Competence only comes from experience, it can't be taught, only earned.

Hidden Falls was a two-day opener and the boats unloaded to tenders at night so they could start the next morning's fishing with an empty hold. The fish from the second day would be brought back to the canneries and receive a few cents more for dock delivery, cutting out the middlemen. That night, as the boats waited at anchor for their turns at the tender, a skiff from another boat came to pay a visit. It was Don Brekke, Anders' father, skipper of the Yorktown. They had been working short-handed and he came over to look at this boy being shopped over the radio.

"Do you know how to weld?" Don asked.

"Yes," Tommy said.

"Do you know how to work on refrigeration?"

"No."

After a cup of coffee and some private skipper talk, Don Brekke offered Tommy a job. Three-quarters share, normal for a greenhorn. And that night he left the Pillar Bay and motored over in the skiff to the Yorktown. And that was how he met Karl and Anders. That's how Torger Torgersen got on a Brekke boat.

Fishing held him for ten years. Salmon money got worse but they tried other fisheries. Winters were spent fishing squid in the Channel Islands out of Ventura. Spring brought herring. He even got an occasional call for a longlining position. Tommy lived the off seasons in

Ballard above the Jones Brothers butcher shop on Ballard Avenue. It was a classic boarding house with small single rooms off a narrow hallway, a small bed and a shared bathroom. He paid for it when he was gone so he would have some place for his stuff although it was just a couple pictures and some books. He spent six years in and out of that little room. Tommy was so young and tough that he didn't even know he was living rough.

And then he met Kim and things changed. She was a neighborhood girl who worked at the grocery store. He would flirt with her as he bought his daily dinner out of the deli case. One night he asked her if she wanted to go bowling, after her shift, next door at the Sunset Lanes, a twenty-four-hour lane that shared the parking lot with the grocery store. She said yes. She was only eighteen and Tommy was twenty-four. She barely came up to his collar bone, but they fell in love and Tommy changed his ways for her. First thing she wanted was for him to get a real apartment. She didn't like walking down the hall to share the bathroom with the other men that lived above the butcher shop. So, he moved down the block to the Curtis building. From his window he could see the cranes at Halibut Flats unloading sand and gravel from barges. His window faced Ballard Hardware and sometimes his skipper would throw rocks at his window to wake him up. One morning still sitting astride him after sex Kim looked down and said, "I want to get married. I want a baby." Tommy looked up at her clothed only in the morning light and one block over a clamshell crane bucket slammed into a barge with an empty metallic clang. They both laughed. The early morning sounds of the working neighborhood had always been an annoyance to the young couple trying to sleep. But now it rung like a bell in church, albeit an industrial church.

Tommy reached up and grabbed her hips, pulling them back and forth. "Right now?" he asked.

"No silly," Kim laughed. "We need to plan. We'll need money and a house."

He fished less and less. Tommy got his Class B license and drove fuel trucks in the winter to stay in the neighborhood. She went to school and got her license to cut hair and then leased a chair. Then their daughter came and he quit going to sea. He went down the street and hired on at Halibut Flats Sand and Gravel to be home every night. They bought a house and then leased her a storefront and she became a boss.

Tommy remembered leaving Kim those first couple summers. In the days before the boat departed Fishermen's Terminal they thought they would die. They fucked constantly and she cried on his chest. Tears came to Tommy's eyes looking at Kim but they never made the jump. Separations are like kidney stones. You think the first one is going to kill you. The second one hurts just as bad but you know you aren't going to die so you just ride the pain.

They put their pain on paper and wrote letters. Tommy called from a pay phone whenever the boat was in port. The letters headed north were addressed General Delivery, Torger Torgerson, Petersburg, Sitka or Craig, depending on the phase of the season. Just after tying up he would race to the post office and hope for a stack of letters. Some would be descriptions of her days, of the customers at the grocery store and of her dreams for their future. If there was a lipstick kiss on the envelope he knew to open it in private. In those she would describe all the things she wanted to do to him and her other dreams for their future. If he was extra lucky there would be a polaroid of her naked body. She laminated these so the salt air would not harm her. Tommy spent hours in his bunk reading the letters and looking at the pictures.

He remembered that first homecoming after their first separation. After the long trip south from Alaska the oil tanks at Richmond Beach appeared and Tommy knew he was almost home. That long last hour and then coming to the locks. Commercial boats skipped in front of yachts, as it should be. Kim was on the terraced hillside as they came in. It was a nice September day and she was wearing a sun dress. When she waved Tommy thought his chest would explode. Even thinking of it now his body warmed.

Anders father, Don, was still the skipper. When they were finally in range he called Anders' mother on the VHF radio. They had an antenna mast above their house on Blue Ridge. Anders' mother then used the phone tree tapped to her kitchen cabinet and called Kim and a couple other wives to say that the boys were coming into port.

Tourists took pictures of the boat coming in and the crew acted the part. They threw hitches and lines around cleats with more flourish than necessary. The Corps of Engineers crew played along and asked how the season was. Tourists listened in, never witnessing such a spectacle back home in Ohio. Karl was on deck giving quiet instruction to take up slack as the water in the locks rose. Anders was on the bow and Tommy had the stern. Kim stood at the fence above smiling, flushed in her summer dress. Tommy lost all his words, everything, built up emotions, thoughts, sea stories, plans all vanished at the sight of her smile. No lewd thought even, which he reflected on as odd. Just a happiness to see her smile.

"Keep it tight back there Tommy," Karl said. Tommy had a round crab buoy in his hand to fend off sloppy yachts. The lock gates opened and they were in fresh water.

Don waved his finger in the air. "Let go bow," he called to Anders. "Bow away," his son said quietly, professionally. The CoE man dropped the line in the fresh water and Anders pulled it aboard through the snot hole. The bow drifted away from the wall.

"Let go stern," Karl called aft.

"I'll see you soon," Tommy said up to Kim. She smiled speechless. The CoE man dropped his end in the water and Tommy started hauling it in. As he hauled he let go of the small line attached to the buoy and it floated away like a soap bubble on dishwater. "Shit," he swore. Karl went for the gaff but Don was already rolling on the throttle. Don noticed the commotion, looked back and saw some of his gear floating away. One of the Corps of Engineers flathats quickly corralled the buoy with his gaff. Kim yelled, "I'll bring it," and waved the boat on. The crew all waved at the young woman, even Don gave her a thumbs up out of the skipper's window. The boat headed for Fishermen's Terminal. Once tied up and on shore power, Don cut the crew free for two days and the boat emptied in minutes.

Tommy waited for Kim in the wheelhouse. She walked up the dock occasionally bouncing the buoy like a basketball. Tommy opened the side window and leaned out.

"Hey baby, want a ride?"

"Do I?"

He went out the door and then down the ladder face first, completely comfortable after three months on the boat. She tossed him the buoy. "Come aboard," he said and then helped her over the rail. And then she was in his arms, her face against his neck, the tears coming.

"I love you. I missed you."

His throat swelled and tears also filled his eyes. He was embarrassed and later ashamed that he was embarrassed. He pulled her into the galley where they held each other until they could breathe and see.

What changed, he wondered. Where did she go? Where did we go? Was it the child? That was the easy answer but no that wasn't it. It was money. It was that damned leased chair that led to clients that led to a leased store. Then Kim's mind changed. She started going to parties by herself. And then she betrayed Tommy. The pain came fresh and he got out of bed.

20.

Monday morning. At least it wasn't raining, Tommy thought. Everyone was supposed to meet at the plant and walk the line together for the first day. But two hadn't shown up for the vote and a couple more had disappeared since the vote. Tommy would learn several things about his brothers during the strike. Some things would just prove his hunches about people correct but others would surprise him. That first morning it was just as he suspected. Those that cheated on their wives were absent from the picket line, and the complainers disappeared. They were the workers who constantly complained about the job, about management, about the union and about their coworkers. And now they would complain about the strike. The ninety-ten rule is the same for stewards as any leader. Ten percent of the people take up ninety percent of your time. It was something that led him to agree with Karl. Modern life was too easy. There was no price to be paid for laziness or stupidity. Poverty wasn't fatal. The junkies camping down by the pre-cast yard endured, they were revived by red bus paramedics and given aid by the city.

Tommy parked and carried three signs to the little group that had already gathered. It was hard work because they hadn't done it before. How do you stop driving and start walking the line? They would have to learn. Just the act was difficult. Do you walk slow like a French Foreign Legion march? Or do you walk fast to keep moving and cover more ground? Should you make eye contact with customers, let them know you see them still shopping behind the line? Or, should you stay within yourself and muster some kind of quiet dignity, some kind of Stoicism where you are sure of your decisions and let others make theirs?

Harold came out of the office and got into his truck. He drove away without looking at the strikers. That was fine because they didn't want to look at him either. They had no personal grievances with Harold but his side of the table was being unreasonable. The operators came out of the plant and asked if it was for real. They went back in the gates to gather their tools and then walked out the gates for the duration.

A few cars honked as they passed the picketers. The neighborhood needed time to come to understand this new rule, this new fact. It would be days or even weeks before the outsider could form an opinion about who was right and who was wrong. It would take a lifetime to realize neither.

Then the warehousemen, who were also Teamsters but from local 117 with strike language, cleaned out their lockers and left. And a little after that the truck mechanics, who were organized as machinists, locked up their tools and went home. The other trades wished good luck. It was the salesmen who were confused and worried. They had to choose their own paths and most chose the money because after all they were salesmen. But one, Johnny, he left. He was raised the son of a union miner in Anaconda Montana and said that his eighty-year-old father would kick his ass if he knew his son was working behind a picket line.

Some salesmen would smile and laugh and shrug their shoulders and pretend that they didn't understand as they worked behind the line but they knew. They knew that those actions defined their souls and defined their character in the eyes of others and the damage they did was permanent. And those that didn't realize this had no soul to offend.

Karl didn't have to work for a couple days so he went out Monday night on a long walkabout. He rambled down First Avenue through Belltown. He stopped at the Frontier Room and drank a couple of Jack and Cokes while being pleasantly abused by the bartendress. Belltown was peopled with the young rich whom he ignored because to him they did not matter or exist. Anyone who spent their lives making money wasn't worth a damn to him. They smelled good but had no ideas of their own. He was sure that they had never read a book and reached their own conclusion and that their epiphanies were merely half remembered conversations. He wondered where he could find the nurses and schoolteachers.

It amused Karl to explore other men's weaknesses. Karl was always disappointed by their fragile visions of the world. Most men readily accepted alien thoughts not realizing that in doing so they signed on for someone else's life. He liked to find out what they had reasoned, concluded and believed for themselves. He found almost every man mentally weak— never putting in the work to think for themselves, to view the opposite, to explore the paths that led to and from their beliefs. Those beliefs were like cabins in the woods with trails leading away to each side. Most men only use one or two of the trails, the same ones their fathers had used. Rarely were men strong enough to ask the right questions, to put in the hard work of cutting a new trail, the hard work of honest thought. And those smart enough for the task, academics, were usually physically weak or cowards unable to act on their own conclusions. Karl had met a very few independent men that were both honest with and about themselves and the world. They were almost always skippers, men who literally captained their own ship. Ahab and Wolf Larsen were always the examples that came readily to his mind but Anders' father was also such a man.

How many writers or thinkers had actually done anything except write or think? Where do men's thoughts come from? Men don't realize the damage done by a constant drone of TV or radio. Words, thoughts, slowly saturating the brain. Like rot, rust or water on an unmaintained boat, the words find a way in.

Karl continued on to Kell's Irish Pub but Brendan Behan was not in. He briefly wondered why there weren't any Norwegian bars but then remembered Norwegians could bore the bottom paint off a boat. In the Irish bar he struck up a conversation with a couple of carpenters. They were a real Mutt and Jeff combo, small-time independents that flew under the radar, dealt in cash and didn't pay taxes. Karl asked if the strike had affected them. The little one swore and went on about a set of stairs that needed pouring.

"How much do they want? Greedy fucking bastards," the little one asked.

And Karl had the original idea of putting his pint glass across the idiot's ear, but then there was the problem of the big one and there wasn't a clear path to either exit.

"It's not about money," Karl taught. "It's about language. Right now, they can't honor other Union's picket lines so if they showed up at a worksite where the electricians or carpenters were on strike they would have to cross the lines or risk being fired. They traded the language away back in the dark days of Reagan— may Odin eat his black soul."

"What's wrong with Reagan?" the little one asked.

Of course, Karl thought. Reagan was the patron saint of tax cheats. Reagan's anti-government populism won over the working class at the same time that the morally bankrupt 68er, hippie, me-first generation decided to grab anything not nailed down. The result was the elevation of entrepreneur over craftsman or worker. He again regarded his pint glass and thought of the little one's ear. It might be worth it.

"Well, that's a good cause," the big one said. "I hope they win." The big one was the brains. They continued to talk about the construction trades and the changes growth brought to the city. Neither of them cared about the port. They might as well have lived in Iowa.

"It's been a pleasure gents, but I feel the need to see some ladies."

Karl stumbled southward again, blessedly downhill. He stopped in front of the art museum and looked at the posters. The traveling show was about Charles Sheeler. The poster was his painting of the River Rouge Ford plant. Karl liked the clean bleakness of the work. It was loneliness without sorrow, machines without men. Unfortunately, the museum was closed on Tuesdays. So he made a plan with himself to return when his boat went off call. He wasn't used to a day job and already had suspicions of not liking it. He was used to full work or full freedom, not this awkward pace of small steps like strolling on railroad ties. He was used to living a month of life in a week on shore. And in that condensed, purified life if he couldn't find love he had to find an approximation, the same with sex. He knew that no one lived thirty days of life in a month, not without death in one pocket and good fortune in the other. The key was simple things like not sleeping too much and not watching too much TV. He always made sure to eat a couple of decent meals and drink quality booze. But this new life tasted of slow death, of suburbia.

He crossed the street to his favorite strip club, The Lusty Lady. He liked that there was a strip club across the street from the art museum. They complimented each other instead of conflicting. Art and beauty because art is not always beautiful and beauty is rarely artful. Or was it high and low thought? The brain versus the balls. Whatever it was, he liked both sides of the street. Outside the door he looked at the performer's pictures and fake names. He looked for someone who looked tough, smart. Someone who could appreciate the same, who could share a moment of compassion with him.

He went inside. He changed a five into quarters and went inside a booth. The mechanical curtain raised on two girls, one on each end of a rectangle room. The booths for the observant lined the outside. Some had reflective glass, in others you could see eyes looking up, following. He imagined the girls with clothes on, what they would look like passing on the street; the opposite of what happens outside. He read their personalities by how they moved. How their legs swung, how a wrist bent, how hips rocked. Maybe the near one had a drug problem, her skin was bad, or maybe she was just young. He imagined them college students paying for knowledge or lesbians laughing with sexual power over the male beast.

"Enough of the abstract," he said aloud to himself and left the little room. Karl walked around the store, for that's what it was, a place to purchase things— desires, memories, pleasures, catharsis. He studied the expressions on the faces of the patrons. Amused college boys, randy and excited. Embarrassed husbands desperate for anonymous sex. Perverts feeding their addiction. Gay men trying to convince themselves otherwise. Sailors over on a ferry from Bremerton enjoying the spectacle of white women dancing. There was a larger feeling of camaraderie as they moved from booth to booth. It was safe and no one was in competition with the other because for all it was impossible. The glass defined that impossibility and nurtured the fantasy. Unlike other clubs where semi-nude girls dry humped patron's laps and the men fought each other with money for the attention of the dancers. Fights which often led to fists, knives and guns.

Karl studied the pictures of the girls outside the private booths. A blonde with big fake tits held no interest for him and a little Asian guy seemed almost feverish as he searched his wallet for remaining green. The next booth had a brunette. He entered and put a twenty in the machine. The screen went up and a naked woman lay on a pile of blankets and towels. And for that night he hit the jackpot- a thick girl with natural boobs.

"Hello," she said sitting up on her knees.

"Hello. I'm Karl."

"I'm Rain." It was obviously a fake Seattle stripper name like Stormy or Moss. "How are you tonight?" she asked rocking forward on her knees and cupping her tits as if offering them to Karl.

"I'm wonderful now. Yourself?"

"Lonely." She asked if he would mind if she played with a toy. Karl could barely accent— his lungs caught in his throat. He admired her thick body. Her arms, her middle, especially her thighs.

"Did you play softball?" he asked.

Her face hardened unsure if he was insulting her. "Why?" she asked.

"Your legs are beautiful, perfect." She smiled, placated. She told Karl to make himself more comfortable, which was code to feel free to beat off. Karl undid his belt and stuck his hand in his pants.

"What position did you play?"

"Catcher."

"Perfect," he said and she smiled amused at this man with a softball fetish.

"Is there anything special you want?" she asked.

"Can you come?" he asked.

She laid back on the blankets and he put another twenty in the machine. She came or at least faked it well and Karl came in his untucked shirt tails and then tucked them in, not wanting to leave a mess for someone else. She noticed him buttoning up and stopped her show. He tipped an extra twenty. "Thank you," he said and went back into the night satisfied, drunk and content. He hoped she would consider him a gentleman.

In the cab on the way home with his own fluids against his stomach he thought of the big thigh softballer. There was something light and laughing in her eyes. Karl wondered who she was but he had a rule against dating strippers. To work on boats for more than two weeks and not know the truth of this would have been idiocy. And no man can avoid some amount of jealousy.

Karl had only made the mistake of following a woman's advice once. She had told him not to go to sea so they could be together every night. The commonality of the experience was laughable. Karl did not punish himself for choosing wrong. It is a young man's path to choose wrong. But not learning would have been inexcusable. She had cost him money and a job on a highliner but he landed on the Brekke boats because of it. He soon realized that she was giving advice that served her own ideas. That was fine. When he realized her error he began to doubt other things she had told him.

Like telling him that all strippers come from abusive pasts and the men who pay them are enabling the abuse to continue. Again, it was an idea that served herself, not the stripper and not Karl. It wasn't enough that he truthfully promised not to look at other naked women while they dated. She wanted him to affirm her thoughts like a religious devotee or a recovering alcoholic. It isn't enough that you tolerate their mantras. You must agree with them, embrace their validity.

Of course it didn't work out and she was released to wreck someone else's life. In that late night semi-drunk, ball empty, cab ride Karl found a magnanimous charity for her. She wasn't all bad. He remembered that although she wouldn't touch his cock she loved to be fucked in the ass while in the shower. He smiled to himself and hoped she was happy. The world was full of mystery and if you don't learn from life then you are doing it wrong.

21.

It was a slow night. The rain had chased the people away. Anyone inside was staying inside. Anders and Kate talked to pass the time. She told him about the parties and shows that she went to. She seemed to do something every night even though she worked two jobs. Her version of punk rock seemed to be anti-everything and a lot more fun.

"I'm going downstairs to do inventory. Call me if you get any orders," Anders said as he pulled one of the laundry bags from the bin and swiped a book from his pack before heading down.

Kate didn't call him. She cooked the two orders for burgers and an order of fish and chips that came in.

Anders sat on a bag of rice and read "La Technique" by Jacques Pepin. He had gotten it from the library on 24th. The librarians had been confused when he didn't navigate straight to the commercial fishing section. Anders had been studying fishing manuals, navigation books and general seamanship since he was a young boy. Most of his knowledge was passed down by his uncles and father but they rarely gave the whys, only the hows. Now he looked for similar books on cooking. What he really desired was a book on cooks, on cooking, on the life of cooks, but none seemed to exist. He was beginning to understand what it meant to cook although he still did not know how to be a cook. He liked being surrounded by the dry storage. He liked being able to browse the walk-in either for a snack or an idea.

He heard footsteps descending the stairs. Anders stood and put his book on a shelf between a gallon of olive oil and a container of cherry peppers. Amanda turned the corner.

"What are you doing Anders?" she said with a smile.

"Inventory," Anders said and then truthfully, "and reading." He pulled the book from the hiding place and showed her the cover. Anders sat down again on the rice.

"I thought you were doing something else but good for you. Be serious about it." Amanda pulled a little brass pipe from her purse. "You want some?" Anders declined and Amanda shrugged her shoulders and then lit the weed.

Anders stopped reading to watch the waitress. Even getting stoned Amanda was sexy. Her thin muscular body made every action look sexual. Holding her pipe bobbing to the muffled music coming through the floorboards her calf muscle climbed and fell. Her shoulder dove to meet a rolling bicep. The week before Anders had almost passed out watching her pump the air out of the wine bottles at the end of a shift.

"What?" she asked. He must have been staring.

"Nothing," Anders lied. "I just want to thank you for getting me into Le Canard," he said truthfully.

Amanda smiled sure of what she did to the young man. "You can make it up to me some time. You still owe me one." She closed the lid on her pipe and put it back in her purse.

"What are you doing tonight?" Anders asked surprising even himself with the question. Where did such confidence or daring come from? He was growing. He was living.

"I've got plans," Amanda smiled. "Maybe some other time." And then she climbed the stairs. Anders' heart beat heavy with blood.

When he finally climbed the stairs, Amanda was gone. Kate worked to close down the kitchen. "I thought you abandoned me," she said as she put one of the bus tubs in the dishwasher. She had already cleaned the work areas and made an attempt at sweeping.

"Wow," Anders said. "What's the rush?"

"I'm going out. I know you love standing around in the kitchen but I want to go dancing." Sweat ran down her neck and arms.

Anders went to the slop sink and started filling the mop bucket. He poured some bleach into the hot water and leaned back to avoid the fumes. "You can go if you want. I'll finish up."

"I didn't say that. We're almost done." Kate pulled a trash bag out of a can and knotted the throat. "You want to come along?" she asked.

Anders was holding down on the lever ringing the water from the mop. He hardly considered the question. "I've got to work in the morning," he said.

"So do I."

Anders ran the mop under the cold station flicking it sideways so the yarns would get bleach water against the wall. He looked up from swabbing after a few strokes. "What's going on?"

The rain had stopped and the brick street shined the reflection of store and streetlights. Anders walked up the street with Kate. "It's a beautiful night," she said and then hooked her arm through his and bumped her hip against his thigh. Further up the street, nearing the Sunset, she skipped and tried to get him to skip with her. He refused out of some misplaced sense of manliness.

There was a crowd milling about outside the Sunset. A ska band was in town from Los Angles and it brought out a different crowd. He recognized some of the guys standing around outside the Sunset. They were older punk rockers, traditional skinheads and the local motorcycle crowd. Friends of Tommy and Karl. The largest and scariest of the bunch was a skin named Pete. He sat on an old Lambretta scooter and held court. Pete was a union Ironworker and his right forearm was tattooed with a spud wrench, the symbol of his trade and his neck sported a skyline of the tall buildings he had built and was proud of.

"Hey Cuz!" Kate called to Pete.

"Little girl!" he called back. Kate dragged Anders into the circle of punk rock thugs.

"Pete, this is Anders," she said not releasing his arm.

"We've met," Anders offered. "I fish with Tommy and Karl."

"Right, right. They coming tonight?" he asked.

"No. Karl's on the water and Tommy is on strike."

"Of course. Tommy is a steward right. He's a man, a good man," Pete summarized.

Anders nodded his genuine agreement. It made his own chest swell to hear his roommate so respected.

"Tell Tommy I said hello and hang tough. Tell Karl I said he was a midget faggot." Pete smiled widely. He was missing a front tooth. Then he turned and said, "Hey Lily, this kid is Karl's roommate."

A woman with a jet-black Betty Page haircut turned round. "Oh really?" in a combination of purr and snarl. She looked at Anders and winked. She wore a tight-fitting flowered dress that was barely up to the job of containing her body. The dress ended just below her knees and she was anchored to the wet bricks by black fishnet stockings and white patent leather heels. Her style was at once modest and overwhelmingly seductive. She was covered in tattoos from the chest down. Anders didn't notice, because he strained not to notice, that her chest tattoo was the same as Karl's. She was a true Siren, a rocky shoal not to be flirted with. Anders would give her a wide berth. Just that wink and smile filled his cock with blood.

"He's with me," Kate said and hugged Anders' arm.

From the door of the bar a horn section blew and everyone smiled. It was time. From the first song until the last they danced. It was white boy ska with a heavy beat. From his position in the crowd a couple of rows back he could see Kate dancing up front with her fists above her head. When their eyes met they both smiled and continued their dance.

After the show Kate hugged him on the sidewalk and the mixture of rain and sweat wetted his neck. Later in his bed he could smell her on him.

22.

The first week of the strike passed. The Business Agent had told the stewards, "If you are going out for a day, then you are going out for a week. And if you are going out for a week, they are going to keep you out for a month to make rent and mortgage payments due and make insurance gap." Unfortunately, that was looking like a truism.

Tommy tried to be at the line whenever he wasn't at the hall but he knew that wasn't practical or healthy for the rest of the guys so by the second week he had devised a rotating schedule where every third day a third of the guys would walk the line. That gave them time to be with their families or work a side hustle. Tommy's truck was paid for, his rent was free and he had money in the bank for his mortgage.

Tommy was tired of answering questions. There were no new answers.

"I'm going to go get lunch," he said and walked out into the rain. Sometimes he needed to get away from the guys. It was impossible to always be positive. He needed solitude to recharge. Tommy drove his truck up 15th to Vietnam Restaurant. It was his favorite pho joint in the city and it was in Ballard. His travels through the neighborhoods of Seattle had taught him a couple lessons about pho. Most of all, it was the broth is that mattered. Vietnam's broth changed throughout the week but Tommy had never been able to determine which were the best days. Other indicators of good soup were: the staff shouldn't speak English and if they did it should be very poor, they should have their own chili paste, not Siracha, and fish sauce although he didn't use much of that. Finally, the bathroom shouldn't be too clean.

The matron was working. She clopped around the restaurant in large basketball shoes with the heels folded in making them into clogs. She wore a stained red sweater with a large Norwegian flag across the front. Obviously, it was a garage sale or thrift store find but excellent for neighborhood relations. Tommy took a seat under the abalone inlaid mural of horses running from a lightning strike and the permanent 'Merry Christmas' sign.

Tommy ordered a 'large pho ga, extra noodle'— basically chicken noodle soup. He added hoisin sauce, chili paste, a squeeze of lime, some sprouts and four jalapeno slices. Tommy kept adding chili paste as he ate the soup until the final remaining broth was red with oil.

The owner was an intelligence officer with the south when we abandoned their country to the communists. It earned him ten years in a prison camp. Who knows, maybe he executed Viet Cong in the streets with a snub-nosed .38 but probably not. Ten years seems pretty lenient by communist standards. Like Werner he was an immigrant of war. Both men had been on the losing side, one an ally, one an enemy.

Anders woke in the basement and could hear the rain pound the concrete outside the small windows. He thought briefly of Ventura and the nice weather. They never woke to rain down there. He pulled on a pair of jeans and a t-shirt from the night before and climbed the stairs. He opened the door to Karl banging around the kitchen in sweatpants and Xtratufs. Karl wasn't wearing a shirt as he made coffee in a French press. A drip coffee maker sat on the counter unused for years. Karl poured the boiling water from a foot above the carafe. Anders sat down

114

in the breakfast nook and studied his housemate. "Going fishing?" he asked. Karl never left the boat. Even on shore he still acted like he was underway. Anders worried about this. It was what he didn't want.

"No, I got to get on the roof and make sure it's ready for winter. I wish you guys did more around here. I put you two on my will to inherit the house in case I go down. But don't plan on it because I'm not going anywhere." Karl smiled at Anders. It was the look of a father, a captain, a big brother and a fellow viking all rolled into one. It was a challenge and a pledge. Anders wasn't shocked by the news of his potential windfall. He had quit being shocked at anything Karl did. Karl poured more water and was splashed on his chest tattoo. "Fuck!" he said and wiped it off with his hand.

Karl had a nuanced relationship to the shore. If a trip was uneventful, if the weather was good and the boat worked well, he didn't feel he deserved much time on land. But if things went wrong, if storms attacked and danger stalked, then he could take a couple of weeks and spend money and live well. Life, the enjoyment of life, had to be earned.

Anders looked out the window and caught a glimpse of Werner through the crane yard fence. Werner would be out for his morning walk. Regular as rain. He wondered if Karl would end up like Werner— old, alone, angry. "I swear he was at my grandmother's funeral," he said to Karl.

"Maybe they met at the shipyard when one of your boats was in," Karl liked to emphasize both Anders' inheritance and obligation.

They had indeed met. It was after Werner had sunk and that experience had changed him. Few know what it is to sink. Karl knew.

Karl poured Anders a cup of coffee and went out to the front porch to raise the Norwegian flag. "You got to remember to put up the flag when I'm not here," Karl said. It bothered Anders that Karl walked around with no shirt on in October. Anders was still embarrassed by Karl's actions at the Hat. Anders was trying to make a home at the Hat and he didn't want to be associated with the drunken fisherman violence of Old Ballard. It bothered him that Karl should be almost forty and pleased with his body. It bothered him that Karl seemed not to doubt, that he seemed comfortable and resolute with his decisions. Karl walked into his bedroom and pulled on a Ballard Oi! T-shirt. It was a play on the classic Ballard Oil logo. It was Karl's short-lived punk rock band. All the songs were about boats or fishing: 'Knute's an asshole', 'There's a fire in the fiddley' and 'Guns at 120 fathoms' were the biggest hits.

"What's the deal with that new waitress?" he asked Anders.

"Amanda?"

"Yeah, whatever. The skinny one."

"She's cool. She's new but she also works at a couple other places. She got me in at Le Canard."

"She looks like a social climber to me. You want that?" Karl walked past Anders at the breakfast nook and went into the bathroom. He took a piss without closing the door.

"Want what?" Anders asked not sure if he meant the job or the waitress.

"To be a cook?" Karl said and then flushed. He didn't know how to get through to the kid. "You're really not going to do any of the winter fisheries?"

"I don't know."

"What about that little dyke dishwasher? She seemed pretty cool."

23.

As Tommy sat on the strike line, in his chair under the tent, he kept his doubts inboard of his teeth. He tried to convey a confidence but he also considered both sides of the street. He approached problems slowly, with caution, doubting himself first. He tried to really listen to people, especially people he disagreed with, because he was often wrong. Once on the boat he had thought it a good idea to dry out welding rod in the oven. For the rest of the season everything baked, every roast tasted like sixty-ten with a hint of seventy-eighteen. Another time he told Anders to 'wash your fucking hands before cooking' because everything tasted like diesel only to realize that it was his beard that smelled like diesel. Therefore, he never thought he had all the answers and never portrayed the other side of the street as the enemy.

Anders was dreaming of Amanda. She was in their shower, their small dirty shower. She grasped the shower nozzle with both hands and looked over her shoulder at Anders. They were both soapy and wet. The phone rang. He heard it in his dream. It kept ringing and eventually he realized it was a real phone, the phone in the kitchen. And then he was awake. "Jesus Fuck! Someone answer the phone!" he yelled at the ceiling and then he got up and climbed the stairs. Both his roommates' doors were open, both already awake and gone into the world of men and machines.

"Did I wake you?" his father asked. Always the same question and always the same answer. Of course not. He wasn't sleeping. He was drinking coffee and reading the paper. Anders held his cock and wished that he could bring back the dream. His father asked him to check the bilge pump in the main shaft well on the Sara. "Have someone go with you and drive around for a while. I want to know when the pump comes on and how much it pumps. Either the float switch or the packing is bad." The squid net was already over the access plates that ran down the center line of the fish hold. His father should have known that.

"I have to work this morning." Anders wished he could pull back the words. He hoped his father was ignoring his words, which he often did.

"I thought you worked nights," Don said.

"I'm helping out at Le Canard in the mornings." Anders didn't lie. There was silence on the line. Too much silence. He would never be smarter than his father.

"Remember what's important," his father said. "Just get it done. Out." His father ended phone calls like he was talking on the radio. Anders didn't even know how odd it was.

"Out," Anders said to the emptiness. He needed to tell his father the truth. It hadn't gone over well with his roommates and they were kittens compared to the Captain.

When Anders got home from work Karl was sitting on the front porch in a teak deck chair reading. There was another book on the table next to a pile of peanuts. A Steller's Jay on the power line screamed for a snack. Karl raised his reading glasses to his forehead and threw a peanut on the sidewalk. The jay swooped on it. Karl looked like the old man he should have been.

Anders leaned Ring Ding Ding against the porch and asked Karl what he was reading. Karl flipped the cover towards the younger man. It was 'Joe Hill' by Wallace Stegner. 'Dynamite' by Louis Adamic was on the table. Anders had seen both books in the shelf but had never read them. He had yet to develop the love of books shared by Tommy and Karl. The older men never went to movies and rarely turned on the TV.

"Trying to get in the mood," Karl said turning back to the written word.

"Want to go for a cruise?" he asked Karl.

"Always. What's up?" Karl asked. He folded over a page and closed the cover.

"Dad thinks something is wrong in the main shaft. Either the float switch or the packing. Hopefully neither."

"Under the squid net," Karl said.

"I know."

Karl went inside to get ready and Anders started his little Isuzu diesel truck. He had bought it used in his sophomore year of high school and hadn't ever thought of upgrading, already displaying the natural Norwegian stinginess. His parents told stories of neighbors with millions in the bank yet still driving Dodge Darts from the 70s as a prideful display of sitting on their wallets. On the back bumper was a sticker that said, "Freemont sucks now— thanks to Suzie". Anders had no interest in Fremont politics but his truck was named Suzie for obvious reasons.

Karl reemerged from the house ready for work. "Did you ask Tommy? Is he walking the line today?" he asked Anders.

"I didn't. I didn't want to bother him."

"Well, shut that thing off. We'll take my truck in case he wants to come."

On the way, they drove to the Dutch Treat on Market Street for coffee and muffins. Behind the counter on the wall was a grid of open-front boxes. The Dutch Treat did a side business as a mailing address for fishermen. Before Karl had bought the house, Karl and Tommy had their mail sent to the coffee shop. It was nostalgic to visit. Karl bought an extra coffee. They stood around and flirted with the barista before continuing on.

They rounded the corner and sure enough about a dozen picketers milled about the gates where usually trucks would be coming and going. Tommy was in a little group of drivers at the far gate but he crossed over when he saw Karl's pickup pull off the side of the road. He walked up to Karl's side of the truck.

"You guys going fishing?" he said noticing their outfits.

"How's it going?" Karl asked and handed Tommy his coffee.

"Thanks," Tommy said. "This shit is boring. I'd rather be working. That's for sure."

Karl put his forearm on the windowsill and looked around, the knot of tattooed muscle rolling up and down the bone, surveying the scene. "Yeah, I can't believe this shit." Karl and Anders felt a little uncomfortable loitering around the strikers. It felt like they were getting in the way of some important business that the picketers were accomplishing. It would take a while before they realized that the only business that got done was at the bargaining table and that giving company to men on a strike line was one of the best things a person could do. Just standing with them was enough.

Anders leaned forward and spoke to Tommy. "My dad wants us to run the Sara. He thinks the main shaft packing is bad or that something's wrong with the bilge float switch. Either way it's turning on and off too much."

"Yeah, the float might not be going all the way down. Does he know the squid net is already in the hold?"

"I'd think so. He's the one that told us to load it. You want to come with us?" Anders asked.

"Shit. I wish. I have to stay here." The other two men nodded. They had known the answer before the question was asked. Karl put the truck into gear. Tommy gave the door two pats and they drove away.

Karl and Anders continued on to Fishermen's Terminal. The afternoon sky was clearing and it would be a nice day for a cruise.

"I couldn't live without the boats," Karl said as they walked up the dock. It was a bait, an offering.

"I know what you're saying," Anders said. "But it's also limiting. Boats mean you are gone. Away from the city and everything it offers— women, food, music, culture." One at a time they took hold of the davit and swung over the side rail. Anders climbed the outside ladder to the wheelhouse and unlocked the door. He started the main engine and then came down the inside ladder. Karl had unlocked the galley door with his key and was sitting at the table. "Don't you miss everything when you're gone?"

"Yeah, I do," Karl admitted. "But... when you get off a boat you have a better appreciation for the shore, for the city. And you have the time to live, to live properly, with intent. I couldn't work every day the way Tommy does. That would drive me fucking nuts. He can plot every day on a calendar for the next twenty years. Oh, it's a Tuesday— I'll be at work. When you live like that you don't notice shit. It all becomes a blur. Just one big day until you're dead."

"Yeah but you miss so much by being gone. And what woman is going to wait around?" Anders asked his voice rising a bit.

Ah hah, thought Karl. That's what it is— women. "Well neither of us have that problem," he said.

"But I want to. Look at what happened to Tommy. I don't want that."

"Kim has always been a bitch. Your mother handled it well. And it's not like the old days. We have phones. Distance makes the makes the heart grow fonder you know."

Anders waved his hand. "I'd like to try a normal life before I dismiss it. A bed every night. Maybe a woman every night."

"Same bed? Same woman?" They both laughed.

They decided to take a long cruise since it was a rare sunny October day. They took the fishing boat for a loop around Lake Union which involved four draw bridge openings. But it was worth it and the cruise gave Karl more time to drill Anders about his intentions. The younger man didn't have all his thoughts lined out but he wasn't afraid of making decisions, of deciding for himself. Anders sat in the captain's chair and Karl stood outside the wheelhouse, on the upper deck, so he could watch for the pump to come on and still talk to Anders.

"Remember when we were off Noyes Island and you said having the right last name shouldn't make you a skipper?" Anders asked.

"Of course, but I wasn't talking about you." Karl remembered it well. After Don had retired, he assigned the skipper positions on his boats to his younger brothers and cousin. Karl and Tommy had been passed over. Don had a clear preference for blood ties. It was understandable. That was Karl's last season fishing salmon. Tommy still had a few more years in front of him. Don had shuffled his fleet when he took off his boots and dried his feet. He had given the Saratoga, the best boat, to his youngest brother Knute. To offset Knute's weaknesses Don had also given him the best crew— Karl, Tommy and Anders. The Sara had the power block attached to an articulating knuckle boom. That meant whoever was running to boom could stack the net by swinging the power block fore and aft. It really meant that they could fish with one less crewman and that bumped the crew shares to twelve percent.

If Knute could have been a better skipper the boat would have been a guaranteed highliner. But he wasn't a good skipper. Knute had only returned to fishing after failing as a construction contractor. Knute was a yeller and he sowed chaos. He drank too much and didn't inspire confidence. He locked himself in his stateroom at night and would wake up angry. He would change his mind, rescind his decisions every morning. Karl had seen it many times on many boats. The yellers were the least competent. They shouted to hide their fear. They didn't trust themselves so they pushed outward. They moved the battle line away from their own minds.

Early in the season Knute had outlawed rolling of the eyes in response to Tommy's near-constant criticism of each decision. They were going to fish inside for pinks— roll the eyes. They would fish the coast for sockeye— roll the eyes. Tommy eventually quit talking to Knute. He went five weeks on a fifty-eight-foot boat without saying a word to his boss. It was obvious that Tommy thought talking with his skipper was not worth the effort and might even be a step backwards. Luckily Tommy knew his job and went quietly about it. Late in the season the boat swung toward open mutiny.

Karl was equally disappointed by Knute's lack of competence but as skiffman he felt compelled to try and salvage some success in the season. Karl, the most knowledgeable fisherman on the boat and de facto second in command, suggested and pointed but Knute's thick head saw nothing.

Things came to a head late in the season when the boat headed for the coast to make their money on sockeye. The weather had turned disagreeable. By that time in the season, the men wore beards as protection from the ground-up jellyfish spraying down from the power block as the net was hauled aboard. The open ocean meant fishing in a swell. It increased the difficulty of everything: fishing, cooking, walking, taking a shit. When the skiff passed the end of the seine to the main boat in a swell, the small boat could be ten feet above the rail one second and then ten feet below a second later. And pulling the net in a swell strained the gear, the hydraulics and the nerves. But the sockeyes running those waters were the money fish.

They were fishing off the haystack. It was a rock just off the shore which acted as a natural funnel for the coastline following sockeye. Puffins and seals covered the wave drenched outcropping. Proper technique for fishing the haystack was to queue up and take turns making sets. The order was first come first serve. Boats would anchor two days before an opener to claim their first or second set status. Many average fishermen made good livings by waiting in line. The crews on those boats could have up to an hour between sets. They cooked, they watched movies, they napped. It was good living all the way around. But Knute couldn't wait in line. That invited the silence of thought and doubt lurked in silence. He fished the second set out from the rock and caught the blow-by from the inside boats. It was the one answer Knute knew by heart, keep dunking the net. The Saratoga set their net sixteen to twenty times a day for the same amount of fish caught by other boats at a leisurely six-set pace.

While pulling the net or between sets, crews watch the other boats, to see their hauls. You can tell the quantity of the catch by watching how a boat struggled to pull in the sock, which is the boat end of the seine filled with salmon. That day they watched the inside boats make their money with a third of the effort on both men and gear. But a half-mile out something completely new was happening. The Alferi brothers were changing the game. They were from California and well respected as kings of the squid game. They made most their money fishing squid at night in the winter off the Channel Islands. They brought three boats up from California and Alaska was new territory for them. They saw the fishery with new eyes. In view of every boat on the coast the Alferis made a season's worth of money in a day. Everyone on the Saratoga could see the Californians' boats lean heavily as they brought their bags aboard. Even Knute could see that. But he didn't alter his course. The Sara continued to pound out second-rate sets because Knute had never fished a half-mile out and none of his family had ever fished a half-mile out. Twice, from the skiff, Karl pointed out to sea at a California boat leaned over with a heavy haul.

Once, as the skiff was pulled tight against the stern in preparation for another set, Karl scrambled across the net and climbed the ladder to the wheelhouse. He picked up a pair of binos and glassed the Alferis. "Are you seeing this?" Karl asked Knute. Knute picked up his own pair of binos. They watched another giant sack of sockeye get hauled aboard. Even greenhorns knew those boats were getting rich. Knute set his glasses down and said, "get back down there. I want to make a set." And they did, in the same place with the same result.

That night at the galley table, after Knute had locked himself inside his stateroom with a bottle, Karl said, "I think we've taken a wrong turn on this whale-road. Knute couldn't lead us out of a cul de sac." And with that Anders switched his allegiance from stateroom to fo'c'sle, from blood to neighborhood.

They floated for a bit and watched two seaplanes land and one take off.

"Anything?" Anders asked out the window.

"No, not really. I saw the pump come on once for a few seconds. I think your father might be wrong on this one. A rare occurrence."

"Well, it was a nice day for a cruise. It would have been a crime to be inside."

"Like in a kitchen?"

"Touché. Point to Karl," Anders smiled and slid the boat into gear. They headed back down the ship canal towards Ballard.

As they crossed the bridge in Karl's truck, Karl looked around the horizon, still no clouds. "We should have a bonfire tonight. You know any girls we can invite?"

"Actually, I do," the young man said. "Stop by the Hat." Karl pulled off the road by the strikers. Tommy walked over to his side of the door. "I'll be back in a few minutes," Anders said and trotted across the street, headed for the restaurant.

"What's up?" Tommy asked.

"Let's make a fire at Golden Gardens tonight," Karl said.

Tommy looked at the clear sky. "Not a bad idea. I'll bring the wood."

"I'll bring the beer and food. Anders is trying to bring the girls."

Anders entered the Hat. There was an employee phone list downstairs in the office. As he passed the kitchen he spotted Kate at the dish station. "What are you doing here?" he asked.

"Hello to you too Anders," she said.

"I didn't think you were working."

"I got called in. Why? What's wrong."

Anders was flustered. "Nothing… nothing, never mind."

Amanda came out of the back room still writing on her order pad. "Hi Anders!" she said with too much joy. She slapped his ass as she passed and it made him jump. With both women accounted for there was no reason to go downstairs to the office so he left the restaurant, confused and stymied.

So, the grand fete was only three men. Around the campfire they talked fishing, boats, the strike and even cooking. Eventually they moved on to sex, the eternal subject. Karl believed in its importance as a mineral or food, something essential to body and psyche. He was worried about Tommy's monkish existence especially with the stress of the strike. "I think it's a ritual of the procreative act. It's our only natural function as a species— to reproduce. Sex tells your body, your inner mind, the subconscious, or soul or whatever, that you are doing your job, that you are a good human. That's why priests are so fucked up."

"I wonder if gay sex can still scratch that itch?" Anders asked. Karl and Tommy looked at Anders. He said, "I'm asking for a friend," and all three men laughed.

"Probably," Tommy said. "Your body doesn't know."

"Oh, it knows," Karl said. "Your mind knows."

"What about masturbation?" Tommy asked.

"I'm not saying it's bad. It's just not the same thing. It's a simulacrum— a poor substitute. I've been waiting years to use that word." They all laughed again. The stories around the fire lasted until ten when a park employee enforced the rules.

24.

Karl worked another four twelves of harbor work. Between assisting vessels in and out of their berths there was too much downtime. He read books in the captain's chair but grew bored and worried about getting fat. For this meager work the crew was rewarded with three days off. It felt cheap and Karl went to bed early.

Karl's soul had recovered some balance by the time the kettle whistled in the morning. He walked barefoot out to the porch carrying his coffee and boots. He sat in a deck chair and watched the Vietnamese net builders yank down on their sewing needles fastening their knots tight. The rain fell lightly. Karl pulled a sock from his boot and dried his foot with it before donning it. Then he pulled on the boot, laced it and repeated the process. He watched the net builders do their ancient work, common work across cultures now transformed into an industry that supplied factory ships manned by immigrants from non-fishing societies, men who worked their whole voyage below decks in a floating abattoir. Karl knew these nets were for the ocean rapers with their mile-long trawls. They were for the boats of the comically named American Seafoods company, a Norwegian owned fleet parked at Terminal 91. Yet Karl wasn't convinced that the future answer was the small boat religion of Pete Knutson. Should the world go back to hand lining? Seining off the shore? The problem was demand— too many damn people. Eventually all these people would overtax the ocean and overtax the neighborhood.

But again, everything changes. Even the neighborhood was changing. The little WW2 bungalows were disappearing. Houses were being bought and sold and everything was getting nicer. His corner of the neighborhood was safe, still comfortably industrial. The importance of the fish economy was declining and that would change the neighborhood even more. The net builders across the street were still busy. Ballard was still the main jumping off point for the Alaska fisheries. But now it was easier to send parts and supplies north on a barge, boat or even a plane. The shipyards in Washington and Oregon still built boats but they could be refit in Juneau or Ketchikan.

He went back inside the house and cleaned the kitchen, mopped the floor and then sat at the breakfast nook and paid the monthly bills. He felt a drunk coming on and needed to put some work in to balance the ledger. Then again, maybe he wouldn't get drunk. Maybe he'd just walk around the neighborhood looking to help someone with something, available for work, love or adventure depending on the Gods' will.

Karl pulled on a wool halibut shirt and headed south on foot towards the ship canal. Before he crossed Leary Avenue he glanced inside the loading dock of a stainless steel metal fabrication company. He could hear the zap and hum of welders as they built conveyors and tables for the fishing industry. He walked under the bridge and then up Ballard Avenue. He passed Kolstrand, makers of deck winches and pulleys. Further up the street he passed Ballard Hardware. The heavyweights of the Ballard marine economy still worked. Across the canal Marco Marine and Seattle Ship Supply plied their trade. The highliners were still parked at Ballard Oil.

Karl walked by the strike line. The strikers stood in the rain like old ladies waiting for a bus. Tommy was there but there was no new news because no one was at the bargaining table. The two sides had scheduled a meeting at the end of the week. Few of the workers believed in easy victories. They had worked too much in their lives, had lived too close to the earth.

Karl didn't like the standing around. He thought the strikers should be doing something, somehow striking a blow, not just waiting for others to act upon them. Karl continued on his walk. He followed the tracks toward the locks. Passing Ballard Oil, he could see what highliners were parked at the dock. Highliners were the top producers, the big money boats. The Brekke boats had always docked in the terminal. Anders' father must have had his reasons. Don always had a plan. Karl walked on to the Lockspot. He drank a beer with his lunch and chatted with the bartendress. She had fucked Karl a couple times years ago and even though there was nothing between them they sometimes side-smiled at each other like they had a secret on the world. That always made Karl feel better, that and the beer. He walked the train tracks back instead of Market Street. There was a plastic grocery bag caught on the blackberries and Karl pulled it off and started filling it with trash. It seemed like the thing to do. It was something. He needed to always be doing. Mostly the trash was cans and bottles left by the bums who hid there. Once the bag was full he tied the handles together and deposited it in the dumpster in front of Ballard Oil. Karl continued on with a sense of accomplishment. Passing Anchor Tattoo he tapped on the window and the owner looked up. Karl went and fetched a couple coffees and they talked about the strike and the neighborhood. The tattooer worked on a sketch for a client coming later in the day. Karl was thinking out loud about the old days, the old strikes he had read about and the differences with Tommy's stagnant line. He told the story of the Minneapolis Teamster strike of 1934 cribbed from Farrell Dobbs' book *Teamster Rebellion*. Those times of street fighting held a romance that warmed his heart, blood shed for class warfare.

Karl looked over the counter at the drawing the tattooer was working on.

"That sucks," Karl said and then sipped his coffee.

"Fuck Karl. Thanks for the support."

"No, the drawing is good but the idea is bad. Who is getting that? No, let me guess— some guy that weighs less than his girlfriend and has been in less fights than her."

"You shouldn't judge," the tattooer said without looking up.

"Why shouldn't I?" Karl asked.

"I don't know. It says it in the Bible or somewhere. You don't know what the kid has been through or what his thoughts are. Not everyone has to be a fisherman."

"In Ballard they do."

"I'm not."

"Yeah, but you serve the community."

The tattooer snorted and continued working on the sketch. Karl looked out at the passing cars and thought.

All Karl's tattoos had meaning. They were stories of work and travel. After ten years of towing he still got fishing tattoos. Towing was devoid of imagery. He couldn't see getting a tattoo of a bollard or a deck winch. They would be confused for a squatty H and a boulder. Even the kitschy four master on his chest meant he was of the sea. Who was he to judge someone else's symbolism? He was the judge, he thought. That was life. Moral and aesthetic judgements. Just as some people choose to live in suburbs and eat at chain restaurants. He had no qualms about judging someone else's symbolism. It was a language and some people spoke poorly. Hell, even Jesus would say that Jeff Koon's art sucks.

Karl continued his walk. He rounded the corner and stopped into the Smoke Shop for a drink. It was an old school Ballard bar and he liked the atmosphere. The walls were covered with pictures and paintings of working boats.

Karl looked for someone he recognized other than the bartender. Simo the Finn was at the bar huddled over a well whiskey. He was a retired merchant seaman who played accordion for drinks up and down Ballard Avenue. Karl spotted him and walked over. Simo's squeezebox sat at his feet like a piece of luggage.

"I thought you were 86'd," Karl said.

"They forgave me," the old man said looking up from his drink, eyes unfocused. "I didn't mean any harm by it. I was only talking the truth."

Karl bought two drinks, one for Simo and one for himself.

"Karl," Simo said.

"Yeah?"

"Don't grow old."

"You grew old Simo. Why didn't you take your own advice?"

"That's it! You don't realize until it's too late. Trust me. Don't grow old."

Karl didn't laugh. He patted Simo on the back. He knew enough not to discount the old man's words. Wisdom was hard to find in the world. Most people ignore the signs, the omens, through life and instead cling to fantasies to ward off the dark. Don't grow old. It was good advice and was uncomfortable enough to taste like truth. Karl clinked glasses with the older man and they both threw the drinks back. "I've been trying to get killed all my life but it hasn't worked out," Karl said and then motioned to the bartendress for two more. Simo's usual conversation was about the pleasures of Estonian women. Karl wasn't used to seeing him so down. "How 'bout some music Simo?"

Simo picked his accordion and played a slow, sad folk tune. The other patrons continued their conversations or stared at the TV. It was a normal occurrence.

Karl carried his drink from painting to painting like he was in an art gallery. He listened to Simo's music and looked at the pictures. He knew several of the boats on the wall. Others were from before his time. Crabbers, trollers, seiners, tow boats and power scows— beautiful working boats. He loved looking at the old boats and imagining the crews. The collection was uncurated. It had begun with a crew bringing in a painting of their boat to watch over and be watched as they drank. It was like planting a flag. The collection grew and became unique. There were no yachts or 'flying dutchmen'. No connoisseur advocated for those works. Karl thought of America's Cup boats or classic twelve meters. They were visually beautiful with almost perfect lines. And they were built for a specific function which made them a tool. But still they wouldn't have fared well on those walls. Racing sailboats were like beautiful rich women— treasured because of their impracticality, cherished for their uselessness.

The music stopped and Karl looked over at Simo. The old man was draining a schooner of beer. The brief silence allowed Karl's earlier thoughts of tattoos to merge with the boats on the wall. That was it! That was the difference in his philosophy be it tattoos or paintings of boats was a simple question. Were they working or pleasure? Were the objects for play or were they real? Children with fashionable tattoos were the moral equivalent of rich people with yachts. Meaningless, irrelevant and more than a little insulting. Karl celebrated his flash of insight with another drink. He left a twenty with the bartender to keep Simo wet before going back to the tattoo parlor. Karl always walked around with a catalog of tattoo ideas in his head. The tattooer was accommodating and gave Karl a new Dutch wooden shoe on one forearm, the symbol for sabotage, and an arched black cat on the other forearm, the symbol for direct action.

Satisfied and happy from burning needles and the accompanying endorphins, Karl walked back down Ballard Avenue to the strike line. It was still raining and Tommy still stood in front of the gated concrete plant, still holding a sign. The other strikers clustered in small groups or sat in camp chairs beneath a portable tent and read paperbacks. Karl showed Tommy his new tattoos but the significance was lost. Tommy knew that it wasn't the time for direct action or sabotage. It was the time for standing around. It was the time for customers to call and complain about missing concrete. The time for foremen and superintendents to call and complain about inflexible schedules being bent and broken. Beyond the plant gates great sums of money would be tied up in construction loans their ledgers slowly turning red. A strike was a contest as to who could bleed slower. But there was always the risk that bosses would call and be sympathetic with a struggle against an uppity union. That was possible, but Tommy could bet that the unity between bosses would always be less than the unity between workers. After all they were competitors and none had the others' best interests in mind. Tommy knew it was the time for standing around.

Karl found the exercise depressing. He had never known or appreciated anything subtle. He left Tommy and walked on. He crossed the Ballard bridge with the intention of walking the loop through Fremont to burn off the daytime cocktails. From the bridge he looked up the canal towards work. He noticed which boats were in. Karl hated to see any boat leave without him.

Karl headed east for a bit until he came to Seattle Pacific University. He then climbed up and over the Queen Anne hill headed for downtown. He walked the sidewalks, nodded at people and looked at the houses imagining all the lives lived in them. He knew that not one of them was a fisherman and very, very few would be involved with the sea or the port. The majority of them bought and sold things. Maybe one or two of them bought and sold fish or boats. They were soft people, land people, warm people. They feared cancer and stock market crashes.

Karl walked down the hill and continued on to First Avenue. He walked through Belltown and could see glimpses of Elliot Bay between blocks where the street plunged toward salt water.

He looked through the fogged glass into Kaleenka. It was a Russian restaurant. The small tables were full. Karl liked to come alone and eat borscht with a dollop of sour cream after a day of reading Dostoyevsky, Solzhenitsyn or Pasternak. Karl enjoyed the solitude of eating alone in a restaurant. Allowing the day's words to digest with the food. But today Karl hadn't been reading Russians.

He walked a couple doors north to the Virginia Inn, a small bistro. The owner, a Frenchman named Patrice, was leaning against the bar. Karl was something of a Francophile after studying French in high school. He had wanted to be an exchange student but his father died and threw the already shaky family into turmoil. He should have come here after a day of reading Celine, Lartéguy or Camus but he didn't. Karl would visit the Virginia to talk. He ordered a croque madame and a glass of red wine. The restaurant was empty and Patrice leaned against the bar reading the paper. He poured two glasses of wine.

"They've got me working in the harbor— a day job. I feel like an accountant," Karl said.

"You wouldn't like owning a restaurant." Patrice closed the paper and brought the two glasses down.

"No, I don't believe I would... No offense." Karl accepted the wine and said, "merci." They toasted and drank.

"Patrice, what do you think of the Legion?" Karl asked.

"The Foreign Legion?" Patrice asked. Karl nodded. "I think westerners join for the wrong reasons, for adventure, whatever that is.

But since the collapse of the Soviet Union the Legion is being flooded by Slavs. The Eastern Europeans and Asians understand that it's a means to an end, citizenship. They get the worst missions too—Sarajevo, shitholes in Africa. You thinking of joining?"

"No, I just watched a documentary. Life just seems too easy, too unimportant. Where is the struggle? Where is the war?"

The men watched two ladies cross the street. They each held on to a strap of a large bag. They were drunks, professionals, lifers. Midway through the crosswalk one of the ladies threw a big loopy punch that missed its target and she stumbled to the ground releasing the bag. The other lady sensing the opportunity started kicking her friend but then she too fell and they proceeded to roll around continuing to fight on the ground. The lights changed but traffic couldn't move. The city watched with mild interest. To Patrice it didn't even warrant a comment, it was too ordinary. Karl smiled as he watched. He knew there were many bad decisions that led these two ladies to now fight and block traffic on First Avenue. But there also had to be one bad decision that started it all. The one unreversible choice. Karl wondered what it was. They probably were dealt bad genetics and family failure but nothing in life was more unequal than natural skill and intelligence. Eventually SPD arrived and broke up the show. "There's your war today," Karl said. Patrice just nodded and continued watching.

Karl entered the Seattle Art Museum. He first went into the bookstore and paged through the books on Sheeler. He bought the exhibition book and went to the café. He gave the book one cup of coffee's time for study before visiting the actual works. He was of two minds. Karl wanted to locate the artist in his own time before looking at the paintings so he wouldn't miss the hidden language, but he also worried about his eyes being clouded by someone else's thought, the writer of the exhibition book. Would his natural reaction be altered by the pointing finger saying look at this? But decisions need to be made and he chose foreknowledge.

Karl had spent many afternoons at the museum and most of the permanent collection was memorized. Again, as he climbed the stairs he thought of the boat paintings at the Smoke Shop. Karl didn't demand that art be representative. But it mustn't be a con. Modern art was made for shopkeepers and bureaucrats. He felt shock was overrated and overplayed. He was conscious of life and death and was annoyed by shock. He wanted understanding and insight, meat and marrow. Beauty on occasion.

He liked what he saw in Sheeler. It was an appreciation for reality, an appreciation for the man-made environment. Sheeler seemed too in love with the machine; losing the relation a worker has to his tools. Sheeler looked at machines as an intellectual and modernist. Karl had loved boats and even hand tools on occasion. But they had never been religious totems. Karl thought even Tommy would fail that jump.

The industrial paintings were the most appealing to Karl. He circled back on *River Rouge Plant*. He looked at it from close and then from far, from left and right. And then he read the description on the wall again.

"This isn't right," Karl muttered. A docent had been shadowing him partly out of boredom and partly out of curiosity.

"Excuse me?" she asked.

"The card on this painting is wrong. It says the picture is of 'Ford's coal processing and storage facility'." Karl pointed at the right side of the painting. "Those are bows. Those are draft marks, although a little screwy. Anyway, those would be Great Lakes ore boats. Coal would have come in by train."

The docent took a closer look. "I've never noticed that. This is a traveling show so the Whitney would have written the labels. I've been staring at these paintings for two weeks and have never seen a ship's bow." She laughed a little laugh, a museum laugh. "You seem to know more about this one than I do but is there a question I can answer?" she asked.

"Yes, why isn't he more popular?"

She laughed again and he reached out his hand. "I'm Karl."

She took his hand and said, "Tema."

"Are you a member?" she asked.

"I am."

"There is an after-hours private showing tonight with a Sheeler expert. You could ask him about the ships. There'll be music and drinks too."

"Are you going?" he asked. He could have been asking for her endorsement or for her.

Karl caught a cab home to take a nap and shower before the presentation. He put on a collared shirt but still wore boots and jeans. A khaki trench coat classed things up. A second cab delivered him back to the museum but he didn't see Tema inside. The presentation was interesting and Karl drank a couple glasses of wine and snacked on the hors d'oeuvres.

"Why didn't you ask about the ships?" Tema asked from behind.

Karl smiled as he chewed a cracker with crab. He rinsed it down with some wine. "Truthfully, it had too much personal interest. But I still can if you want the answer."

"No, that's fine. What did you think about the presentation?" Tema asked.

"That guy kept going on about how Sheeler's art had removed emotion. I don't buy it. I think there's more emotion in those paintings than most. He doesn't scream at you or lay down and cry but that doesn't mean there isn't emotion. I think it's more complex, more meaningful. Simplicity often hides bigger truths." Karl smiled. He was satisfied with his rebuttal of the expert. Tema looked at him unsure, like he might be pulling something over on her. But she wasn't sure and it made Karl interesting. They talked more about the show and about SAM's collection.

"I'm going to walk up to the Alibi Room and get some dinner. Would you like to join me?" Karl asked. "My treat. No strings attached. I don't get to talk seriously with women much and I'm enjoying this."

Tema was hesitant. Karl was an odd man. "And why is that? Why don't you talk with women?" she asked.

Karl chuckled softly. He knew he sounded strange. "I work on a tug boat and before that I was a fisherman. I've spent my whole life surrounded by men and salt water. It gets old. You've already made my day interesting. I'd like to buy you dinner and continue our talk."

"That explains your interest in the ships."

"It does, and my reluctance to ask about it."

Some drug dealers were working the sidewalk as they climbed the hill. It wasn't unusual but alone Tema would have crossed the street. Karl didn't stop talking to her. He didn't stop looking at her. He didn't give them a wide berth. He paid them no notice at all and she noticed. They quit talking as he walked by. She briefly thought about it. He wasn't big. It was something else. Scars, tattoos and a thick neck. He exuded violence, a coiled violence.

As they turned toward Post Alley Karl came face to face with the stripper from the Lusty Lady. She wore glasses and a watch cap but her crooked smile was unmistakable. "Hey," Karl said. She didn't say anything back, failing to place him in her mind. Karl didn't want to lose the opportunity and whipped his mind to think of something to say. "You know, catchers should get more credit. They are the quarterbacks of softball. They run the show." The stripper smiled and laughed, now remembering. "Have a good night," he said and she returned the greeting before walking on.

"Who was that?" Tema asked.

"A softball player I've watched," Karl said.

Tema was a full-time museum employee. She had an MFA from the University of Washington and was a painter. Her eyebrows were thick, her hair was thick, her glasses were thick. She had thick tits, ass and legs. Her mind was subtle and quick. She wore silver rings on her index and pinkie fingers, on her thumbs. She had black hair on her forearms. She seemed Slavic. She was a woman you could call a comrade if that word still had meaning of its own, a woman to work next to on a kibbutz.

Karl didn't believe in art for art's sake. The big tube of toothpaste made him angry. "That's not art. That's an aesthetic argument. Art has to say something. It has to communicate something about the human condition. It should have replaced religion." He didn't ask her opinion because he was enjoying himself. Both his hands waved through the air. The one holding his wine and the other a fist. He enjoyed talking of things other than wind and weather, ships or sex. "Like glass. That's the biggest con ever put down and we're to blame. Seattle's to blame. Glass isn't art. It's craft. Glass blowers are artisans not artists. No one seems to understand the difference anymore."

They drank a couple bottles of wine with dinner and Karl found a smiling audience for his diatribe that wandered from art to work to pets to food to neighborhoods. Tema let him enjoy the ride only pushing back when she spotted holes in his logic.

"Life would be boring, no, more than that— pointless without struggle. And that struggle should be both mental and physical. I don't want friends that agree with me. I want to be challenged. That is the only way you know what your own thoughts are. I still say that most modern art is shit but at least it has made me consider it. Or maybe you have made me consider it. I owe you a debt."

As the food stole the blood from their brains for their stomachs the pace of the conversation slowed. Tema excused herself and went to the bathroom and Karl continued arguing in his head. What the fashion magazines pushed as beauty didn't interest him. Popular culture pushed weakness as an ideal. Strength was a working-class attribute and must therefore be equated with stupidity. The ideal had no scars. Karl thought if men could express what they truly thought was attractive a lot of skinny, vapid, trophy wives would be unemployed. Although he had no first-hand experience, he knew in his gut that they were bad lays. Sex was something that served them, it was the currency in which they traded, and that made it false, a transaction. Which was also an aesthetic argument.

"That's all I can do," Tema said. Karl smiled and folded his napkin on his plate. He left a half glass of wine and a generous tip.

They walked up the cobblestone alley into the evening bustle of First Avenue. Drunks, tourists, club-goers, homeless and downtown dwellers all went their different ways. They had spent the evening arguing about art and music and knew almost nothing about each other except opinion.

"May I?" she asked and put her arm in his. It was the only time ever she hadn't been scared to wait for a bus on Fourth and Virginia. "I'd like it if you came home with me," she said.

"I'd like that too," he said. They rode the bus back to her place.

She was holding his cock as he woke to the sound of his pager vibrating on the bed stand. He picked it up and looked at the number. It was work. "Can I use your phone," he asked. Karl stood naked in the kitchen while Tema pulled on a kimono and headed to the bathroom. I can always trust the boats to save me from happiness, he thought. Karl called the Port Captain.

"Kevin's son died. He has to fly home from Dutch. Can you take his run?"

"Of course, what happened?"

"Got pulled overboard with a pot. Must have been caught on something."

"Shit, the statue gets another name."

"Yeah."

"It'll take me a couple hours. I'm not at home."

"You want me to send the parts driver to pick you up?"

"Yeah, but give me 45 minutes." He winked at Tema and then asked for her address.

Karl could barely hear the port captain say, "Jesus…" on the other end of the line but he thought just because one person is dead it does no good for the living to quit living.

Karl hung up. "A friend's son got killed fishing and I have to fly up to Dutch and take over his boat so he can fly home." She climbed atop

137

Karl and they had slow, tender, parting sex. He came inside her for the third time.

Karl caught a ride back to his house with the parts driver, a member of Tommy's local who didn't even know that ready-mix was on strike. Karl caught a five o'clock flight and spent the night in Anchorage to catch the first morning flight to Dutch. He was onboard by 10:30 the next day.

25.

The phone rang while Tommy was brushing his teeth and admiring a Penthouse Pet from 1974 decoupaged to the bathroom wall. He spit and hustled to the phone. It was the Business Agent from the local. He asked Tommy to bring his truck by the hall on the way to the strike line— the Teamster Hall on the corner of Denny and John was not on the way to the strike line but Tommy agreed and hung up the phone. He then called another brother to let him know that he'd be late on the line. Unexpected chores done, Tommy returned to the bathroom and finished brushing his teeth and gazing at the Pet. They sure were built better back then, he thought, and why bring my truck? Tommy didn't own a car so it wasn't an issue.

As he came out of the bathroom the phone rang again. It was Kim and she wanted to stop by since he was home. Tommy hung up and thought "home" used to mean a house he shared with his wife and daughter thirty blocks north. He dressed for work but didn't put on his boots. Instead he unfolded himself on the couch and closed his eyes for ten minutes. Anders came upstairs getting ready for work.

"How goes the strike?" Anders asked.

"Still on the line."

He wanted to sleep but closing his eyes only made his thoughts go faster. Tommy wondered why so many people were up and disturbing his morning. Eventually, Kim's Honda pulled up and parked in front of the house. He knew the sound of her e-brake and the sound of her shoes climbing the steps. She almost always wore nice shoes now. He kept his eyes shut.

"Striking looks like hard work," she said through the open door.

138

"Twenty-four hours a day."

She sat down on the coffee table facing him. Tommy closed his eyes. Anders came out of the bathroom with a towel wrapped around his waist.

"Hey Kim," he said as he headed for his basement dungeon.

"Looking good Anders," she said to make him uncomfortable. But he did look good. Anders was no longer the boy he was when she first met him as a three-quarter share crewman on Tommy's boat. He had filled out as a man but remained thin.

Kim explained that their daughter needed money for dance lessons and who could argue with dance lessons? Tommy kept his eyes closed.

"How much do you need?" he asked.

"Three-hundred."

"There's a lock box under the foot of the bed. The combination is 174." It was his local's number.

"How original," she said.

"It used to be 722." July 22nd, their wedding anniversary.

Kim went to his bedroom and turned on the light. She thought it odd that an ex-husband would let an ex-wife rummage unescorted through a bedroom. She would have never let him do the same in her bedroom. It was neat and clean. Too tidy actually, hinting at mental instability. The bed was made. Clothes off the floor. A picture of them with their daughter on the dresser and a dog-eared copy of *Iron Coffins* on the bed stand.

She pulled the lockbox from beneath the bed and spun the tumbler and opened it. Inside was a gun, a naked picture of her and nine hundred-dollar bills. The room smelled like him.

"Can I take four?" she called out.

"Take it all," he said from the couch.

She took five and put the bills in her purse. She looked at the picture. She was so young then. She wished she could give him a newer picture. She was in better shape now. Kim put the box away, turned off the light and went back to the coffee table. She sat down. Anders came up the stairs, dressed.

"Off to work?" Kim asked.

"Yeah, another double," Anders said.

"Still at the Hat?"

"Yeah but I'm doing days at Le Canard."

"Good for you. That's a nice restaurant."

Tommy wondered if she had ever been there. He had never taken her. Anders left. He kicked Ring Ding Ding to life and rode off in a cloud of blue smoke.

Kim put her hand on Tommy's shoulder. His eyes were still closed.

"You need to get laid," she said.

Tommy opened his eyes and Kim pulled away her hand.

"I'd settle for a blowjob," he said.

She laughed and sat up straight. "Not by me you idiot." She stood up and straightened her skirt. "Seriously, get out of the house."

"Can't blame a guy for trying," he said and again shut his eyes.

Kim moved toward the door. "I don't need that," she said.

A mechanical click came from the side of the house. Tommy opened his eyes and quickly made for the door pushing past Kim. He went outside and around the side towards the crane yard.

"I got you fucker," he said.

Kim followed. "What?" she asked.

"A rat." He pointed and between the house and the chain link fence a rat ran back and forth captured in a live trap.

"Gross." Kim turned and left. She didn't say thanks for the money because she wasn't asking for a gift.

Tommy stood in the rain, in wet socks and wondered what she meant by 'need'. Did she not need sex? Or didn't she need Tommy in particular? Neither was a good thought so he approached the rat. Tommy had mixed feelings about the little beast. His tail was disgusting but his ears and little feet were kind of cute. It was a Norwegian wharf rat. Tommy had thought the process through when he set the trap. He wasn't going to execute him with the pellet gun. No, Tommy was smart enough to know he would never get a kill shot on the first try and he didn't fancy turning the little guy into swiss cheese. Instead, he would drown him in the 55-gallon drum that caught the rainwater from the gutters. Karl had installed the barrel with the intention of using the rainwater to water his plants but it just overfilled and then washed down the curb. The idea of water conservation in Seattle was ludicrous.

Nevertheless, Tommy's idea was simple: catch rats in cage, put cage in water.

Tommy picked up the rectangular cage. The rat scurried from end to end, its weight making the handle teeter totter. "No offense buddy," he said and then dunked the cage. But the cage didn't submerge. Two inches remained above water line and the rat clung to the air. Tommy watched the disturbing rodent terror and was disappointed in his plan. Tommy grabbed a three-foot piece of stub steel rebar lying next to the foundation and tried to push the rat under but it just dodged the pole. The rat didn't want to die quickly. An uneasiness saddled Tommy. He was not used to being an executioner, not used to determining the fate of others. He pulled the cage out and set it aside. The wet rat dug at the far end of the cage. Tommy poked in the water with the rebar. He could feel something at the bottom of the rusty water. Maybe bricks.

He couldn't let the rat go but he regretted the amateurishness of the delay. Tommy moved the rat out of the way before he tipped the barrel over because even an executioner should be polite. The water rushed down the sidewalk and out into the street. A Vietnamese net knotter across the street heard the crash and looked up from his work. Tommy waved at him. "Don't mind me. Just trying to drown someone in a kiddie pool," he said under his breath. Two heavy, rusted diesel starter motors were at the bottom. He stacked them in a row and righted the barrel. Tommy had to refill the barrel with the garden hose adding another layer to the absurdity. Indeed, even the irony of drowning a fellow Norwegian, if only in name, was not lost on him.

He went inside, sat on the couch and waited for the water. Occasionally he could hear the rat thrash about. Finally, the water overflowed and Tommy shut off the valve. He grabbed the cage and said, "goodbye little square head." When he let go of the handle the cage disappeared quickly. Tommy went back to the couch and waited for a long fifteen minutes unwilling to face any more surprises. He washed his face and put on a fresh shirt.

What to do with the dead rat? There wasn't an unpaved piece of soil for a block to bury him in. He didn't want the dead rat in their garbage can, attracting more rats and cats. He put the body in an empty Rainier twelve pack and on the way to the Teamster Hall Tommy pulled

141

through a boat yard and pretended to look at a seiner high and dry on cribbing before tossing the rat coffin in a large roll-off dumpster.

On the sidewalk outside of the local were 5 burn barrels. Another steward had already pulled up with his own pickup. Tommy pulled in behind him. Halibut Flats already had a burn barrel but these were special. These were engineered, or 'engine nerd' in construction parlance. They were stoves actually and they were lent to the Teamsters by their brothers in SPEEA, the Society of Professional Engineering Employees in Aerospace, the Boeing technical union. No one builds a picket line burn barrel like an aerospace engineer and the men were very thankful. They were impressive little machines made from 55-gallon barrels with hinged lids and a detachable six-inch stove pipe as a chimney. They even had little legs to increase airflow through the bottom. They would find out later that they were a little too engineered and ran like jet engines— with all the vents open they howled and ate wood faster than you could feed it. Tommy took one stove and the bigger plants took two.

He was almost out of gas so he stopped on the way back to Ballard to fill up. The pumps were full so he waited. Tommy kept glancing in his rear-view mirror at the stove. He was proud of his friends and proud of his union. A small black mini-pickup with a child in a car seat had taken the last pump. A young kid in his early twenties got out and went inside to prepay, a cash customer. In the bed of the truck were carpenter tools, an air compressor, saw horses and a small job box. Tommy invented his story. It was a trait of being a city driver. At each stoplight he tried to read the people. He really should have been a cop. The shitty truck and lack of stickers said he was non-union. It's a shame Tommy thought— this guy doesn't know enough to help himself out by helping others. Tommy suspected that the young carpenter would cross a strike line because he didn't know any better. But, then again, maybe he cheats on his taxes and steals his neighbor's paper.

While Tommy pondered the carpenter a new black sedan circled the pump island. It backed in at a right angle between the small pickup and another car. A man in dress shirt and pleated slacks got out and started pumping gas. What an ass! Tommy thought, slightly impressed by his arrogant aggressiveness. This guy had to be going places. He'd own the town someday. A salesman for sure. There was no doubt about his cheating on taxes, or stealing papers. Tommy saw the kid come out of the store and approach the salesman. Tommy got out of his truck to watch. He wanted to hear the salesman's reasoning. He moved close enough to hear.

"Hey that's my gas," the kid said.

"No, it's not," the salesmen said flatly.

"I just paid for it."

"No, you didn't."

"I just..." the kid pointed at the station.

"I don't care." The salesman looked him square in the face. He was no coward. An ass and a bad citizen but no coward. He would go far in life. Both of them were a couple me-first motherfuckers on opposite ends of the food chain. What wasted effort.

Maybe it was too much and maybe the carpenter recognized this. The salesman was the guy who won the game the carpenter wanted to play. The carpenter's arms flew from his side and landed on the salesman's throat. They sat for a second and then released. It was a fluid, practiced action, the movement of someone familiar with choking. Tommy doubted the happiness of his home life.

"You assaulted me," the salesman said. "You assaulted me. I'm calling the police."

"Don't do that. I'm sorry. It was my turn."

The salesman pulled out a phone attached to his car by a long cord and made the call. The carpenter walked back to his little pickup and put his hands on the tailgate. He was resigned like someone familiar with losing. The child in the car seat waved his arms around pointlessly. Within minutes a police cruiser pulled in and the salesman hustled over to close his deal.

Tommy drifted over to the carpenter. "I saw him push you first," Tommy told the carpenter, but the carpenter didn't respond. He didn't get it. "I saw him push you first. I'm a witness," Tommy said again. The carpenter still didn't get it. He understood the words but didn't understand the meaning. "I'll wait," Tommy said and went back to his truck and read the copy of 'Borstal Boy' Karl had given him.

The cop talked to the salesman and then to the carpenter and then finally came over and talked to Tommy. He took Tommy's statement and his info. The salesman looked over to Tommy, seething with the injustice of it all. Neither of them deserved punishment or mercy.

Tommy left not gloating or victorious yet not ashamed either. He wanted to tell someone. He couldn't tell Karl because Karl would be too delighted and would accuse Tommy of not pushing far enough. Anders wouldn't understand and would wrongly focus on the lying.

The barrel was a great morale builder and they fired it up right away. Harold came across the street to see his former employees' new toy. He feigned an interest in the design but it was obvious to Tommy that striker comfort worked against Harold's interest and he saw Harold frown reading SPEEA cut into the side with a torch— cross union solidarity.

"What are you going to do with it at night?" Harold asked. "What about the crackheads? I'm sure they'd love a fancy stove like this."

"Hmmm, you've got a point." Tommy pondered. "I guess I'll take it home."

"I don't think hauling a hot stove is a good idea either. But don't let me tell a Teamster how to haul." Harold smiled, and it was his first smile in a month. "You can lock it up behind the gate at night and then get it out in the morning."

"I thought you changed the lock," Tommy said.

"I did but just ask a salesman to open it for you." Harold returned to his side of the street.

Tommy smiled and thought Harold was smart. He had just made Tommy dependent on Halibut Flats, again. But after almost a month of striking they seemed to be settling into a semi-permanent Christmas truce. Not enemies, just fellow combatants stuck in a machine that continued on, driven by unseen others.

The next morning when Tommy pulled up to the strike line a retired cop car was parked outside the plant. The car had been repurposed by a security company with a yellow light bar instead of blue.

"What's this shit?" Tommy mumbled as he pulled up next to it. The car was empty. Tommy shut his truck off and got out. He spotted the guard behind the fence.

"Hey," Tommy yelled. "What are you doing back there?"

The guard approached the fence carrying a long flashlight like a baton. "Can I help you?" he asked with professional coldness.

"Yeah, what are you doing back there?"

"I'm doing my job. Halibut Flats hired my company to protect their property."

"From what?" Tommy asked.

"From whatever. I heard there's some labor issue."

"Yeah, no shit Sherlock." Tommy walked away disgusted and then stopped. "Hey," he called the guard back again. "I need my burn barrel over there."

The guard smiled and said, "They told me you would be coming for it."

Tommy hated to be outmaneuvered but there was no denying it—Harold had played him like a fool. Tommy accepted it and each day asked the guard to check in and out his burn barrel. It was petty and effective.

26.

A week later Karl's boat returned from Alaska. It was a good crew and they went about their business with minimal direction from the wheelhouse. After tying up, cutting the crew loose and finishing the paperwork, Karl went up to the Port Captain's office to see what his next assignment would be. He led the conversation by telling the Port Captain that he didn't want to return to harbor work. The boss wasn't fazed by the pronouncement because there wasn't any port work available. He went to a large whiteboard that covered one wall of his office and tracked all the boats and their assignments.

"Well, there just isn't a ton of work right now," he said to Karl while studying the board. "No skipper spots for sure. Not even for mates. I can't pay you your wage to cook plus you'd drive everyone nuts. It'd really help us out if you used some of your vacation,"

"How much do I have on the books?" Karl asked.

"You don't know?" The Port Captain was astounded. "One sec…" He picked up the phone and called downstairs to payroll. "How much vacation does Karl have? No shit? Okay, thanks." He hung up the phone and looked at Karl. "You have seven weeks."

"No shit," said Karl.

Karl agreed to take three weeks at a minimum, maybe more if he found something interesting to do. Three weeks of paid vacation with nothing planned is a dangerous road. He'd go out of his mind if he stayed around the house or even the neighborhood.

"Come on, I'm buying, but we should probably walk."

Karl and Tommy went to the Hat and well diluted their blood. Even Tommy smiled after six drinks and it wasn't his worried smile. Tommy brought Karl up to speed on the progress or lack of progress in the strike. Management kept refusing to even discuss strike language. Halibut Flats had changed all the gate locks and hired a night security guard following the other companies' suit. Supposedly there had been threats of vandalism. It was a bullshit power posturing move. Everyone knew it. Anders brought them out a couple of plates of chicken-fried chicken and sat down in the booth.

Amanda walked by. "I could have brought that out." She was ignored by two of three men. After nine Tommy glanced more and more at his watch. He had to be back on the line by eight.

"Go ahead," Karl said. "I can drink by myself and Anders gets off at midnight."

"Sorry," Tommy said and Karl waved his hand to dismiss the apology.

Anders came out of the kitchen but didn't want a drink. He had a cup of coffee. "I told Amanda I would help with her car."

"Tonight?"

"She's broken down in a no park zone. You can come along and help."

Karl shrugged his shoulders. He had a full stomach and was pleasantly drunk. He didn't really want to stumble around Ballard and an adventure downtown was appealing. Amanda sat down in the booth next to Anders. She looked at the young man.

"You're still going to help me, right?" She put her hand on Anders' forearm.

Karl noticed and smiled. She was good. "What's wrong with the car?" he asked.

Amanda turned to Karl with eyes not cold yet not warm either. He could sense that she wanted to hate him but had yet to find the reason. "The clutch is broke," she said. "I can push the pedal but nothing happens. Anders is going to help me push it to a parking spot where it won't get towed."

"Can you feel the spring when you push it? Is there resistance?" Karl asked.

"I think so," she said putting one finger to her thin lips. She tapped her lip and repeated, "I think so."

"You want to leave it there?" Karl asked.

"Not really but I have to do something."

"We all have to do something," Karl said and took a sip of his cocktail. "Fuck, let's grab my truck. I have tow straps in the toolbox. Anders has to drive though." Karl raised his glass as an excuse.

"I'll be back," Anders said and left the table. A few minutes later they could hear his two-stroke motorcycle go by.

Karl looked at Amanda. "Why you messing with that boy?" he asked.

"I'm not messing with him. I like Anders. He's smart and he wants to learn. That's rare."

"Is he going to be your boyfriend?"

"Oh god no," she laughed.

"Does he know that?"

She frowned. "He knows what he wants. Why don't you let him live his own life?"

"Because he is on the verge of really fucking up."

Anders parked his bike and then went inside to get Karl's keys. Karl's truck was beautiful and it barely moved. It was a five-year-old diesel one-ton but didn't even have ten thousand miles. Karl had bought it new. Anders waited for the glow plugs and then rumbled the truck to life. He enjoyed the luxury. It was a truck of someone who worked and was a pro at it. Anders drove to the restaurant and stopped in the no parking zone with his flashers on. Karl and Amanda climbed into the cab. They sat three across with the woman in the middle even though it was a crew cab.

Anders pulled the truck in behind Amanda's car. Karl used the back tire as a step and climbed into the truck bed. He opened the toolbox and pulled a headlamp out. He put it on and then searched through the box in the narrow cone of light. Out came a long yellow nylon strap with two loops, a couple of marine-grade, US made, Crosby shackles and a bag of tools. He handed Anders the strap and shackles and climbed down carrying the tool bag.

"Let's take a look first," Karl said to Amanda. "Pop the hood."

She did and sat in the driver's seat as Karl said, "push the pedal… release the pedal."

"Anders, get me the orange shackle from the right side of my toolbox."

"Here, I have these, right here," Anders held out one of the gray shackles.

"No, I need one without a threaded pin." Anders went to the truck.

Karl looked around the hood to Amanda. "I think we can fix you enough to drive home. You're missing a piece of linkage. I'll patch you up but you're going to want and get the right piece."

Anders returned with the shackle. It had a two-inch pin and was stamped for twelve tons. "It's a little big," Anders said.

Karl smiled. "Yeah, no shit." He took the shackle and then grabbed a pair of lineman's pliers from the bag and pulled the cotter pin out. "This is what I really needed," he held the small pin up.

"Why didn't you say so?"

"You going to explain every little thing when you're the skipper?"

"You're not the skipper here," Anders protested.

Karl stood up straight and smiled again. "I'm not?" And then he disappeared under the hood with the pin and pliers. After a few grunts he told Amanda to work the clutch pedal. "That'll work," Karl said and closed the hood.

Amanda started the engine and put the car in reverse and then first to test the fix. Satisfied she set the brake and got out of the running machine. She smiled and said, "thanks guys," and then gave them both a hug.

"What are you going to do?" she asked, making conversation.

"Find someone to play with my balls," Karl said.

"Excuse me?" She thought she really hadn't heard him.

"Get Fucked," he said and then there was silence. Anders wanted to say something but he feared ever taking sides against Karl. "I meant get myself fucked. Not for you to get fucked." Karl smiled at Amanda, putting on a show. Overacting himself to make the woman uncomfortable.

"Oh," she said.

"Thanks for the ride," and Karl walked off into the rain.

They watched Karl walk off in the swirling mist his hands thrust deep into the pockets of his mechanic's jacket.

"You going back to the bar?" she asked.

"No. I have to take Karl's truck home." Anders lied. He was thinking of the dishwasher. He didn't want to walk into the bar with Amanda. Life was getting confusing. Possibilities jostled with each other like punks in the pit. He had two jobs and was almost on the verge of having two women. Anders knew it was impossible yet Amanda's presence drew him. Her smallness was like a delicious scent from the kitchen. He wanted to know what she felt like pressed against his body. He wanted to pull her close, absorb her. But mostly he wanted her to take him seriously, to see him as a man, not a boy. He faked an indifference. "I spend too much time there. I'll probably just go home."

Karl climbed the stairs to the 211 Club at Second and Bell. It was one of his secret hangouts and he only went to it alone. A mediocre pool player who didn't even own a cue, he never won or lost much money but enjoyed sipping beers and talking with hustlers and old-timers. That night a Chinese lady was laying waste to all comers. Karl passed on a few offers just to watch her play. She never smiled and Karl wondered if she was accepting applications for a galley slave. He walked back to Ballard and took a shower. It had been a good night and he looked forward to a sleep in a bed versus a bunk. It was four when he came out of the bathroom. Tommy was sitting at the table drinking coffee.

"Sorry man. Did I wake you?" Karl asked.

"No, I couldn't sleep." Tommy had grown old in the strike. There was nothing youthful about him. Karl went to the kitchen and poured himself a cup of coffee. He could sleep anytime.

"How long have you guys had that Pinkerton?" Karl asked.

"The what?"

"The guard at the plant. I don't ever remember you guys having security."

"No, that's new. I think Harold just got one because all the other owners have them."

They sat drinking coffee at the small table under the single light. Outside, the industrial night was sleeping quietly in the mist. The cranes, the nets and the trucks all waiting for the next day of work.

"Well, I'd hate for him to waste his money," Karl said and pushed back his chair. Tommy finally smiled.

They dressed all in black like French commando frogmen and grabbed two neglected bicycles from the side of the house and rode into the old part of town. Everyone with any sense was still asleep. Only criminals and cops prowled these strange hours. They stashed their bikes in an alley behind a dumpster and closed on the plant.

They watched the two gates into the plant from the shadows across the street. The piles of stored cement block and chimney liners made a good hiding place and provided seats to wait. They talked about how easy and natural it was to fight in your own neighborhood. They understood guerilla wars and insurgencies.

"I wonder if resistance work was this much fun?" Karl asked

"I doubt it."

"Still we should have French names, code names. I'll be Claude and you can be Marcel."

"Why Marcel?"

"Because you're absurd," Karl chuckled.

They debated tactics and ordnance. In Karl's backpack they had bottle rockets, roman candles and M-80s. They ruled out the rockets and candles because those would have given up their ambush position too easily. They decided on M-80s launched from wrist rockets. It was a classic. True, a quick fuse could take off part of your face but "Who Dares, Wins." They planned. They would put the first two shots over the guard's head. The next two would be on the gate line, boxing their prey.

Karl handed Tommy a cigarette. "Here mon ami, for the lighting."

Tommy took it and smelled the brown stick. A clove. "Nice touch," Tommy said.

"It's the details that make it special Marcel." Karl chewed on his and Tommy stuck his in his watch cap like a pencil.

Being still a little drunk Karl's attention wandered and he looked up at apartment windows across Ballard Avenue and he wondered who lived behind the curtains. Tommy knew the Pinkerton's schedule. He would come out one gate, locking it behind him, check the rail cars and then enter the other gate locking it behind him. He probably only kept this steady route to keep from falling asleep because nothing would ever happen, until now.

"We should have come by boat from across the channel," Karl said still looking up at the darkened windows. Karl loved the romance of difficulty. A task needed to be challenging.

"Next time," Tommy said without taking his eyes off the gates. He saw the cone of light from the guard's flashlight. "Heads up." The Pinkerton was unlocking the west gate. Tommy put his cigarette in his mouth. "Light up," he said.

"No. Wait until he is behind the rail car."

Karl readied his lighter, the one he always carried, engraved with an anchor and "Yorktown." He carried it to light cigarettes for ladies even though he didn't like ladies who smoked. The guard went behind the car. His light searched the tracks and wheels.

"OK. Light up but keep your cherry hidden," Tommy said

"Like an eighth-grader." They were both giddy with excitement.

"First shot high overhead," Tommy said just to say something.

"Oui Marcel."

The guard unlocked the gate and slipped his fat body through and then relocked the chain.

"Ready Jean?"

"Claude."

"Whatever."

They stepped around the corner of the warehouse into the streetlight.

"Ready." They pulled tension.

"Light." They leaned in, puffing on their art student cigarettes. The fuses hissed to life.

"Fire." The two bombs sailed into the night sky trailing their little comet tails of sparks from the fuses. Neither insurgent watched the first shot as they busily reloaded. They should have because it was spectacular. Tommy's shot made it almost to the sand bunker before exploding. Karl's exploded with a muffled thud because it had ricocheted off an access catwalk on the plant, and flown through a rust hole into the main loading hopper. The Pinkerton, shocked and confused, turned from the explosions and ran towards the gate and he could see clearly the outlines of two men firing their second shots. One hit a rail just outside the gate and bounced straight up. The other caromed off the gate and flew toward the guard exploding ten feet away. Seeing his attackers, the Pinkerton retreated but as he turned toward the plant he was swallowed by a billowing gray cloud. Karl's first shot had scored the impossible win. He had slain a monster with an unaimed arrow. The gods had guided the ricochet and it was with the luck of Loki, a questionable good fortune. The confined concussion had knocked loose seventy years of built up cement dust. Every bolt, fixture and wall gave up its collection. An avalanche of ancient Portland cement fell. An inverted mushroom cloud rolled from beneath the plant. It spread and grew. Karl and Tommy watched the Pinkerton disappear in the gray wall.

Tommy stood up straight. "No fucking way."

"That was more than I expected," Karl said. The cloud consumed the plant and the gate. It continued to grow in every direction through the windless night. "We should go." They were almost to 15th when they heard every siren in the neighborhood start up. Fire trucks, ambulances, police cars, even the fire boat across the canal came to life. Every boat and car within five hundred yards was covered when the dust finally settled.

Tommy could finally sleep and he slept hard. He didn't hear the phone in the kitchen ring at eight. On the fourth call Anders climbed the stairs swearing the whole way because he didn't have to work a double and wanted to sleep in. He answered the phone and then woke Tommy. It was Ben, the morning picket captain.

"Harold's looking for you."

"Negotiations don't start till noon," Tommy said still without coffee.

"No, not about that. The security guard got assaulted last night. They hauled him out on a stretcher. He took 14 stitches across the forehead."

"That didn't happen," Tommy said, but he didn't go by the plant.

He drove down to the hall at eleven, an hour early for the scheduled negotiations, to nose around and talk to the other brothers, business agents and office girls.

The other stewards arrived and they made a game plan for the day. The Business Agent, their lead representative, looked tired. His job was to end an unwinnable war. He didn't want any more unsolicited advice from the stewards. He was tired of democracy.

"Just keep your mouth shut. No matter what they say don't respond. Only I talk. We will take breaks where we can all swap ideas but it's important that we come across with a unified voice. Got it?"

"Roger that," Tommy said.

The union reps were headed for the meeting room when Harold spotted Tommy in the hall. Harold threw it in passing gear and hurried over to Tommy.

"What the fuck Tommy? What the fuck was all that shit about?"

Tommy backed a little away, only slightly confused. "What?"

"Don't play stupid." Harold was red. "You fuckers assaulted my guard and opened the cement valve on the plant." Harold pointed down at Tommy. "When I find out who it was they're gone. No questions just fucking gone."

Now that's the wrong thing to say to a Union man. Workers could be fired but there was always a process. Unions were the defenders of civilized rule. "I'm sure I don't know what you are talking about." Tommy was on his heels.

"Half the neighborhood's gray and you don't know nothing about it." The other stewards heard the commotion in the hall and came up behind Tommy. Harold glared at the motley bunch behind his employee. "This has nothing to do with any of you," he snarled at the assembled group.

"Everything has to do with everyone. We're Union," the Business agent replied calmly.

Tommy found his voice. "Granted I've only worked there for six years but I didn't think you could open the cement valve without air pressure so you're saying that we snuck into the plant and turned on the air compressors? If we really wanted to fuck you we'd just call OSHA or the EPA. Shit, Barney Fife probably did it himself worried about job security. Asshole should join a union." The men behind Tommy laughed.

"Fuck you Tommy." Harold was still pointing at Tommy. He swung his finger around the assembled bunch. "Fuck all you guys." Harold strode off and left the building. Obviously, he wasn't in the mood to negotiate.

"That doesn't seem good," Tommy said to the BA.

"Nah, that's ok. But I don't want to know what you did."

"I don't know what he's talking about."

"Shut up Tommy." Then the BA turned and walked away worried at yet another snag. He stopped and turned back to Tommy. "You still want to work there when this is done right?"

"I love Halibut Flats," Tommy said automatically. He loved his job. He loved work. He loved only two other things in life— his daughter and his ex-wife who didn't love him.

Negotiations went on without Harold for a day. The black soul lawyers that represented all employers' groups in Seattle refused almost everything and offered almost nothing. Their arrogance was obvious. The Union said it would trade away demands for funeral leave for domestic partners and matching pay for deployed reservists. The employers caucused and returned with the offer of forty-eight-hour strike language meaning that drivers could legally honor a picket line for a maximum of two days. "That's the absolute max," the black soul lawyer said.

The union representatives left the room to caucus. It was a short meeting. "What do you guys think?" the Business Agent asked. Another steward made the jackoff hand sign. They all laughed and knew the strike would go on.

27.

Karl made it into the afternoon before the threat of three weeks of idleness spurred an attack of stir-crazy. The only standing invitation he had was from a traveling nurse in Ketchikan. She still had two months on her contract. Karl wondered if she could choose Key West for her next contract. But he finally decided to keep his first foray small— a clockwise tour around the Olympic Peninsula.

He went into his bedroom and looked for Tema's number. Maybe she would want to go to the coast for a couple days, drive down to Astoria, visit the maritime museum and climb the tower. It would be interesting to get her out of the city. Tema the urban. Tema the urbane. But she declined, she had to work. Karl noticed a hesitation in her voice. He'd let her make the next call.

Therefore alone, Karl drove down the five to Portland and ate a steak dinner at Mary's Club before he reversed course and headed North again, oddly down river, on the Oregon side of the Columbia. Mary's originally catered to the merchant seamen crowd and Karl liked to imagine his towboat and fisherman forebearers enjoying a meal, a drink and the outstanding scenery. Every visit always led to the question: why weren't there more restaurant strip club combos?

He made it to Astoria, checked into a motel under the bridge and still made last call at the Desdemona Club where he knew the bartendress. She seemed pleased to see him and upon hearing that he was staying the night kept his glass full. Finally, Karl had to walk away from an unfinished Jack and Coke. He left a fifty under the glass and was headed towards the door when she caught his arm.

"Hey stranger," she said. "At least tell me your room number before you walk out." She had always been aggressive and a little crazy. Karl appreciated the mix but knew it too well.

"Are you seeing anybody?" he asked.

"Yes, but it's not serious." She had never been a liar.

"Sorry," Karl said, "but I'll have to pass."

"I never could understand your morality."

"Yes but it's mine. Unfortunately, I'm the judge of my actions and I can't cuckold someone."

"You can pretend I didn't tell you," she said with a wink and a squeeze of his arm.

"You don't know how much I wish I could," he said and kissed her on the cheek. Later, only regret shared his bed. The next morning Karl visited the maritime museum before crossing the bridge back into Washington. Two days later he was in Port Townsend visiting wooden boat shipwright friends. They let him sleep in the Tordenskjold which was up on stilts in the shipyard. She was built in Ballard in 1911 and still fished hard. Karl had spent two seasons in her fo'c'sle.

28.

"Do you know anything about bicycles?" Kate asked while scrubbing a double boiler with steel wool.

Anders looked up. "Not really. What's wrong?"

"I don't know. He won't shift. I had to ride the bus to work."

"Your bicycle is a boy?"

"Of course not. It's a man."

Anders laughed.

Anders descended the stairs to call in the next day's order. He completed his paperwork and sat in a chair thinking. Anders met Kate as he climbed the stairs out of the basement. She blocked his way.

"Want to see my new tattoo?" she asked.

"Sure." He thought it an odd time and place for show and tell.

Kate pulled up her apron until she held it in her mouth. She then pushed her t-shirt up with her thumbs and pushed her pants down with her last three fingers. On her lower stomach, below her belly button was the Hobart logo transformed into a tattooed belt buckle. The outside lines were still red and raw, fresh. Below the buckle her pubic hair curled around her straining fingers. "Can you see it?" she asked through the apron. She was looking up to keep her clothes clear.

"Yeah," Anders said. He wanted to touch it. His hand moved a couple inches and then retreated. "Very cool." On the steep stairs the buckle was at eye level.

Kate let the apron fall from her bite. She caught it with her still straining hands. She looked down to admire the new addition. "It'll look like hell when I'm old and fat but what won't?" She laughed a short laugh. She looked at Anders's face. He was still concentrating on the tattoo. She let go of her clothes and they covered the tattoo.

It was Sunday night and Anders and Kate were the only two in the kitchen. They talked of the future. "I want to have children," Kate said. "I want to be able to be at home for them. My mother always worked. She had to. But I want something different."

"How are you going to do that washing dishes?"

"I didn't say right now and it takes two people to make babies. I want someone that can provide for our family. I guess I shouldn't say that."

"Not very punk rock," Anders said as he pushed the pumice brick across the flat grill.

"Really?" she asked. "I thought punk rock was about being truthful and going your own way. You know, DIY. I know what I want as my family and I'm going to get it someday. Not today or tomorrow but someday."

Anders didn't say anything. He thought about what she said. Kate continued to amaze him. She said things…

It was only a quarter past midnight when Anders leaned Ring Ding Ding against the porch railing. He dug his keys from his pocket and opened the door to a dark house. Tommy's door was shut, asleep probably and Karl's door was open and his truck was missing. Anders dropped to the couch but left the TV silent. He was lonely without his roommates. He was lonely without work. Anders considered riding his bicycle over to Fremont or the U-District but even in a crowd he would be alone, even more so. He really wanted to be back in the kitchen. He wanted to be working next to Kate, to be talking with her about nothing, to listen to her stories and laugh at her adventures. He wanted to know more about her. He had never met a young woman so sure of herself and of her place in the city. Anders considered Kate young because he was still at the age where small differences in birth seem important. At Tommy and Karl's age everyone within twenty years on each side was considered a friend and outside that window a mentor or student.

Anders opened the front door and looked out at the concrete yard. Across the sidewalk were Tommy's truck and Anders's truck. Anders's truck was three miles away from turning over 100K. It was going to be a special moment. He thought it was something he could share with Kate. The idea just jumped into his head proving that some nascent brilliance existed in Ballard. Maybe they could make some food and drive out to Golden Gardens and look at the salt water. But then he worried that she might have other plans. The odometer was too close to risk an empty drive into the neighborhood. But now he was thinking of Kate and it was too late to change that thought. She was still at the restaurant when he left. He remembered that her bicycle was broken and she had ridden the bus. He could give her a ride home but again the risk of rolling the odometer over without proper ceremony. He grabbed a second helmet and kicked Ring Ding Ding to life. He hoped she would still be there. He rode by the bus stop just in case.

Anders parked the bike outside the Hat on the sidewalk. He went inside carrying one of the helmets. The kitchen was empty. Amanda was totaling her register. "Look at you motorcycle man," she said. Anders wondered why she had to be that way— always slightly mocking.

"Did Kate leave already?" he asked.

"She did," Amanda said counting her money again. "Why?"

"I was going to give her a ride... Her bike is broken." Anders looked around, maybe Kate was there.

"You can give me a ride," she said looking over her shoulder. She turned to him and reached for the helmet. "You still owe me."

Mistakes were made.

Amanda rode on the back of the bike down the block to her apartment. She wanted to change for the ride. She invited Anders up and it was the first time he had been in her apartment. It was nice. It was above a machine shop, hidden, accessed by a stair off to the side. But she had made it her own. Amanda went to the small kitchen and pulled a couple of beers from the fridge. She had a large collection of vinyl and spun some Clash and danced down the hall to change.

Amanda came out of her bathroom dressed the part with jeans and boots on. She pulled a leather jacket from the closet. Anders had never seen her like that. "You clean up nice," he said for once being on the sending side of the mockery.

"Wait," she said as he moved to the door. Amanda pulled her little brass pipe from her purse and lit it. She looked up at Anders with her one open eye as she took a drag. "You want some?" she asked without exhaling.

They left Ballard and headed south across the bridge. Anders thought that it felt good to do something with Amanda that didn't involve talking. He always seemed on the defensive when she talked.

They climbed up on the Viaduct just after the Art Institute. The harbor with all its lights and black water was beautiful at night. A boat was being unloaded at Terminal 46. Anders signaled and they turned left on South Lucile and rode through the dark to Airport Way and Georgetown. He put the kickstand down outside of Jules May and they started their walk from there. Amanda had cocktails and Anders had coffee or water.

On the ride home Amanda squeezed tight against Anders, tucked into him avoiding the shadow of cold salt-water air. Northbound from Georgetown on 99 they could see the lit-up city skyline grow as they climbed onto the elevated highway. Again the harbor was beautiful and from the upper northbound deck they could see three bulk carriers at anchor waiting their turns at the grain terminal. Anders thought about all that Montana wheat headed overseas.

Amanda's hand slipped down to Anders's thigh and then rested in his crotch. He concentrated on the road and traffic as she messaged his inseam to his more and more obvious appreciation.

Anders didn't know how it would end. He wanted to keep riding around the city, being with Amanda in the night without others or language. The lights on the Ballard Bridge turned red as they approached from the south. The gates came down and the deck slowly rose. Anders stopped the bike, put down the kickstand and killed the engine. When he got off the bike he put his hands in his jeans pockets and smiled. They walked across the empty southbound lanes and looked down upon Fishermen's Terminal. "That's my boat," Anders said and pointed. Anders explained what each boat did, which fishery they were built for.

"You are a lot cooler than you seem in the kitchen," she said.

Back at Amanda's apartment Anders talked about restaurants. He thought that was interesting to her. But Amanda didn't respond. Finally, he looked into her bedroom. She was asleep on the bed, face down in just her underwear and a t-shirt. Anders stood in the doorway looking in at her. One knee was slightly cocked up and her arms were above her head, her hair spilling over her face. Anders stood there for a few minutes unsure what to do. He wanted to climb onto the bed next to Amanda. He wanted to hold her small body in his arms. But hesitation seized him. How was it supposed to be done? Should he just lie down? With his boots and jeans on? Amanda was asleep on the covers. Anders wanted to hold her to him under the covers. If he climbed into bed with Amanda he faced the problem of clothes. He faced the problem of waking up. What if she woke up and wondered why the hell he was in her bed? He had better keep his pants on.

He went to her kitchen and opened the fridge. Anders had a beer because he didn't know what else to do. There were too many questions. How should he lie with this woman? He examined the pictures on the fridge. Amanda was camping with some other girls. Amanda was in Paris alone. Amanda was on the beach with some guy. Amanda looked sad. Amanda looked happy. Amanda drunk. She was in every picture.

Anders put the empty bottle in the sink and grabbed another one. He retired to the couch to think. It was then that a muse visited him. What he really wanted was for Amanda to want him. And for Amanda to want him she had to at least think of him. True, if he stayed the night and woke up next to Amanda, her first thought would be of him but it might be, 'why the hell is he in my bed?' But if he left, her first thought of the day would be of him. 'Where did Anders go?' He went into her bedroom to take another look at her. She slept now curled up with her knees drawn up to her chest. It was difficult to be smart. He wanted to climb into her bed. Maybe he could just hold her for a while and then slip out.

So, he drank another beer. Life seemed so good. He was making decisions. He was captaining his own life. He looked in on Amanda and decided that she needed the blanket from the couch. He wrapped it around her. She purred.

Anders left the bottles on the counter not wanting to seem like too much of a pussy. On the back of a receipt he wrote, "You were beautiful. Call me," and his number. He would be her first thought of the day. He was pretty sure he was a genius.

A slight mist was blowing as Anders slipped out the door. It was just after three in the morning. Anders put on his helmet and kicked Ring Ding Ding to life. He didn't let it warm and took off east towards their little house. Anders smiled to himself inside the helmet, sure of his brilliance. He was thinking of the future when Amanda would rub his cock on every ride and beg him to come to bed with her. He smiled and felt warm even in the cool mist. He was still smiling when the bike took a hard left out from underneath him.

He had only ridden two blocks when he clipped the curb in front of the Kirsten pipe factory. The bike skidded to a stop in the middle of the street and Anders bounced off the far curb. He lay still for a moment wondering if he was dead. His second thought was of Amanda's ass in the dim light of her bedroom. He wished that ass was pressed against him. Why wasn't he still there? Maybe that muse wasn't on his side.

Anders wiggled his fingers and toes and was relieved to not be dead or paralyzed. He sat up and the face shield dangled off the helmet. Anders looked around to see if anyone had noticed his fall. The streets were empty. The bike lay on its side, left turn signal blinking. Anders slowly stood. Everything seemed to work and he was not yet sore. His body vibrated and he knew the pain would come. He walked over and uprighted the bike. His right arm ached. He pushed the bike to the curb and then tried to kick start it. It wouldn't fire. Anders removed his helmet and surveyed the damage. One side of his helmet was scratched and the hinge that held the shield was broken. One of the turn signals was broken and Anders went into the street and kicked the broken plastic towards the gutter. He sat on the curb flexing his right hand. It worked but was painful.

A cop car turned the corner. It stopped in front of Anders. The window rolled down. It was Bruce.

"Everything thing all right here?" he asked.

"Yeah. I think I'm going to walk home. Bike problems and I've had a couple of beers. Better not risk it."

"That's a good plan," Bruce said and then drove on not wanting to know more.

Anders walked home and woke a few hours later to the sound of a heavy rain outside his small window. He remembered the night before and questioned its reality but then he sat up and was sure. His whole body ached. Either he had crashed or someone had worked him over with a bat as he slept. His right hand barely worked. He could make a fist and open it but something was wrong. He remembered before the crash. The image of Amanda in her underwear was bright even in his dark basement. He smiled, again convinced of his genius. Although it was only five in the morning he thought of Amanda waking up and wondering where he was. Thinking about him. That would be worth the pain of the crash.

Then he remembered his bike. Anders had left his bike on a side street for anyone to steal or vandalize so he rolled out of bed. His jeans and boots were still on which was lucky because his right arm didn't seem up to the task of tying laces. Anders climbed the stairs and opened the front door. It was pouring rain. Small rivers ran from the gutters headed towards the sound. Anders reluctantly pulled his rain gear from the peg next to the door and put it on. He wondered how many years had he lived in PVC fishing gear? Literally years. He slipped out of the house with the damaged helmet. He had left the other helmet at Amanda's. It was another reason for her to call.

The bike was still against the curb its left rear turn signal broken and hanging by the wires. Anders held the throttle with his left hand and tried kicking it. No luck, so he started pushing. His right forearm ached dully but with every push it shot electric pain up through his neck. Even so Anders continued pushing. Instead of going down to the crosswalk on Leary or up to Market Street he pushed straight across 15th Avenue. It made him feel like a crackhead— pushing a broken machine across five lanes of early morning work traffic. Neither Tommy nor Karl would have ever done something like that.

Tommy was standing on the front porch drinking coffee and surveying the sky as Anders pushed the machine up the street. He didn't come down to help. He didn't say anything. He continued drinking his coffee. Anders leaned the bike on its stand.

"What gives?" Tommy finally asked.

"I crashed last night. I think I might have broken my arm."

Tommy nodded and climbed down off the porch to look at the bike. The rain soaked the shoulders of his sweatshirt instantly. He inspected for damage. "Doesn't look too bad," he said and sipped more coffee. Anders thought Tommy looked old. The month of strike had aged him at least five years. More than old he looked tired. They climbed back onto the porch, under the protection of the overhead.

"Look at this," Anders said and pushed up his sleeves. There was a small knot on his forearm just below the wrist. "I can still move my hand but it hurts like a son of a bitch. Do you think it's broken?"

Tommy shrugged his shoulders. "You might want to see a doctor." He knew Anders didn't have insurance. In Alaska he could have walked into any hospital and been taken care of by the Fisherman's Fund but in Seattle he was just a cook. He and Karl had tried to convince Anders to enter one of the trades if he wanted to take a break from fishing. But Anders didn't listen to the older men. Now he had to worry about going to the hospital. But neither of them ever thought Anders would stop fishing, not with his family's history. The older men didn't listen to Anders.

29.

The negotiations didn't start until eight but Tommy was on the road by 6:30. A light mist swirled around the streetlights. He warmed the old truck until the heat blew hot on his boots. He had recently put in a new fan and relished its power. He drove slow watching the sleeping neighborhood. A woman waved to him from the bus stop at Eighth and Market. She was wet. Her hair hung long. What the hell, he thought and pulled over. He leaned over and unlocked the door. She jumped in.

"Thanks. I don't know when the next bus is. I just need to get up the hill." She moved too much when she talked. She moved too much when she didn't. Drugs. Tommy had just picked up a working girl. Well, her habit was something a cop couldn't fake. Wouldn't that be great— missing a negotiation meeting because he was busted in a prostitution sting.

"You going to work?" she asked and Tommy said yes. "You lonely?" she asked and Tommy lied. Her skin was bad from drugs but could see that she used to be pretty. Choices, everyone made choices and choices had consequences. And it wasn't an either-or. There was a myriad of bad decisions. He could have stayed fishing. He could have stayed married. No one had good choices because the end was the same for everyone. But choices had consequences. "You get the 'nice guy' discount for picking me up," she offered with a bad tooth smile. Tommy laughed and shook his head. She had used his name without knowing it. There had to be some reward for being nice but he declined and let her off at Aurora Avenue. She climbed out of his truck and he noticed the ass of her sweat pants was dirty. He understood the functionality of sweatpants as her work clothes but it was the most unattractive thing a woman could wear. Tommy longed for something he had never seen— a whore in a dress.

"See you around," she said.

"Yeah, maybe," and he drove off. Tommy had done his good deed for the day. He had given a wet hooker a ride.

That was the city— brief interactions with strangers that would never be seen again. He thought of the old Vietnamese man and wondered how the driveway turned out. But the neighborhood was different. Those were relationships even if only with the grocery clerk and pho lady.

He was still too early for the meeting so he drove south past the Hall, through the Battery Street Tunnel and onto the Viaduct. He could smell the salt water. The city was quiet but the harbor was working. The container cranes at Terminal 46 swung in and out picking their loads. The can haulers idled in lines outside the gate waiting for their chance. The Teamsters had tried several times to organize those guys but he doubted it would ever happen. The bosses gave them leases on the trucks that shielded management from paying any benefits. In effect, they became their own bosses except the guys who really owned the trucks still arranged all the loads and provided the maintenance of the equipment. It was a scam. They were warring immigrant groups that were played off each other. But maybe it was a stepping stone, a way up. Tommy had lost his ability to see black and white.

Tommy drove out on Harbor Island passing Terminal 18. Just north of the Fischer Flour Mill he turned left and parked next to the seawall looking at the West Duwamish and Terminal 5 beyond it. He liked the mixture of water and industry.

A Port of Seattle cop pulled up next to him and rolled down his window.

"Everything alright?" he asked.

"Yeah, just thinking before work."

"Not many people come to Harbor Island for fun."

"Yeah, I suppose not." Tommy smiled.

"Hey, I know you. You drive a cement mixer." The cop said sitting up a little.

"For Halibut Flats," Tommy said.

"My uncle is Ole Hegelund. I sometimes help out on my days off." Ole was an old-timer that did small concrete finishing jobs, mostly in Ballard.

"Ole's a good man," Tommy said. He was although not the nicest guy.

"Yeah. He's definitely worked his whole life. He dropped out of school in the sixth grade and has been doing construction ever since. That'd never happen nowadays."

"Those old guys are tough."

"Yeah," the cop agreed and satisfied that Tommy wasn't stealing or shooting up he left him to his thoughts.

Anders woke less sure of his genius. It hurt to move his fingers and there was an odd new bump sticking out of his forearm. He wanted to talk to Amanda. He wanted her to wake and think of him but it wasn't yet seven. He doubted she woke before noon. Anders wanted to speed up time as most people want to slow it. He wanted the pain to be skipped and the woman with short bangs to wonder where he was.

He looked at his forearm again. He flexed his hand. It worked although painfully. He had never broken a bone before and supposed that the hand would not function if the arm were broken. Maybe it was broken and maybe the broken arm would work in his favor. Amanda might feel sympathy for him. But how would he work? He was supposed to be in the kitchen at Le Canard at nine.

One thing was for sure— he was not going to fall asleep. Anders again climbed the stairs to the now empty house. And then he did something neither of his roommates could have done. He called his mother. Thankfully she was home and they chatted about small things. They discussed his sister, a junior at the University of Washington. She was the achiever in the family. His mother did not mention fishing or boats and that was purposeful kindness and it was noticed. Anders finally told his mother about his arm. Obviously, he did not tell her about the events leading up to the crash and when explaining it gave a much truncated— "I crashed my bike on the way home from work."

"Motorcycle or bicycle?" she asked.

"Bicycle," Anders lied.

Anders didn't know what to do. He didn't want to go to the emergency room because he didn't consider a broken arm, if it was broken, an emergency. His mother agreed because she knew her son didn't have insurance. A benefit of living in Blue Ridge was that they had a neighbor who was a doctor. She would call his office and then call Anders back. Anders thanked his mother and then felt like a child as he waited for her help.

His mother called back with an appointment arranged for an hour later. "Can you drive there or should I come get you?" she asked. Anders could steer but didn't know how he could shift so he asked for a ride. Truthfully, he didn't want to waste rolling his truck through a hundred thousand miles on a trip to the doctor.

Anders called Jules and said he wouldn't be able to come into Le Canard that day explaining that he may have broken his arm. Jules merely said okay. Anders wasn't vital to the kitchen operation, but he was expected. He waited to call the Hat until he had some word from the doctor. If he missed a shift at the Hat someone would be pissed.

The bosses walked out of the conference room their shoes quiet on the carpet. The Teamsters sat in silence careful not to start talking while the other side was still in hearing range. They waited long enough for them to drive away because no one had anything to say. The strike was floundering. They needed help from the outside— political or economic pressure. The regional and national Teamster organizations were supportive of the action. It was no wildcat strike over hurt feelings. But the men at the table were out of ideas. They had played their cards and now had empty hands.

"Tonight's the King County Labor Council meeting," Tommy said.

"It is?" the BA asked.

"Yeah," Tommy said. He was the 174 delegate to the council and went to all the meetings. He was also a member of the Building Trades Council. "You want me to say anything?"

"Absolutely! Ask those bastards to call the Mayor and City Council. Maybe get something on TV, anything."

Tommy left downtown and went by the line to break the bad news to the guys— no progress, strike continues. The men continued to surprise him. The young and unencumbered failed to show up for their shifts but middle-aged men with mortgages and dying parents were on the line even when not scheduled. They accepted the bad news with a shrug and offered words of encouragement to Tommy, a confusing boomerang. At five Tommy helped put the tents away and then drove to the Labor Temple on First Avenue for the meeting.

Tommy sat in his truck thinking. Harold and the other owners weren't the enemy. The system wasn't the problem. This strike, conflict and war weren't symptoms of something broken. It was a natural cycle. Conflict was eternal and should not be avoided. Wanting to put your boss out of business was like wanting to kill your spouse during an argument. It was childish. It was shallow thought to think that labor could 'win'.

Tommy pulled the council president to the side before the meeting and gave him the negotiation update. "We need help from the labor council," Tommy said. "We need pressure to come from other angles." Everything ran on Robert's rules of order. He would have to wait for new business.

Tommy found a seat next to a large tattooed Ironworker named Big Pete. They had run in the same punk rock crowd as kids. Pete sported spud wrench tattoos on each forearm. The building trades sat as a group. They exuded a potential violence that made the other unions nervous.

"How goes the line?" Pete asked.

"Sucks," Tommy said truthfully.

"I hear ya."

The meeting started with the singing of the Internationale and everyone was supposed to know the words. It was embarrassing and uncomfortable. The council was dominated by young college graduates, no doubt labor studies majors from Evergreen College. Labor was not their cause. It was their means. They found jobs right out of college representing service workers and government employees and were used to negotiating from weakness. They thought more of folk songs than punk rock and conveniently ignored that the building trades used to beat the hippies in the streets during their idyllic 1960s.

Tommy had learned a few things in the Labor Council. The easier the journey into the Union the weaker it was. Those with four-year apprenticeships were the strongest. The Teamsters were close behind because the drivers had to go to school to get a commercial license and then, most often, work shit jobs for a couple years to build experience before getting hired on at a Union shop. But unskilled labor had no solidarity because there was no buy in. It cost nothing to walk into a job that only required your presence and therefore they could walk away just as easy, or be replaced.

The meetings ran according to Robert's Rules of Order and no one paid attention during past business. Tommy's mind drifted to the strike line. He thought he should bring his gas grill down to the line. They could cook burgers. It would be good for morale.

Big Pete elbowed him and brought his consciousness back into the building. "These cunts don't give two shits about the construction trades. They just want our endorsement and money in exchange for wearing a Che Guevara tee shirt in college. Fucking pussies have never worked a real job in their lives," Pete said loud enough to be heard a few rows away.

Tommy laughed, enjoying Pete's unanswered taunts. Tommy asked in a more polite volume, "what do you bet there's a 'subvert the dominant paradigm' bumper sticker in the lot?"

"Who even talks like that? Fucking cunts."

He watched one lady, outside the circle of building trades, squirm in her seat. After a life of engines and hard work he often misjudged the ability of soft people to hear at greater distances. Tommy considered it a good day when his tinnitus didn't howl its garage rock feedback as an accompaniment. Hearing aids were de rigueur for retired Teamsters.

Finally, they got to new business.

The President of the council came to the microphone. "Brothers and Sisters, the construction Teamsters of Local 174 are on strike. Brother Torgerson is on strike! He's come here tonight to ask for our help, for our support!" he said and pointed at Tommy. "He's fighting for the oppressed!" Tommy was sure as fuck not oppressed. The Teamsters weren't oppressed. These were empty, meaningless words that people accepted like religious totems.

Tommy leaned towards Pete. "I think I just threw up in my mouth," he said. Pete laughed.

More empty words followed and then finally the council President asked the other unions to reach out to their elected officials to help educate them about the struggle. And they were reminded not to cross picket lines, which was nice.

30.

The strike continued. Tommy was unloading pallets gathered from the neighborhood— fuel for their stove. They would break them down and stack the wood according to size along the fence. They carefully policed up all the nails with a magnet.

"Head's up," Bill said and nodded across the street toward the office. Harold was coming their way, crossing the road at an old man trot, probably as fast as he could move. Tommy didn't know what to make of it, so he stood, it seemed the only thing to do. When Harold got close enough he panted out, "fire at precast." That was all that needed to be said. Tommy turned and jumped in the driver's seat of his pickup.

"Get in!" he shouted to the other drivers and they all piled in the back. Tommy dropped the column shifter into first and one wheel made smoke as they headed for the other yard. Harold followed in his truck. As they rounded the corner flames danced thirty feet in the sky above the hobo camp. An RV was engulfed and tents were burning with pieces floating in the super-heated air, spreading the fire. The whole of the blackberry patch was smoking with visible flame jetting and disappearing. The flames were closing in on the parked line of mixer trucks. Tommy skidded to a stop next to the gate and the drivers in back were piled into each other against the cab. Luckily Harold had not changed the lock on the precast yard and Tommy opened the gate with the key on his chain. Most of the other drivers already had their keys out focused on saving their own trucks first.

As soon as the engines started the drivers pulled the hand throttles wide open to build air as quickly as possible to release the brakes. Most of the trucks pulled away from the flames still dragging a tire or two. Three trucks sat empty, their drivers having the day off from the strike line.

"We need the spare keys out of the operator's shop," Tommy said to Harold and pointed at the locked door.

"Break it open," Harold said. And Scotty sent the lock and hasp flying with one swing of the chip hammer ready in his hand. Two trucks were started and moved to safety but 70 wouldn't turn over. A couple men looked in the shop for cables and Tommy backed his truck in front of 70 and ran chains between them.

A propane tank inside of an RV detonated.

Mike said, "Fuck this shit. I don't even work here." But he didn't leave.

Tommy put his truck in low/low and locked the axles. The chains came tight and he pulled against the dead truck but with all its brakes locked Tommy's truck just bounced its rear end in the gravel, threatening to snap a drive line. Tommy's engineer brain kicked in. He had a fifty-foot air hose behind his seat that he used to fill tires and spray dust off. He hooked the hose between the two trucks' tank drains and opened the valves sending air to the dead truck. Flames reached for the stranded truck and the rubber on the right tag axle tire started to smoke. Eventually they built enough air to grudgingly pull it clear, the dead pusher axle turned at an angle like a plow. It took two men to work the steering wheel of the last truck.

The fire trucks arrived and within a couple minutes they had three hoses working the fire. The drivers and Harold watched the show. All of them thinking for a moment— I should have been a firefighter. When the flames turned to smoke and steam the men returned their trucks to their parking spots but left 70 in the middle of the yard. The fire station Captain walked down the ramp into precast and said the fire was due to a 'domestic dispute'. It was a classic story. The jilted lover burns down the house or in this case briar patch.

The men piled back in Tommy's truck and he returned them to the line at a much more civilized pace. Harold parked his truck and was headed to the office but he circled back to address the crowd.

Harold said, "You guys did good. Thanks. Tommy, that was real smart about the air hose." A 'thanks boss' came from each of the men.

Tommy said, "I think we've had enough for today. We'll see you tomorrow," and the men drifted off to their vehicles to go home like striking was a normal job.

31.

The phone rang. Anders put the book down he held in his casted hand and got up off the couch to answer it. He wanted it to be Amanda but it was Kate. Anders was confused. He had missed two shifts at the Hat so far and the restaurant rumor machine probably wasn't doing him any favors. He wondered how much of the story Kate knew. Too much was a safe bet.

"Do you need anything? Soup, aspirin?" she asked. He said he was fine and thanked her for asking. She gave him her phone number in case he needed anything. Anders went and lay on the couch again. He was an idiot. Both women were showing their moral compasses, one good and one bad. Amanda didn't call. She would never call. Anders called Kate back.

"Hey, my truck is going to roll over one hundred thousand miles. I was thinking about driving down to Golden Gardens tomorrow to watch it click over and celebrate. Maybe make some sandwiches. Do you want to come?"

"Are you inviting me on a picnic?" she asked.

"I guess so."

"Then why didn't you say— do you want to go on a picnic?"

Anders was silent, on his heels.

"Yes Anders. I want to go on a picnic with you. Give me your address and I'll ride over."

The next morning it was cold and clear as Anders walked up 14th to Ballard Market. He bought a couple of fresh bolo rolls, some fresh basil and provolone, and a few roma tomatoes. On the way out he thought, what the hell, and bought a bottle of red wine too. He made the panzanella sandwiches and put them in a wicker picnic basket that Tommy had bought at a yard sale and had lived above their fridge ever since. Underneath the sandwiches he put a roll of paper towels, the bottle of wine and a couple Styrofoam cups.

Anders had told Kate 'around one' for their picnic and she knocked on the door at exactly one. It was the first time she had seen his broken arm.

"You look about useless," she chided.

"I feel useless," he said.

Anders opened the door wide and invited her in but Kate wanted to lock up her bicycle first.

"I thought *he* was broken," Anders said.

Kate giggled at Anders' memory. "He still won't shift but your house is downhill. Broken men seem to be a theme in my life right now."

Anders smiled. "Well, let's try and fix one of them." Kate brought the bike up on the porch and Anders diagnosed the problem with one hand. The front derailleur was stuck. I wasn't broken just unmaintained. The bike lived outside and hard use and the elements wouldn't let the spring return to the first gear. He used a can of brake cleaner to get rid of the grease and debris. Anders suggested they let it dry while they picnicked and lube it later.

Kate locked her bicycle to Ring Ding Ding and they went inside.

"Where are your roommates?" Kate asked.

"Tommy is on the strike line and I don't know where Karl is. He's on vacation so he could be anywhere."

Anders went to the sink and struggled to wash the grease from his fingernails. He couldn't hold the nail brush with his broken arm and scrub. Kate noticed and laughed. "Let me help you with that," she said. She held his hand and gave the fingers a good scrub with the brush. Anders had never felt so well cared for.

"Can you drive?" she asked.

"I guess we'll find out. You might have to help shift."

The cast covered from his knuckles to the middle of his upper arm. Anders could shift by moving his shoulders and waist but it was awkward and painful. Kate had never driven a manual transmission. She didn't own a car but had taken driver's education in high school. So they went slow and learned to dance together. At first, Anders told Kate when to shift but a few blocks into the trip she needed no prompts.

After parking, Anders pulled blanket and basket from the bed of the truck and they walked to the point. Anders spread the blanket on a log and they sat down to look at the water but it was cold and they figured the blanket would be better used around their shoulders. It was a challenge to hold the sandwich and cup of wine while keeping the blanket on their shoulders but it was a pleasant excuse to press against each other.

Anders explained the job of each passing ship or boat. Kate asked questions and he was happy to continue the lesson. Then a fin came out of the dark water, then a spout of water and air. It was close enough to hear.

"Whales!" Kate said.

"It cost me a lot of money to arrange that," Anders said with a straight face. Kate laughed and leaned over and kissed him on the cheek.

"Anders, you're a good man if you could just get out of your own way." He smiled, unsure of what she meant but very happy for the kiss.

When they got back to the house Anders lubed the derailleur with a Teflon spray explaining that it wouldn't pick up grime like oil. She asked how he knew such things and Anders merely said, 'boats'.

"Do you want to come in?" Anders asked.

Kate laughed and threw her leg over her bike. "No, you are still in the doghouse. Today helped but I'm not going to sleep with you because we saw some whales." Kate wouldn't give herself away, she wanted love and loyalty. She had grown up rough. She knew she was cute, not beautiful, and that cute had a very limited life span. She wanted to find someone and stick.

"I was looking for you," Anders said.

Kate looked him in the eye. "But you went with her."

"That was a mistake," he admitted.

"I'll tolerate that once. That was your mistake, your last one." And then she rode away.

32.

Tommy sat in a camp chair under their tent on the strike line. They had the stove running but he wanted to read the paper. There were no negotiations that day and he had seen Harold leave the office after lunch. He hadn't returned. The strikers were just waiting to call it a day.

A hippie, spelled 'hiker' in the paper, was washed off the rocks on the coast while posing for a picture and dashed to death on them. Definitely not a pleasant way to go and a death that served no end except vanity yet Tommy felt no sadness. Tommy rooted for nature

175

when it killed civilians or tourists— when mountains coughed and swept away skiers or climbers, when sailboats were swallowed whole. The best, the thing that warmed his soul most, was mammals eating mammals. A bear or a cougar eating a suburban housewife was the pinnacle of cosmic truth, or the good.

Most Seattleites had a completely false sense of nature. They thought it benevolent, a mother. That was an urban myth created by someone who had spent little time living in nature. Nature wanted you dead. She wanted you as fertilizer or food. There were millions of crabs scuttling round the floor of Bristol Bay and the Bering Strait waiting for a snack to be dropped from a boat whether it be in a pot or wrapped in rain gear. The woods too were full of rapists and murderers, and that wasn't the loggers. Tommy was sure the delicate urbanites that believed in these fantasies looked away from ducks having sex in the park because it was rape. Tommy knew to never look away from nature. She was the original crazy bitch with a taste for murder.

"Time to call it a night Tommy," Ben said. He drenched the firebox in the stove with water and then shoveled the ashes into a metal pail with a wooden-handled entrenching tool from his Vietnam tour.

"Yeah," Tommy said. "I think I'm going a little batty from this lack of work. I'm not made for sitting around."

Ben laughed. "No, no you aren't."

Tommy opened the door. A young woman with copper hair stood on their stoop holding a tinfoil casserole pan. He recognized her as the dishwasher from the Hat.

"Is Anders home?" she asked.

"He is. Please come in." Tommy opened the door wide for her and walked to the stairway and yelled down to Anders that he had a guest.

"I didn't want you to starve so I made you dinner."

"I hope you made *us* dinner," Anders replied.

Kate smiled. "You're getting better Anders."

They put the casserole in the oven and then went for a walk around the block. Anders stopped by each business and explained what they did. At the net builders Anders explained the different meshes, floats and lines. At the crane yard he explained how small cranes assembled the large cranes. There wasn't much to see from the outside of the lamination or cabinet shops.

As they climbed the house steps Anders asked, "what if I wasn't home?"

"Well, that was my gamble. And what if you had another girl over? What if you were drunk or stoned at five in the afternoon?"

"So, it was a test?"

"Yes. And you passed," she said.

Inside, Tommy sat on the couch reading *The Last of the Vikings* by Johan Bojer. Anders and Kate went to the kitchen to check on the casserole. It was warm and Kate asked Tommy if he'd like to join them for dinner.

"I'd be delighted," Tommy said and closed his book. Anders was already setting the table for three so Tommy went into the kitchen and opened a bottle of wine. They didn't own proper wine glasses and instead used old jam jars. "Smells delicious," Tommy said as he set the bottle in the middle of the table.

"It's tuna casserole," Kate said. "I know that's probably not the right dish for a couple of real fishermen, but it has a special place in my heart. We didn't have much money growing up and this was a standard. It's cheap and easy— unlike me," she said, and stage winked at Anders. Tommy laughed. Kate wanted to freshen up before eating and went into the bathroom. Anders and Tommy looked at each other wondering what the young woman would think of their walls laminated with vintage pornography. It had been a long time since a woman had been in their house. Ex-wives didn't count.

Kate emerged smiling. "Your bathroom is interesting," she said.

"Yeah, it kinda a dude's house. Sorry," Anders said.

"I didn't say I didn't like it. If they were modern girls I probably wouldn't. There isn't a fake boob in the bunch. And, they're old ladies by now," she said as she slid into the nook next to Anders.

"To Vanebo's arm!" Tommy raised the toast.

"To Vanebo," Anders saluted.

"What is that? I hear you say Vanebo at the bar," Kate asked.

"Vanebo was a fisherman that got his arm caught in a gurdy while setting gear. It destroyed his arm and he cut it off himself before throwing it overboard. The arm waved at him as it sank," Tommy explained. "It means the old guys were tough and we should try to be like them."

Kate looked at Anders and said, "no one will mourn your arm."

Tommy giggled and Anders said, "no, I guess not."

"To Vanebo," Kate finished the toast.

The three of them had a pleasant dinner, civilized and family-like.

The house was very small and Tommy wanted to give the young couple some privacy so he excused himself after dinner to go read. As Tommy went into his bedroom for the night, he caught Anders' eye and gave him the thumbs up, endorsing this bold young woman.

Anders washed the dishes and Kate dried. When they were done, when there was nothing in the drying rack, Kate reached up and pulled Anders into her kiss. "I like you," she said. They sat on the couch and talked about work and coworkers and told little stories about themselves.

"Will you walk me to the bus?" she asked when the conversation slowed

"You don't have to go."

"Yes I do. Plus, I didn't bring stuff for a sleepover."

As they walked up to Market Street, Kate asked Anders why Tommy and his wife had broken up.

"She cheated on him. Maybe they could have survived that. Tommy has a pretty strict sense of honor and trust but I think, more so, that he saw where she was headed even if she didn't. She likes to hang out with fancy people. I've been to parties with her friends— they talk about money. It's gross. Tommy must have seen that too."

"I like him," she said.

"I thought you liked me," Anders said.

She squeezed Anders' good arm. "Not in the same way. I like Karl too. You have good friends. They are good people. That's important. You are the dirty hands, clean money crew. I want to be part of your team."

The bus pulled up and they kissed one more time.

33.

Karl returned from the coast to a dark and empty house. Only the port and starboard lights burned and the flag was still up. He assumed Anders was working and he headed down to Ballard Avenue. It was a cold rain, with snow forecasted, so he drove his truck. Tommy was at the terminal making sure the Brekke boats and the Nadine were squared away in case it snowed. The Nadine had a piece of plywood covering her fish hold but it seemed stout enough to handle a snow load. Tommy wished the carpenters hadn't already removed the aluminum hatch cover. Tommy was a man of steel and iron, of gas and diesel. His saw was a torch. He distrusted carpenters and their wizardly craft.

Karl strolled down Ballard Avenue. Amanda almost walked into him as she exited the Hat.

"Hey Karl," she smiled.

"Amanda," he nodded to her but kept walking.

"Hey, I owe you a drink for fixing my car. Can I buy you one?" Amanda pointed palm up back at the restaurant.

"Is Anders in there?" Karl asked.

"Yeah, but he's not working," she said but didn't mention why he wasn't working.

"Then let's go somewhere else."

Amanda smiled and they walked up the street. They had a drink at the Smokeshop, where they sat side by side at the bar, and then a beer at the Sloop, where they faced each other in a booth. It was snowing by the time they migrated to the Lockspot, where they sat side by side in a booth. They played pool and continued drinking. Karl knew Amanda was poisoning Anders' mind. She was the reason he didn't want to go fishing. They weren't in love. Anders was blinded by his first adult pussy.

"What have you done to that boy?" Karl asked.

"I didn't do anything except show him some options."

"You showed him your ass."

"What's wrong with my ass?" she asked.

"Nothing. Absolutely nothing. That's the problem." They both laughed.

It was snowing large, wet flakes when they came out of the bar. Karl scanned the sky as Amanda zipped her coat to her neck. Snow was rare in Seattle. The saltwater chased it away. "It'd be a good night for a fireplace," he said. They walked the train tracks back towards The Hat. It was quicker. They both balanced on a track like drunken gymnasts. Amanda had more skill.

"I've got to piss. Don't go too far," Karl said.

She continued on and fifty feet down the track a man stepped from the bushes.

"You got twenty bucks so I can get something to eat?" he said. It wasn't a question, it was a demand.

Amanda stepped back. "What? No." She looked around but Karl was not there. "My friend," she said. "He's..."

"He's what? Just gimmie twenty bucks," the man insisted. Another man stood up out of the blackberry bushes. He was larger, with a full black beard.

"What gives?" Karl said emerging from the shadows. He was smiling and had his hands in his jacket pockets.

"The lady was going to give me some money for food. You mind your own business."

Karl continued smiling. "Oh, that makes sense. I can hook you up." He reached into his back pocket, handed his wallet to Amanda and whispered, "Just keep walking."

Karl escorted Amanda past the two men, "Go," he said quietly.

He turned smiling, his hands up. "Now, no one wants..." Karl snapped a left jab that struck the nearest man's throat followed immediately by a right that flattened his nose. The man stumbled back off the rail bed and fell into the blackberries.

The larger man pulled a filet knife from his belt. He was already breathing hard and his eyes were wide. He stumbled on the large rail bed ballast rocks. "Whoa, don't hurt yourself with that thing," Karl gently chided. The wild-eyed drunk looked down at his comrade rolling in the blackberry thorns adding to his injuries. He locked eyes with Karl but Karl's eyes were smiling, soft and calm.

"You're going to pay for that," the bearded man said and took a half step forward but slipped again on the loose rock. Karl stood firmly on the cross ties.

"No, you're out of your league my friend." A short, sharp click announced Karl's knife ready.

The bearded man looked at Karl's knife and then back at his struggling partner and then at Karl's eyes. He put the filet knife back in its sheath. "I'll find you someday and make you pay. Maybe I'll call the cops and say you assaulted us."

"Let's call the cops right now. Let's see what they make of you two. Drunks and druggies living in the briar patch, stealing from women who cross your path in the night. Would you have stopped at her money or taken more?"

"Fuck off. Just go away." The bearded man went to help his partner.

"You should really think about your life decisions friend. No one would give two shits if I killed the both of you. And I would too, if I didn't have a nice lady waiting for me."

"Fuck off."

"Well, you guys have a nice night," Karl said and turned to walk away listening for footsteps that he was sure wouldn't come.

He caught Amanda by Pacific Fishermen's shipyard. She was upset. She was confused. She was standing in a phone booth pushing 911 over and over not noticing that the cord dangled from the handset. Her call went nowhere. Karl took the handset from her and returned it to the cradle. He then took both her hands and held them.

"Breathe, breathe deep," he said in a calming voice. "Hold it for 5 seconds and let it out, all the way out. Good. Now concentrate on a four count. Four seconds of breathing in, hold it for four seconds, breathe out for four seconds and hold it at the bottom for four seconds." Karl messaged her hands and did the breathing exercise with her. After a minute her heart had calmed. The snow fell heavy and wet.

"If I was alone..." she said seeing a reality hidden barely out of sight.

"The key is not being scared. If you're not scared you can focus on solutions. It just takes practice. I learned it on boats. That was a chance to die well, for me, not you. Those are rare. But two drunken slobs aren't worthy."

"You and Anders seem to forget that you live on land, constantly talking about 'boats'. I don't understand it. What's so special about boats?"

"Come on I'll show you." Karl led Amanda by the hand and they turned toward the ship canal.

"Let's borrow a ride." Karl led them into a marina and punched a code into a gate. They walked down the dock. Next to a pleasure boat was tied a dinghy. Karl lowered himself into it and then helped Amanda down. He sat her in the bow. Karl locked the oars and rowed them across the canal. From the canal they could see the city turning white. It had already become quiet. Amanda rubbed her legs, the snow dampening her jeans.

"You used to run track?" he asked.

Amanda smiled. "Cross country."

"I can see it. You're an athlete. You could be tough."

Karl rowed to the Saratoga and climbed on the stern while holding the dinghy's bow line. He tied the small boat off and then pulled Amanda aboard. She was light. Karl laughed as he set her down. "You should eat more cheeseburgers. I'm surprised you don't fly away in the wind."

Karl didn't have his keys. He went to the forward hatch next to the anchor windlass and pulled the T handle out. He tried to turn it but it didn't budge. "Fuck, they have to remember to grease these threads once a season." He got lower and laid into it. "Fffuuuuccckkk." Finally, it broke loose. That was more likely the way he would die— blow a blood vessel. His father had died of a heart attack. Karl set the hatch to the side and lowered himself down into the fo'c'sle. He switched on one of the bunk reading lights. Amanda looked down at his shaved head, the halo of remaining hair barely visible. Bunks were stacked three high on either side filled with oil filters still in boxes and orange tubes containing survival suits.

"You ready?" Karl asked. He waved her to follow.

But to Amanda it seemed wrong. Like entering a whale through its blow hole. Snow swirled about her and she looked down through that black hole. Where would it lead? She just shook her head. It was too much for her. Karl thought it was the violence on the tracks. She wasn't used to violence. She was fully civilized, comfortably lulled by rules and laws. Fists and knives weren't part of her landscape. No, that wasn't it. The violence she sensed earlier was directed towards her. The demand for money from a couple of drunk deadbeats could have turned into something much worse. It was something not in Karl's landscape. She was prey. Karl had never been prey. Even when the sea was trying to kill him he was always an equal to the battle. Maybe he would lose but he would always be game for the fight. Karl looked up at Amanda and knew now was the time to be generous.

"I'll open the galley door. Go to the back deck."

It was cold inside the black steel boat and Amanda was shivering. The adrenalin was wearing off and Karl knew she'd be hungry soon. He went to the hooks on the bulkhead where the crew stored clothes. "Here, put this on." He handed her a halibut jacket and wool cap. She did as told and was swallowed by the too-large gear. Karl rubbed her upper arms. "You'd make a good fisherman. You're tough. A little small but tough." She smiled. Karl lit the diesel stove. "It'll be warm soon."

Amanda looked around the galley. There was a laminated typewritten note taped to the wall, the bulkhead. She read it.

The ship is foundering. What then have I to do? I do the only thing that remains to me—to be drowned without fear, without a cry, without upbraiding God, but knowing that what has been born must likewise perish. For I am not Eternity, but a human being—a part of the whole, as an hour is part of the day. I must come like the hour, and like the hour must pass! ~Epictetus

"What does it mean?" Amanda asked.

"It means shut up and die," Karl said. "Everyone dies, so if this boat goes down do everything you can, the best that you can, until all that's left is dying. Then do that well. Don't be a bitch around your crewmates. Anders' father, Don, has that on the galley bulkhead of all his boats. I like it."

Karl gave her the tour while the stove warmed the galley. Amanda was more interested in the head than the wheelhouse. It was a combo— shitter, shower and sink.

"Ever had a girl as a crewmate?" she asked.

"No," Karl said. "I've known other boats that do but they are mostly the daughters of skippers. Women on boats are supposed to be bad luck but like most religious taboos that probably grew out of lessons learned, like Jews not eating shellfish. Anyway, we have ways of appeasing the Gods. I think it's something deeper than crewmates fucking or the jealousy that a lady could create. If women were on boats there would be no reason to go to land. Plus, I can't imagine sinking with a woman on board."

"You think we'd panic? Get hysterical?"

"No. I think I would panic. I'd lose my acceptance and go down ungracefully."

Karl made a couple 'white trash mochas'. They were half chocolate milk and half coffee, with a topper of whiskey and a favorite of the crew during long days on deck— sans the booze.

"Why do you want to fuck with Anders? He needs to concentrate on fishing, not kitchens."

The galley had warmed nicely. It was comfortable and even beautiful with the snow falling outside the port holes. Amanda pulled off the hat.

"I never forced him to do anything," Amanda said. "He was already cooking. I just opened the door to better things."

"That's the problem. He's young and young people are too stupid to deal with options. They get overwhelmed by bright shiny things. Or waitresses with nice asses."

"I'll take that as a compliment."

"Please do but take it seriously."

"Why are you so concerned? What's Anders to you?"

"He's family and I love him," Karl said with a flat serious honesty.

She was taken aback. In Amanda's world men didn't proclaim brotherly love. And, it didn't exist in the world apart from strenuous professions and the military. Shared danger enabled brotherhood.

"What about you? What have you got?" she asked.

Karl knew what she meant. She was asking about a wife or family, those things that make you want to come to shore. "Soul," he said. He could have said honor or respect or dignity but soul fit.

"What do you want?"

"War."

And she was too smart not to take him seriously.

The snow fell heavy and fast. "I don't think we are going anywhere soon," he said.

"Good," she said.

He got up and turned off the overhead light leaving only a string of Christmas lights as interior illumination. The bright snow outside became more visible. He pushed play on the cassette player.

"For being punk rockers, you guys sure listen to a lot of The Smiths."

"The Smiths is punk rock."

They got to the subject of books. The shelf over the galley table was crammed with books. London, Conrad, Bukowski, Hemingway, Hamsun and Orwell. She accused him of being a Hemingway fan. "I don't care for his prudishness but I guess it was era appropriate. I do approve of how he went out. He could no longer write or get a hard-on so he ate a shotgun. That was according to his philosophy. The only other choices were to be a coward or a liar," Karl said and raised his glass in toast to the dead man.

The snow fell. It was a night where he would kill two men but neither had yet died. One was dying but the other still had a chance to make the right decision.

His vision was limited by the small port window above the galley sink. The waitress was pressed against the sink, her legs wrapped tightly around his waist. She bit his neck, his ear and exclaimed to her god. Karl fucked with a noble purpose— to make her forget about boys. "Can you come again?" he asked. She turned around and held the spice rack below the port hole. She had herring scales stuck to her back, like glitter or sequins, from their roll on the floor. It was probably the most honest thing she had ever worn. As he drove her towards her second orgasm Karl was struck by brilliance, visited by a muse. Everyone was learning about life. The storm and strike were letting life teach lessons fast and hard. Morrissey crooned, 'It took a tattooed boy from Birkenhead to really open her eyes'.

"Come inside me," she whispered as her fluids ran over him. He did as instructed and at that moment was struck by a vision of glorious violence. He would sink the fucking yacht.

Karl left Amanda standing, or rather gently swaying at the sink, and grabbed blankets out of the skipper's stateroom and made a bed next to the hot stove. They collapsed on the floor. He pulled her close and kissed her face.

"Are you alright? You had tears in your eyes," he asked.

"Yes, I was just overwhelmed. That second one was a doozy and I thought about what might have happened on the tracks if you weren't there. It's not often that you get to sleep with your savior. I mean young girls fantasize about firemen... not punk rockers on fishing boats."

"I'll take that as a compliment."

He held her tight and soon she was asleep under the Christmas lights. Karl was warm inside because he had a plan. Eventually he replaced his arm that she slept on with a pillow. She didn't stir. He slid out from behind her and wrapped the blankets tight.

Karl went to the head and took a long piss thinking of what needed to be done. He didn't want mistakes. A little planning saved a lot of headaches. It was something he had learned over a lifetime of doing difficult work. He opened the medicine case and pulled out a new razor blade. He kept running through his plan, mentally walking through each step to the level of where his hands would go, where his feet would stand. He took the razor blade and returned to the galley. He set it on the counter and then quietly slid his wallet, keys and knife from the toes of his boots. He dressed quickly and then stepped out the galley door onto the work deck. Snow was falling heavily and all the boats already had a thick blanket. He slid over the rail to the dock and walked towards the Nadine.

Karl stopped at the base of the light pole that held the security camera that covered dock six. He took the razor blade from his pocket and pushed it through the coax cable until he could feel the solid wire core. That would short out the cable and kill the feed without permanent damage. He left it there and continued to the Nadine. He stopped at the Nadine's rail. Without turning his feet towards the boat he jumped sideways and landed solidly on the deck below. Tommy's lock was on the door. The snow reflected enough light that he easily spun the tumblers to 0174 and opened the door. He left the galley dark but again the reflected light through the port windows led him to the hatch in the floor leading to the engine room. He descended the ladder and closed the hatch above his head. Only then did he turn on the engine room lights. He opened Tommy's toolbox and took a three-quarter inch socket and extension before mating it to a half-inch drive. Karl then started cracking the bolts on the sea strainer until there was an even, steady flow of water coming from the flange. Tommy had mentioned that she needed new batteries and Karl double checked that the large marine cells had been removed from their racks and then returned the tools to the box. He then shut off the light and opened the hatch and climbed out. He closed the hatch and re-padlocked the galley door upon leaving. His approach tracks in the snow were almost gone. Karl climbed on the pin rail and matched his first left foot on the dock to the tracks leading to the Nadine. He brought his other foot down at a normal pace and continued walking to the end of the dock before circling back. If anyone did notice the quickly disappearing footprints they would look like some drunk out for a stroll or maybe a thief looking for a target— not a saboteur. As he walked up the dock he tripped the breaker supplying the Nadine with shore power. He heard the bilge pump turn off. Karl removed the razor blade and the job was complete. He tossed the blade into the black water.

Karl undressed and slid in behind Amanda. He pressed against what should have been her ass. It was almost nothing. Her hip bone poked through her skin, sharp. Only her muscles prevented her from appearing starved. Karl pulled her hip against him until he grew hard.

She stirred. "More?" she asked barely awake. "More," Karl said. They made love that way. Slowly and gently under the Christmas lights and reflected snow.

Afterward they sat naked on the blanket in front of the stove. The boat was fully warm, comfortable.

"You look great in this light," Karl said. Amanda smiled. "Can I take your picture?"

"Naked?" she asked.

Karl smiled. "Just your face. It's beautiful. Maybe sometime else we can take other pics."

"Not likely," she said.

Karl reached for the polaroid on the shelf and snapped a close-up. The flash was harsh but not unflattering. "Let me see," she said and grabbed the developing picture from his hand.

"I should get you across the canal. It doesn't look like this snow is going to stop." He dressed her in the halibut jacket and watch cap. Before he locked the door, Karl put the instant picture of Anders' confusion in the box with the others. One more woman offered to the boat. All footprints were long buried. The Nadine already sat lower in the water. Karl rowed them back across the canal through the snow. He felt like a soldier in the rebel army attacking the Hessians at Trenton or more likely, Max Manus.

It was four in the morning when Karl returned to the house. It had been a good night— a little drinking, a little fighting and a lot of sex. Karl still thought Amanda was bad news and too skinny but she was good at fucking. Maybe he would rethink his prejudice against skinny women. No, not yet. Karl cherished his prejudices because they were his own and based on experience. For day to day thinking these prejudices kept someone alive, healthy and sane but if you tried to codify or institutionalize them like racism, sexism, classism they fell flat.

Karl opened a beer. He thought of Amanda and felt like fucking one more time. There was so much that they hadn't done. He'd let it drop to Anders that they had spent the night together.

Just after five the house phone rang. It was Harold so Karl woke Tommy.

Tommy came out of the bedroom to the phone. It was a sight Karl had seen many times on a fishing boat— the sudden appearance of Tommy in boxers, in the middle of the night because the engine or genset RPMs changed or some other mechanical noise pierced his half sleep, a feeling that they were dragging anchor or an odd cycle in the RSW. Tommy seemed happier on a boat.

34.

"Tommy, can you go check on the Nadine? This snow just sank a bunch of boats in Edmonds. Boat sheds collapsed."

Tommy looked at his watch. He wasn't going back to sleep. He thought of what this would look like. He wasn't a Quisling. He would be angry if any of his guys would even consider this.

"I shouldn't," he said to his boss.

"I know," Harold said. "I'd go but it's my wife... she's not doing well."

Tommy could hear the tiredness in Harold's voice. "I'll head over to the Terminal."

"Thanks Tommy. I owe you one."

"Hey, don't tell anyone about this."

"I hear you. This is going to end."

"I hope so," Tommy said. That was the first good news he had heard in a long time. He hung up and went to take a piss.

"Why are you sitting in the dark?" Tommy asked as he came out of the bathroom.

"Just thinking about that waitress Anders likes. She's got some spirit to her."

Tommy pulled the curtain back and looked out at the snow under the streetlamp. It was still coming down. There was a foot already covering his truck. "You know Anders likes her. He broke his arm coming home from her house the other night. Riding his bike drunk."

"No shit? When?"

"Last..." Tommy thought. "A week ago? He's got a cast and everything."

"No shit. Small world."

"How so?" Tommy asked.

"He's a fool. She almost got him killed. She doesn't give a fuck about him. He's just a kid to her. Hopefully I ended that though, in both their heads."

"Yeah?" Tommy continued looking at the snow pile up.

"Her picture is in the box on the Sara."

Tommy smiled. Of course.

"Want a beer," Karl asked holding one up.

"No. Maybe coffee," Tommy said. He noticed the cuts on Karl's knuckles. "What happened to your hand?"

"Ah," Karl said admiring his own wound. "Some skraelings tried to attack Amanda. They didn't see me. I hope they learned their lesson."

"You're full of action tonight. A regular humanitarian. More Loki than MLK though."

"I hope so. Did you know that MLK fucked around on Coretta? That's fucked up. Come on, have a beer. They'll be no strike line today."

"I can't. Harold wants me to go look at the Nadine. He said a bunch of boats sunk in Edmonds from the snow."

"Don't do it," Karl said. "It'd be good if the Nadine went down. He's sacrileging her by making her a yacht. Fuck that. Let her sink." Karl got up and went to the kitchen. He returned with two beers.

"Hmmm. Maybe I'll lay down for a bit," Tommy said, still not sure if checking on the boat was the right thing to do. He went back into his room and closed the door.

Karl sat there in the silence. Why did Tommy always have to be the nice guy? It'd get him killed someday. Karl couldn't quit thinking about Amanda. He set the beers down and grabbed his keys and went out to his truck. Maybe he was wrong about her. Maybe his prejudice against skinny women was wrong.

Karl knocked on Amanda's door. It was 6 am. He knocked again. The door opened with the security chain still fastened. "Karl!" she said. Amanda undid the chain but kept the door narrow. She was wearing a short silk kimono and it was open across her flat chest.

"I couldn't sleep. Want to go to the Smokeshop and get some breakfast?" he asked.

"I can't," she whispered. "Sorry," she nodded inside. "I've got company." She raised her eyebrows and shrugged her shoulders.

190

Karl smiled. He hadn't been wrong. "Of course," he said and turned and quietly walked down the stairs hoping her lover would be none the wiser.

Tommy couldn't fall back asleep. He lay on his bed and stared at the ceiling. Eventually he heard Karl's diesel pull away from the house. He thought about what Karl said but felt that the boat was his responsibility no matter what her future use would be. He could hear the Nadine calling him like a siren. At least he could shovel her deck. Or rather he could shovel the decks and clear the scuppers of the Brekke boats and then, while he was there, also the Nadine. It was a little moral sleight of hand, a compromise with his own mind and heart.

He dressed slowly, carefully— long johns, wool socks and a fleece top. There were some almost new insulated Xtratufs in the back of his closet that finally got to work. He put his rain gear on and then went out and started his truck turning the heater on full blast. Because he didn't own an ice scraper, Tommy used the broom from the porch to clear his windows and then went back inside and made coffee while the truck warmed.

Tommy shoveled their sidewalk and then shoveled Werner's too. The snow came down so fast that cleared path was again painted white seconds later.

Can a machine try to save your life? The old two-wheel-drive truck didn't want to leave the house. It spun its one drive wheel and went nowhere. Tommy got out and shoveled a path for the wheels and then rocked the truck back and forth, forward and reverse, until she began to make some forward progress. Once moving he kept her moving, plowing through the wet snow and not stopping for sign or light. His wheels spun climbing the bridge. Instead of parking in his normal spot by Seattle Ship Supply, Tommy parked next to the west wall because it was more open and flat. It would give him more room to get his truck moving once his chores were complete. Large snowflakes continued to fall. He pulled the shovel from the truck bed and headed towards the boats. Because of his unusual parking spot he passed dock six first. It was where the Nadine was berthed. Tommy decided to take care of her first, inverting his moral logic.

The stern sat very low in the water and the plywood that had covered the fish hold hatch was floating in the harbor water. Wet, heavy snow coated the deck and house. He jumped on board and slipped in the wet snow. He landed on his knees next to the open hatch and saw that the hold was half tanked down. Tommy looked at the galley door and noticed his lock was backwards. Tommy always ran the hasp from left to right. And then it was very clear what Karl had meant when he said, 'Let her sink'. Tommy knew Karl and knew what he would have done. He opened the galley door and went inside. The galley lights didn't come on. He reached down and flipped the hatch to the engine room. The snow reflected enough light to see black water already halfway up the ladder. Tommy grabbed his headlamp from the hook to the right of the wheelhouse door.

Tommy looked down into the black water and made a choice. He descended into it. He worked quickly understanding what had to be done. He needed to stop the bleeding, to stop the in-rush of water and then focus on removing the water. The water was just above his waist. His feet searched for the grate that covered the bilge. He carefully side stepped forward towards where he knew the sea strainer would be. He touched it with his boot and then reached his hand down submerging himself to the neck in the oily dark water. He felt around the flange— all the nuts were still on the bolts. His fingers followed the rubber gasket round the flange. Tommy could feel the water flowing in. Karl had only cracked the fitting, it was smart— that and turning off the shore power— smart.

Tommy knew the bolts were three-quarter inch. He side stepped back to the toolbox and pulled out a box wrench, a socket, a driver and an extension. The trip back to the flange was slightly up hill. The Nadine was sitting heavy to the stern— water flowed from the engine room to the fish hold through the cut-off piping of the removed refrigerated seawater system. The water had made its way through open hatches into the lazarette. The stern turning submarine.

Again, he reached under the black water to find the bolts on the flange. To tighten the outboard three he had to go under the dark water. He worked purposefully, professionally, without panic or wasted movement.

He moved with a purpose, with a confidence and competence that most men never find in a lifetime. Tommy was happy, happier than he had been in years. Driving a truck had paid him well and being the shop steward had given him purpose but being on a boat and being a good engineer had made him happy, content. His happiness was pure because it was underpinned by pride and unreflected.

On the Ballard side of the canal a boat shed covering four yachts collapsed under the weight of the heavy, wet snow. Tommy heard it. First a metallic screeching as the steel supports began to twist and then a deep thud as the roof came down solidly on the play boats. Tommy concentrated on his task. The impact sent small waves out and across the canal, they bounced off piers and boats, off the bridge and some even made it into Fishermen's Terminal. One made it all the way to the Nadine. A two-inch wave killed him when it pushed the canal water over the lip leading to the hold.

It sounded like someone turned on a shower in the fish hold. Tommy was just finishing tightening the bolts on the sea strainer. His job almost complete. The shower got louder and then the sound got deeper as the weight of the water finally pulled the stern down to where the hold could drink deep. By the time Tommy heard it roar like a waterfall it was too late. The stern settled and the rear cleat was ripped from the wooden boat. "Fuck me," he said quietly. He didn't drop the wrench. He had the intention of returning it to the toolbox as he waded through the water towards the ladder. When the forward line came taught it imparted a spin into the boat and the old girl rolled to her side. Tommy was thrown against the pipes that ran along the engine room ceiling. His headlamp came off. Then something landed on him pinning him to the engine. It was the genset, unbolted from the hull and ready for removal.

So this is how it happens, Tommy thought. The water covered Tommy's face. He struggled against the genset until he could hold his breath no longer. He opened his eyes and saw the light from his head lamp floating in the darkness. He wasn't angry. He wasn't angry at Karl or Harold or the strike or the world. He thought of his little girl, of that last day they rowed the canal. Then he thought how odd it was that he should die on a boat, after all these years and still tied to the dock. *The ship is foundering. What then have I to do?*

35.

Karl left Amanda's and went to the Smokeshop. There were few tracks on the streets. He looked in the door and saw the waitress walking around an empty restaurant. He knocked on the window and caught her attention. She opened the door. "Sorry Karl, I don't think we are going to open today. No one can get in through this snow. It's just me so far."

"You want some help? I can wash dishes."

She laughed. "Sure, come on in."

Karl put on an apron and fixed breakfast for the both of them. Afterwards, they drank coffee and just talked, catching up, as no customers ever arrived. Eventually Karl cleaned up the dishes and straightened the kitchen before heading back to the house, his good deed done for the day.

Anders only heard the knock at the door because it was loud and persistent. The painkillers had made his brain fuzzy. At first, he wondered why his roommates weren't answering but when he tried to roll to his side and was blocked by the cast reality came crashing back on him like driftwood hidden in a wave. He looked at his arm and he remembered the woman. "Amanda!" he said aloud. Every pain killer deluded sexual fantasy started running through his head at once. He looked around his room and quickly straightened the bed. He left one lamp on in the corner. Mood lighting, he thought. He pulled on a pair of jeans and stuffed his half-swollen cock against his thigh. He grabbed a t-shirt and put the cast arm through the hole before taking it back off. He'd go casually shirtless. He imagined Amanda hugging him, her face against his chest. The front door knocked again, louder. "One second!" he shouted up the stairs. Anders wished he could have brushed his teeth. He climbed sure that finally she had arrived.

Anders was half naked, half-mast with one arm in a full cast when he opened the door expecting love and instead faced a cop. Fate didn't get tired of kicking him in the nuts.

"Where's Karl?" Bruce asked.

Anders quickly scanned the sidewalk covered in snow. Both Karl's and Tommy's trucks were missing although it was obvious that one of them had parked overnight. "Don't know. Probably somewhere in the Gulf of Alaska, maybe Inside Passage. Then again, he drops anchor all over town. I never know. Why what's up?"

"I need to talk to him. A vagrant got killed on the tracks by the Lock Spot last night. He needs to talk to me first or stay gone for a while."

"What do you mean?" Anders asked.

"Just give him the message," Bruce said. The other bum's description was too perfect to be anyone else. *A mean little guy with a shaved head and hand tattoos. He jumped us for no reason. And threatened me with a knife!* "You break your arm the other night when I saw you sitting on the curb?" Bruce asked.

Anders knew it was pointless to lie. "Yeah. I had a great idea that didn't work out."

"You always dress that way?" the cop asked with a smile.

"Truthfully, I was hoping for someone else."

"Aren't we all." Bruce climbed down the stairs and then turned back towards Anders. "And I probably wasn't here, right?"

"I don't know what you're talking about," Anders replied.

Bruce smiled and got in his cruiser. The back tires spun as he navigated through the rutted snow.

Anders went downstairs and pulled on a hooded sweatshirt over his cast. He was positive that Amanda wouldn't come. She would never come. He returned up the stairs and made coffee thinking of how he could go back to work with the broken arm. There was another knock at the door. It was a heavy knock.

When Anders opened the door, another cop in blue stood with his hat on. Anders didn't recognize him. He wasn't from the neighborhood.

"Is Karl Eide here?" the cop asked.

"No."

"Do you know where he is?"

"Probably on a boat somewhere. Why?"

"Nothing too important. We just need to ask him about last night. He may have witnessed an assault last night." The cop handed Anders a card. "Have him call me."

Karl sat in his truck a block away. He had pulled into a parking spot when he saw the cruiser in front of his house. That bad feeling came to him. He usually got it right before a piece of rigging broke. Sometimes there was a hum that only he could hear, other times a silence came that made the sound of engines fade away.

As Karl waited he imagined what may have gone wrong. The camera trick with the razor blade— he had not tested it. It was just something he had read about, not empirical. He had trusted someone else's knowledge. Up the street walked Werner, with his old man's gait, struggling through the wet snow in his galoshes, too proud to use the cane he carried. Werner walked by but then stopped and looked at Karl, his old man brain sensing that something was odd. Karl put two fingers to his eyes and then pointed toward their houses, at the idling cruiser. Werner nodded and continued homeward.

"Excuse me sir, do you live here?" the cop asked.

Werner held his gate. "Yes, for almost forty years. Where do you live?"

"That's not important."

"Yes it is."

"Have you seen Karl Eide recently?"

"I think he works on towboats," Werner said and stepped through his gate.

Karl waited until the cruiser drove away and then he shut off his truck and walked to his house.

Karl closed the door and Anders came out of the kitchen with a cup of coffee in his hand.

"What the fuck was that about?" Karl asked.

"I don't know who that guy was," Anders handed Karl the business card. "But, Bruce was here earlier and said a vagrant got killed by the Lock Spot last night. He said talk to him first or disappear for a while. The second guy wanted to see if you witnessed an assault."

Karl and Anders each went to a window on either side of the front door. They watched the snow continue to fall.

"Where'd you park?" Anders asked.

"Up the street." Karl's brain was moving fast. He still had four weeks of vacation left. "Where the fuck is Tommy?"

"I don't know. He shoveled our walk and Werner's walk and then drove off. He's probably up shoveling Kim's."

Karl laughed a little. "Yep, sucker." He went to the kitchen and finished the french press that Anders had made. "Hey, Bruce said killed and the other guy said assault?"

"Yeah," Anders replied.

Bruce wouldn't have said that if it wasn't important. "I might go away for a little while. My life has been lacking adventure lately. Might be an omen to shake things up."

"What about the vagrant?" Anders asked.

"Don't ask questions that you don't want answers to."

Karl went into his room and thought of where he might want to go. Bruce making a personal visit seemed serious. He couldn't think of any reason either of the skraelings should end up dead other than OD but obviously something was stirring in the storm. Karl would have liked to go somewhere warm but air travel and driving weren't clean. Karl knew how to disappear and his mind started chopping through options.

36.

The Port Captain looked out his window at the shipyard. Only two workers had made it in through the snow. One had made a makeshift plow out of a forklift and an empty metal scrap box. He pushed the snow to the side of the yard. It wasn't pretty but at least he was making the effort. The other worker was on the boat in drydock. The snow had collapsed all the tarps that sheltered the welders. A boat was scheduled to sail that day but the Port Captain had his doubts even though the Mate had called and said he would pick up the crew and bring them to work. The PC had started their boat hoping they would arrive. The radio in his office came alive with a conversation across the ship canal between a Foss tug and their Port Captain. They were going to take the 300, Foss' steam powered crane derrick, over to Fishermen's Terminal to raise a sunken boat. The Port Captain hated to see his rivals make smoke while all his boats stood idle.

A police car pulled into the cleared area of the yard and parked. The cop got out and walked to the door on the first floor. It blocked any more plowing and the Port Captain could see the forklift operator swearing at the empty car.

"Anyone here?" a yell asked from the first floor.

"Yeah, come on up," he shouted back.

Across the canal, the Foss 300 signaled that she was backing out.

"Is Karl Eide here?" the cop asked.

"No."

"Is he expected?"

"Why? What's this about?" the Captain asked.

"Nothing serious. He may have witnessed something and I need to get his statement."

The answer was too vague. Too reassuring. The Port Captain looked at his board. "He's not even scheduled for a trip." The Captain realized his mistake and quickly turned his attention back out the window towards the shipyard. But the cop noticed the board. There were columns of workers: names, home phones and pagers. The cop wrote the pager number down, thanked the Port Captain for his time and left.

A large blue diesel crew cab pulled in. It belonged to the Mate who lived up in Sedro Wooley. He logged during his land time and his truck bed was filled with saws, gas tanks and rigging. Three men piled out laughing and holding coffee mugs. It was most of the crew that was supposed to sail at noon. They were a good bunch, no complainers.

198

Karl pulled a duffle bag from his closet and thought about a plan. If it were summer he might go for a couple week walkabout through the Olympics or Cascades but that wouldn't work in December. The only way out of town looked maritime. He could hitch a ride with the northbound boat leaving that day. The off-duty employees often used the boats as transport for fishing or hunting trips to the great wild north. Karl headed to the bathroom to pack his dopp kit.

The phone rang. Karl looked at Anders and said, "you better answer it."

"Hallo."

"Is Karl there?" the voice on the other end asked.

"No," Anders said.

"Hmmm. This is the Port Captain calling. Well… The cops were just here looking for him so… if you…"

"I understand," Anders said, rescuing the man.

"Ah, good. OK. Thank you." The caller hung up.

"That was work. The cops were there too. This new guy is efficient."

"Yeah," Karl said and then his pocket began to vibrate. He looked at the number on the pager and didn't recognize it. He pulled the card Anders had handed him and compared the numbers. "Yeah, a little too efficient."

That accelerated the timeline and complicated his plan. He needed to keep his circle small. Anders already knew too much. Karl couldn't just walk down the dock and jump on board the departing boat. It would put the Port Captain, the company and the crew in a bad spot. Yet, he knew of a way to make it work. It was going to be a lot less comfortable, and considerably more difficult. Karl went to the front window and looked at the snow coming down. He looked at his watch. If it could keep snowing for an hour and a half. He had an idea but it was going to be cold. The boat leaving today was towing a new fuel barge destined for Ketchikan or Kodiak. He couldn't remember the outbound board. He knew the destination started with a K. Karl hoped for Ketchikan where he knew a woman that would welcome his visit.

She was never satisfied with his short stays— too short to even get some decent sleep.

"Anders, I'm going to need you to help me out but don't ask a bunch of questions. Just do what I say. We're going to head over to the Terminal as soon as I'm packed."

Anders nodded. The phone rang again and Karl watched Anders pick it up.

"Hallo…" It was Anders' father. "Yep, I'm already headed there, just about to leave. Okay. Out." Don wanted Anders to go and shovel the decks and clear the scuppers of the boats. Anders dressed for the weather. He cut one sleeve off a waffle long john top and slid his cast through the hole. He layered a sweatshirt, a halibut jacket and his rain gear to fight the snow.

Karl went into his bedroom and turned on his scanner. It was a good crew and they would leave on schedule. He packed a small backpack with the essentials— passport, three thousand dollars cash, a handheld VHF radio, a headlamp with plenty of spare batteries, first aid kit, a reflective emergency blanket, toiletries, two novels and a stainless snub-nosed 357. Before snapping the buckles shut, Karl went to the kitchen and opened all the cupboards to do a quick survey of his options. He grabbed three cans of sardines and a fifth of Jack Daniels to add to the backpack. Into a sea bag went a five-gallon bucket, a 50' line, a cold weather sleeping bag with gore-tex bivy, all the cans of beans and pasta they had on the shelf, another headlamp and more batteries. Water would be the challenge. They had a couple one-and-a-half-gallon plastic jugs of water as part of an earthquake cache in the basement. That would be plenty for Ketchikan but if the tow continued on to Kodiak, Karl would have to call the crew on the radio and alert them to their stowaway. He cut two six-foot pieces of poly line and tied bowlines around the water jug handles and then joined the lines on a large oval carabiner. He would have liked to splice the poly line but bowlines were sufficiently nautical and speedy. Karl looked at his small kit and was satisfied. It was minimal but light and he would be able to move quickly.

The little diesel rattled to life and Anders awkwardly locked the front hubs with his left hand. He used the broom from the porch to push a foot of mash potato snow from the cab roof, windows and hood. The small cab warmed quickly and Anders kept the wipers running to fight the falling snow.

"Will she make it?" Karl asked as he emerged from the house carrying the water jugs.

"Have faith. Suzie's a tough little girl," Anders said.

"Well, one thing's for sure— we won't see any more cop cars in this shit." Karl put the water in the bed and then went back inside for the seabag and backpack.

Anders tried to pull the transfer case into four-wheel drive with his casted hand but finally had to use his left hand to get the leverage. He put the transmission into first with the broken arm, not asking Karl to shift as Kate had done. They climbed over the wet snow and into the street. The ruts grabbed the wheels and the little truck was tossed side to side like a small skiff running with the tide. There wasn't another car to be seen moving about and the snow continued to fall. They passed several abandoned cars on streets and on the bridge.

They parked next to Seattle Ship Supply. The little Isuzu was the only rig in the lot. "Well," Karl said. "Tommy's not here."

"I was hoping he'd beat me to the job," Anders said.

"I'm surprised he didn't."

Anders carried the water jugs and Karl carried his luggage down to dock three where the Brekke boats were moored. Once inside the Saratoga, Karl turned on the marine radio and tuned to the work frequency. Anders lit the stove and then left to light the stoves in the other two boats. When he returned, Anders said, "sounds like something is going on over by the west wall."

Karl was sitting in the skipper's chair listening to the radio. "Yeah, this snow has sunk some boats and collapsed some boat sheds across the canal. Foss has a crane moving in to start salvage. They'll be busy for a few days."

"I'd like to walk over there and see what's going on," Anders said.

"No," Karl said, pretty sure he knew what was going on. "Don't be a misery gawker. Just clean your boats and go home. Plus, I need you here. Go warm up the skiff. We're almost done." Anders did as he was told and soon Karl was handing Anders his luggage and water to place in the bow of the little boat.

They waited next to the fuel dock, engine running, each man holding a piling. The snow hid everything further than fifty feet.

"How long are you going to be gone?" Anders asked.

"I still have four weeks of vacation. I'll keep checking in but follow up with Bruce. No, have Tommy follow up with Bruce."

The tug horned for the bridge to open and was answered. A few seconds later the bells rang. They both wore wool watch caps and the snow stuck to their eyelashes. Karl's eyes tried to burn through the wall of white. He finally spotted the boat's lights flicker past and then a large green mass pulled tight. "Let's go," Karl said quietly and pushed off the bow. Anders rolled slowly on the skiff's throttle. Karl had already explained his plan and Anders' headed for the stern of the barge, toward the flush ladder that should be there. The stern loomed up and the skegs cut through the black water. A little more forward was the ladder. Karl wore his backpack on his chest and the seabag on his back. He held the carabiner joining the water jug lines in his right hand. Anders pushed the skiff gently against the hull and held her steady. Karl clipped the water to a rung of the ladder. He turned to Anders, "Thanks. I'll see you." Anders just nodded. Karl climbed up a couple rungs and Anders chopped the throttle and watched as the water jugs were pulled free of the skiff. There was a quiet thud as they bounced against the hull of the empty barge. Karl then climbed the ladder and once on deck quickly stowed his bags by the pump house. He returned to the ladder and climbed halfway down to retrieve the water jugs. He was inside the pumphouse by the time he felt the tow slow to enter the locks.

Anders returned the skiff to the stern of the Saratoga and got to work clearing the decks and scuppers. He used a plastic shovel they had for icing fish but it was still a pain in the ass because his dominant arm wouldn't bend at the elbow. At least he wasn't hiding on a fuel barge for the next week.

37

Chores done, Anders made some instant hot chocolate and sat at the galley table and watched the crane derrick being positioned by the tug. The snow was finally thinning and he could see a pair of divers in dry suits readying to rig the lift. As he drank his hot chocolate, he reached for the box of polaroids. He opened the lid and Amanda stared out at him. "Son of a bitch!" Anders said to the empty boat and shut the lid. He sat for a minute and then opened it again and pulled her picture out. She was sitting on the floor next to the galley stove wrapped in a blanket off the skipper's bunk. Anders had never seen her naked and now never would. Fuck, he thought, she never even called after he broke his arm riding home from her place. She just asked, 'does it hurt?' when they saw each other at the Hat.

After cleaning his mug and shutting down the stoves in each of the boats Anders walked up the dock towards his truck. The snow had stopped. He thought about what Karl had said about being a misery gawker. His family's boats had survived this little freak storm without so much as a bent antenna. There were probably lessons to be learned about maintenance or responsibility. Hell, there were probably lessons to be learned about waitresses.

Despite Karl's warning Anders drove by dock six. He slowed his truck as he came perpendicular to the dock. A crowd was standing at the far end and he couldn't see anything worth seeing. A worker came in reflective yellow rain gear came out of the port bathroom headed for the dock. Anders rolled down his window.

"What happened?"

The man stopped. "Ah, some old wood seiner sank. Rolled on her side. Probably popped a board. Those old boats make me nervous. Sure, they don't sink but they're not real good at staying on the surface either."

"I hear ya. I'm a steel boat man myself. Hey, what boat was it?"

"The Nadine."

"No shit. She just retired. Rough go."

The worker nodded and continued down the dock. That was the boat Tommy was working on. That wouldn't make him happy. Anders didn't want to gawk but he could probably watch the crane lift the boat in the warmth of his truck from the west wall. He drove that way. The little four-wheel-drive Isuzu was light and nimble. It was like driving a mountain goat.

And then he saw Tommy's truck covered in eight inches of snow.

Anders parked next to Tommy and walked back to dock six. He searched the crowd gathered next to the Nadine for Tommy but didn't see him. He then looked at the Nadine. She lay on her side, the galley door open. An oil boom was already circling the boat and inside its seine-like circle floated a Styrofoam cup with NGT written on it in magic marker.

The Foss tug started backing the crane derrick away. The worker Anders had talked to earlier was standing next to him and Anders asked what was going on. He was told that the crane would start on the other side of the canal because those boats were still above water although covered with a collapsed boat shed. They could still be saved. Anders couldn't give words to his thoughts.

A tall man was talking to a Port employee at the end of the dock. He was explaining that he'd get one of 'his' barges over into the Terminal to set the Nadine on when the crane came back to pick it out of the water. Anders recognized him as Tommy's boss.

"Mr. Pedersen?" Anders interjected when there was a pause in conversation.

"Yes?"

"May I speak to you for a moment?" They walked a few steps away from Harold's wife. "I'm Anders Brekke, a roommate of Tommy's. His truck is in the parking lot, covered with snow."

Harold looked at the Nadine and understood why the galley door was open. Tommy would have never left it open or unlocked. Anders watched the color drain from Harold's face. Both men knew the unspoken.

"I'm going to take my wife home," Harold said.

"Yes sir. Do you want me to do anything?"

"No. There's nothing to be done. Not today anyway."

Anders went home to a very empty and quiet house. He sat on the couch and listened to the water drip from the snow melting off the roof. Across the still neighborhood Anders heard the steam whistle from the 300.

Early in the evening Anders heard a truck crunching through the rutted ice. He went to the front window and saw a white F-150 park in front of the house. Bruce got out still in uniform. Anders opened the door.

"I have some bad news," he said.

"Tommy?" Anders asked.

"Yeah, how'd you know?"

"I saw his truck at the terminal and guessed. He was working on that boat for his boss."

"What's his wife's name?"

"Kim."

"You got a number or address for her?"

"Yeah, just a second. Come on in Bruce. It's cold out there."

"No, it's better if I don't."

Anders went to the kitchen and wrote down Kim's info.

"They let you guys drive your personal rigs?" Anders asked.

"No, not officially but those crown vics are fucking pointless in the snow."

Again, alone, Anders was unsure of what he should do. He was unaware that the news was already moving through the neighborhood. Of course, Harold knew before Anders and he called Anders' father, Don, because Harold knew that Tommy used to fish for the elder Brekke.

All Don could say was, "Jesus Christ, in the fucking port." Don had never lost a man and never even had one seriously injured. Don and Harold would later combine forces to get Tommy's name on the memorial. It was argued that even though the Nadine had ceased to be a commercial boat that Tommy was acting as an engineer when she turned over.

38.

Kate called and asked Anders for a ride to work. The buses weren't running and her bicycle wasn't built for snow. He drove her to work, not saying anything about Tommy or Karl. The news reached the Hat during her shift. When Anders picked her up Kate hugged him around the waist and just said, "I know," and then, "let's go to your house." That night they slept together in his basement room but didn't have sex. In the morning they did.

The strike ended two days later. Harold walked into the meeting and told his side of the table that he was giving his guys the strike language and sending them back to work. Everyone knew about Tommy and no one wanted to argue about money with the old Norwegian. Tommy's death gave the bosses a reason to fold their hands— they weren't beaten, they were being compassionate.

Four days later Karl learned about Tommy. He read about it in the Seattle Times. Tommy was mentioned in two articles— one about the end of the strike and the other about the storm. Karl's nurse friend was at work and he sat silent for an hour in her apartment in Ketchikan. He went to his backpack and pulled out his pistol. He sat on the couch with it on his leg for another hour and then returned it to the pack.

Anders was drawing Kate a bath. He had just picked her up from her night shift at the Hat and chauffeuring her to and from work seemed like the only helpful thing he could do. The cast would come off in five weeks. Kate was outside, lowering the flag, when a cop car pulled up. The passenger window rolled down and the cop asked if Anders was home. She went in and got him. Anders emerged wearing his bathrobe. He had hoped to be asked to join Kate in the tub.

"Hey Bruce," Anders said.

"You've always got an interesting style Anders," Bruce laughed and then continued, "hey, where's Karl?"

"I don't know... gone."

"Well, when you talk to him tell him some bum got run over by a bus in Fremont today. He'll know what it means."

"Okay..." Anders said.

"Shouldn't you be leaving for squid?" Bruce asked.

"Can't," Anders said, waving the casted arm under his bathrobe.

"You don't need two arms to be a skipper. Ahab did it with one leg." Bruce put his cruiser in drive and pulled away leaving Anders on the curb thinking a new thought.

A week later Karl called from Dutch Harbor. He said it was his fault that Tommy was dead and that he had signed on to the worst boat in the fleet and hoped it would go down. Anders told Karl what Bruce had said but Karl just replied, "I don't care."

Before Karl could hang up Anders said, "Tommy chose to get on that boat."

"Yes," Karl said through the wind-blown static. "No one can deny him that honor."

39.

Eventually the cast came off and Anders returned to the kitchens. He and Kate worked and loved and made the little house theirs but always expected Karl to return unannounced. They moved into Tommy's room after Kim had taken what she wanted— only the lockbox and picture. Three months after the Dutch Harbor phone call, a postcard arrived from France. It was from Karl. It read, "I've decided on my punishment. I'm going away from water for five years. Take care of the house. Karl."

Anders showed it to Kate. She was on the way out the door to take leftovers to Werner next door. "I guess the house is ours. It sounds like Karl's going to jail," Anders said.

One morning they lay in bed after making love. Anders asked Kate to marry him but she said no. She wouldn't marry a cook or even a fisherman. But she would marry a skipper. That's how Anders Brekke returned to the boats.

Made in United States
Troutdale, OR
12/13/2023